PITY PLAY

WHITNEY DINEEN

Made in the United States. March 2025

Print ISBN:
E-book ASIN: B0DBGSX36X

https://whitneydineen.com/newsletter/

33 Partners Publishing

ALSO BY WHITNEY DINEEN

Ain't She Sweet

It's My Party

You're So Vain

Head Over Feet

Queen of Hearts

At Last

She Sins at Midnight

Going Up?

Love for Sale

The Accidentally in Love Series (with Melanie Summers)

Text Me on Tuesday

The Text God

Text Wars

Text in Show

Mistle Text

Text and Confused

A Gamble on Love Mom-Com Series (with Melanie Summers)

No Ordinary Hate

A Hate Like This

Hate, Rinse, Repeat

Visionary Fiction

The Celestial Contract

Conspiracy Thriller

See No More

Non-Fiction Humor

Motherhood, Martyrdom & Costco Runs

Dedicated to everyone who loved a boy who didn't know they existed.

CHAPTER ONE

LORELAI

"Hang on, Noah." I put my cell phone down while giving the teenager leaning against the counter a sympathetic smile. As I ring up her telltale order of salty cashew nuts, a chocolate bar, and a travel-sized bottle of Midol, I can't help but think, *I've been there, sister.* Consulting my mental calendar, I realize I'll be there again in approximately three days. I can already taste my go-to culinary comforts—sodium-riddled cheeseburgers followed by a chocolate pudding chaser. The boxed variety, because I'm classy that way.

I pick up my phone as the anguished-looking girl shuffles away. "Okay, I'm back. What were you saying about Luke Phillips?" I'm pretty sure I heard my brother the first time, but my heart started to beat so loudly, the resulting thumping in my ears may have affected my ability to process the news.

Noah shouts in the background, "You throw that basketball like my grandmother! Scratch that—Nana could shoot circles around all of you!" Noah is a high school basketball coach. Apparently, his motivational style is to make his team feel inferior to our eighty-year-old arthritic grandmother, who as far as I know has never even held a basketball, let alone shot a three-pointer.

"Hold on, I'm going into my office." Moments later, Noah grumbles, "I swear, these kids have the attention span of hyperactive gnats."

"Speaking of a lack of focus," I tease. "Are you going to finish telling me about Luke?"

"I already did. His dad had an accident and won't be able to work for a while, so Luke's going back to Elk Lake to take over at Pop's until Mr. Phillips is up and running."

That's *exactly* what I thought he said. Confirmation results in my senses bursting into overdrive. Hot bolts of electricity shoot through my nervous system and make me wonder if I might be having a stroke. Although currently I'm so excited even a major health event couldn't diminish my unabashed joy.

"Word on the street—aka my neighbor's cat sitter—is that Mr. P fell off his roof. What in the world was he doing up there?"

My brother snorts. "He thought he saw an injured raccoon and he was going up to see if it needed any help."

There is so much wrong with that statement, I don't know where to begin. I start with, "Why would you corner an injured raccoon on a roof? It could be rabid."

"I guess it's a good thing it wasn't a raccoon."

"What was it? A giant squirrel? A possum? A furry alien?"

"It was a branch that had come down in the last storm."

That isn't surprising, as parts of Elk Lake are very wooded. Our spring storms can pack quite a wallop as my dad likes to say. "So, he fell trying to remove the branch?"

"He fell trying to kick it off the roof."

"Kick it …"

"You know Mr. P. He likes to think he's still a kid. I guess he was going to show that stick who's boss."

I pull a bottle of glass cleaner out from under the counter and spray down the area in front of me. Wiping in wide circles, I ask, "How badly was he hurt?" I've heard a variety of gossip around town that varies from "lucky to be alive" to "just bruises."

"Luke doesn't know yet. All his mom said is that he'll be in the hospital for several days."

"So, pretty bad."

Instead of answering, Noah shouts, "So help me, Greyson, if you don't turn around and get back on the court, I'm going to bench your butt for the entire season."

"But coach …" I hear a voice in the distance. "I've gotta … you know … go."

"Go where? To the moon? You need to go shopping for a new swimsuit? You late for a nail appointment?" My brother is as warm and fuzzy as a barracuda.

"I've got … you know … stomach troubles."

"You've got to poop? For the love of … Fine. Hurry up and go, but you're going to stay late for five minutes for every minute you're gone."

Noah's team must despise him. However, I don't give that much thought because Luke Phillips is front and center in my mind. From what my brother has told me, his lifelong bestie and his dad have barely spoken in years. That has something to do with Luke not moving back to Elk Lake once he graduated from culinary school. He had other plans. Like moving to Chicago and becoming a big deal chef at a Michelin-starred restaurant, like the one he currently owns.

"Is Luke staying with his folks while he's here?" Before he can answer, I conclude, "That ought to give them plenty of time to clear up any misunderstandings."

"It might if Mr. Phillips knew Luke was going to cover for him at Pop's."

"They're not telling him?"

"Mrs. Phillips doesn't want Mr. P to know yet. She wants him to think Luke is just coming to see him."

"I'm confused," I tell my brother. "Hasn't Mr. P always wanted Luke to cook at Pop's?"

"Mrs. P doesn't want Mr. P to think Luke's doing it out of

obligation. She doesn't want Mr. P to be more stressed out than he currently is."

"But he's sure to find out. I mean, Elk Lake is a small town. People talk." I cite the time I accidentally ran into the McNallys' mailbox with my old Volvo. I was sixteen; it was dark, and I didn't think anyone saw me. Yet when I got home, the first words out of my mom's mouth were, "You owe the McNallys an apology and you're paying for a new mailbox out of your own money." Turns out Mrs. Franken, the McNallys' neighbor, saw me. She called her daughter, who called her cleaning lady, who rang my mother. There's no way Luke is going to be able to keep what he's doing a secret.

"I'm sure he'll find out," Noah concurs. "Just make sure *you* don't spread the word."

"Why would I tell anyone?" Although I could whisper it to a dog sitting on the street corner, and word would likely spread.

"Lorelai …" I can practically hear my brother's eyes rolling all the way from Chicago. "You were madly in love with Luke from the first moment you saw him and you were only five years old. I'm pretty sure you maintained your unbridled devotion until he left town."

While this is true, I have no idea what it has to do with anything. Also, it makes me feel pathetic. "That was a long time ago, Noah. I've gotten on with my life," I say as I shamelessly plot how many times a day I can eat at Pop's without people wondering what I'm up to.

"Says the girl who's still living in her parents' house and is working in a hotel gift shop."

Ouch. "I take care of Mom and Dad's house for them while they're in Florida. I'm performing a service." I know I sound defensive but that's because I am. Before my brother can respond, I ask, "What's wrong with my working in a hotel gift shop? The Elk Lake Lodge has become a big deal, you know. *Travel Wisconsin* magazine just ran a huge feature on us." *Plus, it's not all that I do.* I knit blankets for the neonatal ward at the hospital; I walk dogs at the Humane Society; and I pitch in with Meals on Wheels for the old folks when one of their drivers is down. Yet I don't think Mr. Judgypants would consider any of those things to be valuable contributions.

"There's nothing *wrong* with it," Noah says. It's clear he wants to say more but he seems uncertain if he should.

"But …" I prod him.

"I can't help but think you're settling."

My hair trigger reaction is to hang up on him. Instead, I demand, "What about my life seems like I'm settling?"

He doesn't answer right away, so I can only assume he's compiling a laundry list of reasons. When he finally speaks, he says, "I just can't see you being content working in a gift shop. You used to always talk about opening a bed and breakfast. You wanted to be a businesswoman."

"I'm twenty-eight, Noah. I can still own a B & B someday if I want to."

"Of course you can. I shouldn't have said anything."

No, he shouldn't have, but I don't tell him that. I know my brother is only looking out for me, so I remind him, "Michael and I broke up three years ago. The dreams I had then aren't necessarily the same ones I still have."

"Why, because Michael didn't want you to have them? I don't want to see him take anything more from you."

"He's not taking anything from me. It's been *three years*. I'm totally over him."

"*If* you're over him, why do you still live in Elk Lake? We all thought you'd move back to Madison."

"I didn't move back because Mom and Dad decided to spend half the year in Florida, and they asked me to mind their home while they were gone." For a hot second, I wonder if Noah's right, and I've given up on my life. But then I remind myself that I'm very happy. In addition, I'm busy contributing to my community. So, I tell him, "My life is very fulfilling."

"Good," he says. "But I'd still like to give you the opportunity to see if you'd like to run a B & B."

"It sounds like you're coming home and you're trying to get me to cook for you."

"Not me," he says. And that's when the purpose of this call hits me. He may not be coming home, but Luke Phillips is.

"You want Luke to stay at our house?" The thought of the two of us under the same roof causes my scalp to tingle with anticipation. My hands practically itch at the thought of touching that thick, gorgeous dark brown hair of his. Who am I kidding? The junior high school girl inside me is doing back flips at the very thought. I spent my entire eighth-grade year looking through my brother's bedroom keyhole trying to catch a glimpse of "Luscious Luke" Phillips.

Noah casts a line that drags me back to the present. "It would really help him out."

"Well, I mean …" I don't want to sound too eager, so I force a deep breath before saying, "I guess he can stay here."

"Good." Noah pauses a moment before yelling, "Everyone in the shower and make sure you use soap! This gym smells like a barnyard!"

I need to know. "Does your team hate your guts?"

"Maybe. But who cares? We're number three in the state. I'm clearly doing something right."

I interrupt what I'm guessing is about to turn into a monumental bragging session. "When will Luke be here?"

"Tomorrow morning around ten."

My heartbeat accelerates at the thought of everything I need to do to prepare. "Way to give me notice," I sarcastically drawl.

"I couldn't very well tell you sooner. It's not like Mr. Phillips knew he was going to fall off his roof."

He's got a point there. "Fine, but I can't promise to have everything ready in time."

"What is there to do? Just throw some clean sheets at him and point him in the direction of a spare bedroom."

"Yeah, cause that's the way to run a successful B & B." You'd think my brother was raised by wolves.

"Oh, and I should tell you that Luke just broke up with his girlfriend, so be extra sweet to him. He's pretty low."

While I should be sympathetic that my childhood crush just went through a breakup, I can't help the slow smile that starts to form on my face. Luke Phillips is coming home. Not only that, but he's single, and he's staying at *my* house. I feel like I just picked the winning Powerball numbers—with the kicker.

When I was little, my mom used to watch that old TV show, *Gilmore Girls*. She was always carrying on about how Lorelai and Luke were perfect for each other if only they'd open their eyes and see it. Of course, that show had nothing to do with why I used to write Lorelai + Luke in the middle of a heart on all my notebooks. The reason for that is on his way home to Elk Lake, and I can hardly wait to see him again.

CHAPTER TWO

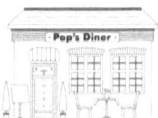

LUKE

I love owning my own restaurant, but no one ever tells you that most of the work isn't creating fabulous culinary feasts, which is the reason I became a chef. It's bookkeeping. My brain starts to fog over as I shuffle through a stack of receipts. I don't look up until I hear the voice of my general manager, Eve. "Leave those. I'll have Charlie tally everything up when she does payroll on Thursday."

I indicate the chair across from my desk for her to sit down. "I don't know how long I'll be gone, but it could be a month or longer."

"Don't worry about us. We're going to be fine. Just keep us posted on your dad. Maybe send some pictures of your family restaurant so we can see how far you've come."

As Eve crosses one long leg over the other, a flash of our two poorly-fated dates pops into my mind. All we could talk about was work, and you know what they say about all work and no play. Toward the end of our second outing, Eve confessed that she didn't think we were meant to be more than friends and great business partners. I agreed with her, but I still thought it was too bad we didn't click romantically. It's hard to find time to date like a normal person when you run one of the best and busiest restaurants in Chicago. As such, it's been years since I've so much as had a steady girlfriend.

"I appreciate everything you do around here, Eve. Capon would be nothing without you." That's not false praise, either. Restaurants are only as good as the front of the house. It's well known that diners come to your establishment for the food, but they return for the hospitality. Eve is nothing if not extraordinarily hospitable.

"I've got a call out to the culinary school to bring in some temporary help while you're away. Extra hands doing the grunt work will give the line cooks a chance to take on more responsibility. And you know how cooks are. Always looking for opportunities to enhance their station."

Nodding my head, I tell her, "That's perfect. I don't want to hire someone full time if we won't need them for long."

Eve smiles endearingly while swiping a lock of her long blonde hair behind her ear. "The school loves to brag about being able to place their students in restaurants like ours, so it's a win-win."

"Just make sure the kitchen keeps a close eye on them. We don't need any newbies cutting off their fingers while peeling potatoes." I reference the first student the school sent. He cut off the tip of his finger because he was more focused on flirting with my pastry chef than on chopping onions.

Eve laughs before saying, "I'm sorry about the reason you're going home, but I think the change of scenery will be good for you."

My GM is always hounding me to take more time off, but there's a reason executive chefs aren't known for how many vacations they take. We have too many demands on our time to worry about our own pleasures. "I suppose it'll be something of a break, flipping burgers instead of grilling filets," I grumble.

Ignoring my surly tone, she decides, "It'll be nice for you to be home. How long has it been, anyway?"

Eve knows I haven't been back to Elk Lake in the two years since Capon opened. I don't really want to divulge that it's been longer than that, so I simply tell her, "It's been a while."

"You know that's pitiful, don't you?"

I usually like Eve's straightforwardness, but that's not currently the case. "Look, I work hard and when I get a day off the last thing I want to do is go home and listen to my dad rail at me for not going into business with him."

"What about the rest of your family?" she demands.

"I talk to my mom regularly, and my sister visits me twice a year from California. My family life is fine." I really need her to stop giving me crap. I'm nervous enough about the reception I'll get from my dad.

Standing up, Eve concludes, "You're going to have a great time. I just know it."

"Uh-huh. Listen, if you need me, I can take the train into the city for a night here and there." The train will be easier if there's bad weather. And let's face it, spring in the Midwest could mean anything from a tornado to a snowstorm.

"We won't need you," she assures me.

"But if you do …" I don't have a chance to say anything more because my cellphone rings. Looking at the screen, I see that it's my friend, Noah. I answer his call with, "Hey, buddy. How's it going?"

Not bothering with pleasantries, he says, "I found you a place to stay."

"Thank goodness." The last thing I want to do is stay at home.

"Lorelai is going to let you crash at my parents' house with her."

I grimace thinking about my friend's freckly-faced, rusty-haired little sister. I would have been a moron not to have noticed how she was always hanging around when I was at Noah's house. While I suppose it was flattering, it was also low-key irritating. "Are you sure that's a good idea?" I'm only semi-teasing.

Noah scoffs. "Lorelai is twenty-eight years old, Luke. I guarantee she's not still holding a torch for you."

"Good. I mean, you know, it was kind of intense there for a while." I cite the time she proposed to me when she was in the sixth grade. She even created a PowerPoint presentation for why it would behoove me to wait for her.

Grunting, he says, "Her mind is currently elsewhere." He pauses for a moment before adding, "Lorelai and her boyfriend just broke up. She's pretty shattered."

"That's too bad." Although, I'm secretly happy her thoughts won't be on her past infatuation with me. I suppose it's kind of egocentric of me to assume she'd still be interested, and I suddenly feel like a real heel.

"You might try being extra nice to her," Noah suggests. "I promise it won't hurt your tough guy image."

"What tough guy image?" I demand.

"Aren't you touted as the most challenging chef in Chicago?" He clarifies, "At least according to *Chicago* magazine."

"There's a difference between being discerning and being difficult."

Noah laughs. "Call it whatever you want, just be nice to Lorelai. Oh, and don't tell her that I told you about her breakup. She's got this thing about people pitying her."

"Why would I say anything?" If I have my way, I won't be spending any time with her. I'll just sneak in and out and keep to myself.

"Things have a way of coming up and I promised her I wouldn't tell anyone."

"Don't worry about me. I'm going to have enough on my mind."

"You nervous about seeing your dad?" he asks.

"Obviously. But more than that, I'm worried about working at

Pop's without him knowing. There's no telling how he'll react if he finds out."

Instead of addressing my concerns, Noah decides, "I think it's a good thing you're going home. It's time." I love how no one seems to comprehend the level of anxiety I'm feeling. All they think is that it's time I make things right with my dad. But I didn't cause our rift. He's the one who refused to come to my graduation from culinary school. He's the one who thought my future was up to him, not me. In fact, as soon as I told him I'd taken a job in the city, he started acting like I wasn't even his son anymore. Things have only gotten worse since then.

"So, I just go to your house when I get to town?"

"Yeah. Lorelai works at the Elk Lake Lodge in the gift shop but she's off tomorrow and the next day."

"I've heard that place is doing gangbuster business," I tell him. "I'd like to check out their restaurant while I'm there."

"I'm sure Lor can help you get a good table."

"You don't think I could manage that on my own?" I snort. "Being a James Beard Award-winning chef does have its perks."

"I thought you liked to keep your anonymity. You know, not wanting everyone to bow to you so you get to see what it's really like to eat at other restaurants."

He's got a point. When fellow chefs find out I'm dining at their establishments, they tend to go overboard. And I do like to see how their average guest is treated. "Maybe you can come home for a weekend while I'm there and we can go together."

"I have plans to take the team to first place this year, which is going to mean constant work. I won't be able to get time off until school ends."

"Good luck with that," I tell him. My friend is nothing if not driven to have the top-ranking team in Illinois. With his work ethic, I know that's only a matter of time.

"We don't need luck. We just have to run our butts off. I swear every year these kids get lazier."

"You sound like an old man," I tell him. "It wasn't that long ago *you* were the one playing high school ball."

"It's been long enough to know that kids today expect their wins without putting in the effort. We knew what it took, and we put in the time."

"Okay, grandpa," I joke. "I need to get going and tie up business here before I leave tomorrow. Thanks for finding me a place to rest my head."

"No problem," he says. "Keep in mind that Lorelai wants to open her own bed and breakfast someday. I bet she'd love any tips you might have."

"I don't know anything about running a B & B."

"No, but you know something about cooking. You could show her how to whip up some winning recipes that'll knock people's socks off."

"Maybe …" That idea doesn't seem at all appealing, but I don't want to come off as ungrateful. "I'll call you in a few days," I tell my friend.

"Good luck, Luke. You've got this."

I hope he's right because at this moment I don't feel the least bit certain things are going to go well. In fact, the only reason I'm going back to Elk Lake is because my mom begged me to. She dropped a guilt bomb the likes of which I didn't see coming. She told me that someday she and my dad would be dead and gone and then it would be too late to make things right.

My dad is only sixty-three, so while I don't expect that grim event to happen anytime soon, he did just fall off a roof. That alone might have been enough to usher him into the next world. I may not think it's my place to fix our relationship—and I don't—but it's clear he's not going to make the first move. If this feud of ours goes on much longer, we may never put things right.

Leaving stacks of papers all over my desk, I push my chair back and stand up. I close my eyes and take a deep breath. I can do this. I know that life isn't always easy, but if this works and my dad and I somehow find our way back to being friends, it will all be worth it.

The bottom line is that I love the old guy, and I miss him. If I have to eat a little crow, I guess that's just what I'll have to do.

CHAPTER THREE

LORELAI

My eyes pop open as soon as the alarm on my phone goes off. There's nothing quite as menacing as the opening strains of "Phantom of the Opera," which is the tune I've programmed to help me greet each new day. The haunting composition adds drama and helps compensate for the placidness of my existence. While I love my hometown, it doesn't exactly ooze excitement.

The first question I have after opening my eyes is *Why is it still dark out*? I never wake up this early. Or is it late? Did I take an afternoon nap? Looking at the clock, I discover it's five a.m. It takes several more seconds to figure out what day it is, and I'm more confused than ever when I realize it's my day off. That's when it hits me: Luke Phillips is coming back to Elk Lake today and he's staying at my house!

Jumping out of bed, I hurry to run a brush through my hair before tying a do-rag around the fiery-colored mass. It's been ages since I last cleaned, and I'm bound to stir up a storm of dust. With all the work I have ahead of me, I'm not sure I'll have a chance to shower before Luke comes, and I want to look my best when he sees me after so many years.

I don't bother getting dressed before tearing down the stairs. As soon as I hit the landing, I scan the living room to assess the damage. It's not messy as much as it is dingy. My first stop is the kitchen where I put on a pot of extra-strong coffee before gathering my cleaning supplies.

Once the Italian roast comes down, I pound a cup back before retracing my steps to the living room. If this were my house, instead of my parents', I would decorate very differently. As in, less traditionally and with a brighter, more modern flare.

Picking up old family photos, I run my feather duster over them. They're still in the wooden picture frames they were first put into many years ago. I gave my parents a digital photo frame one year for Christmas thinking they'd like a wider variety of memories flashing before them. After several months of not seeing it, I offered to set it up for them. My mother hemmed and hawed and tried to change the subject several times before finally confessing she had given it to charity. That's when I had to accept my parents were happy being trapped in the last century and were not looking to embrace anything new.

I make quick work of the living room and get everything done except for the fireplace. If it were up to me, I would replace the old wood-burning element with a nice gas insert so I didn't have ashes to clean up. But again, my parents like things the way they've always been. Which means I have a messy job ahead of me. I decide to put that chore off until I'm done with more important things, like cleaning the bathrooms and figuring out which bedroom to put Luke in.

If he were a paying client, I'd set him up in my parents' room, but those quarters are currently being used by me. Even though I'm thrilled Luke is going to stay here, I'm not motivated to make the effort of hauling all my stuff out of my current digs. That leaves either Noah's old room—which still sports a pair of bunk beds along with the faded aroma of a teenage boy—or mine, which has a queen-size bed. I decide that regardless of the frilly pink décor and Spice Girls posters, a grown man would appreciate something more than a twin-sized mattress—especially a man as tall as Luke.

After climbing the stairs, I open the door to my room, and I'm immediately filled with the comforting familiarity of my early years. I've thought about redecorating now that I'm an adult but being that I spend as much time living in my parents' room—when they're in Florida—as I do here, I haven't quite pulled the trigger. Also, I'm twenty-eight, and even though I tell Noah there's nothing wrong with me still living at home, I have started to wonder how much longer I'll be here.

Once again, I let my feather duster take flight and when it gets to the posters, I perform a ritual from my teenage years. I swipe it across Mel B's face and sing, "I tell you what I want, Luke Phillips. I wanna, I wanna, I wanna, I wanna go out on a date with you!"

I'm so busy jamming around my room that I jump when the doorbell rings. It can't even be eight o'clock so I have no idea who it is. I know it's not Luke because he won't be here until ten. That leaves old Mrs. Bing from next door.

My bluish-haired neighbor isn't generally a bother, but ever since her husband went into the nursing home, she regularly stops by when she needs a jar opened or a spider killed. One time she told me that our weeds were growing out of control and kindly offered to send her gardener over. I let her do that once but then she hit me with a bill for a hundred and fifty dollars. Now we all just live with the weeds.

I run down the stairs with the Spice Girls still ringing in my head, and apparently out of my mouth because as I swing open the door, I practically shout, "If you wannabe my lover …" And that's when I realize Mrs. Bing isn't my guest.

All six-foot two inches of Luke Phillips is standing in front of me, and man, does he look good. It's March in Wisconsin so he's dressed for winter in a bomber jacket and wool scarf. Nicely fitted jeans showcase every gorgeous inch of his long legs.

I know I should say something to him, but my mouth pools

with so much saliva that if I don't swallow it soon, I'm liable to drool on the man. *Swallow your spit, girl.*

Once I manage that monumental, and embarrassingly audible, task, I blurt out, "Hey … Hello … Hi there!" Oh yeah, I'm a real orator.

"Hi." Luke's beanie-covered head tips to the side. His gorgeous brown eyes narrow like he's inspecting a moldy piece of cheese. "I'm looking for Lorelai Riley."

This is my chance to tell him she's not here and that he should come back at ten when he was supposed to arrive, but my synapses aren't firing. That must be why I throw my arms into the air and practically shout at him, "I'm Lorelai!"

Luke takes a step backward like he's going to make a run for it. Instead of fleeing, he moves his gaze from the top of my purple bandana all the way to my bare feet. This of course means he's aware I'm wearing a pink flowered flannel nightgown from Lanz of Salzburg. A favorite with grannies everywhere.

"Hi," he repeats. Yet he makes no move toward the door. In fact, there's no movement at all. It's like he's turned into a marble statue. He even stays put after I step back and gesture for him to come in.

Well, this is awkward. I start stammering, "I didn't expect you until ten. I mean, that's when Noah said you were coming so that's why I'm not dressed." He looks borderline terrified, so I hurry to add, "I was cleaning. Getting ready for you."

He lifts his foot like he's going to take a step forward, but the action is so slow it's like he's trying to push his way through a wall of frozen molasses. "I can find a hotel or something …"

"What? No! Come on in! You're staying here!" The image of Kathy Bates from that old movie *Misery* pops into my mind. From the look on Luke's face, he's thinking something similar. I want to assure him that I won't hobble him, chain him to the bed, and keep him as a hostage, but I think that might scare him more. Instead, I go with, "I'm going to close the door if you don't come in. My feet are getting cold."

That seems to startle him out of whatever haze he's in. "Sorry about that." He cautiously comes into the house which gives me a chance to check out the other side of him. Luke has always rocked a pair of jeans, and it's clear he still does. *Wowza!*

"I was just tidying up your room. Can I get you a cup of coffee while you wait? Maybe some breakfast?"

He looks more relaxed as he drops his bag next to the stairs. "I wouldn't mind both. I got an earlier start than I was expecting, and I didn't eat."

Leading the way to the kitchen, I once again tell him, "I didn't think you'd be here until ten. You must be excited to see your dad."

He ignores my comment, and says, "So, you still live in Elk Lake."

Not him, too? Prickles of anger stab at the back of my neck. "A lot of people who grew up here still live here. Is there something wrong with that?"

I turn around in time to see him grimace. *Good. He should feel bad for trying to make me feel bad.* "I didn't mean anything by it. I was just making small talk."

I suppose that's possible, so I let it go. "Noah says you opened your own restaurant." The truth is my brother didn't have to tell me anything. I've been cyber stalking Luke on and off for years. Less so when Michael and I were together, but even then, I checked out his social media at least bi-monthly. At the time I told myself it was out of curiosity.

"Capon," he tells me, though I obviously already know that.

"I thought it was pronounced Capone, like Al Capone?"

"Nope Cay-pon, like the chicken." Luke shrugs out of his jacket before sitting down at the counter. He teepees his fingers under his chin and focusses on me with a laser stare.

Hurrying to the cabinet, I grab the closest mug. It's one of the many art projects I've made at a local pottery place. It says, "I'd rather be in Barbados," and it's accompanied by a snowy scene I painted on the front. The thing about Wisconsin winters is they can last nine months. Around month five, I'm ready to walk to the nearest tropical island.

"How do you like your coffee?" I ask Luke as I pour the remains from the pot into his mug.

"One sugar."

Tearing open a little green packet, I ask, "Stevia okay?"

He shakes his head. "I prefer sugar."

My hand stops midair before pouring in the fake stuff. "I'm not sure I have any." I turn around and open the door to the pantry before stepping inside. Being so close to Luke after all these years is seriously messing with my equilibrium. I inhale deeply before looking at the shelves. That's where I find a five-pound pack of unopened granulated sugar which must have been purchased by my mom. I pull it off the shelf and carry it to the kitchen counter.

"Not much of a baker, huh?" he asks.

"Not really." Is he judging me for my lack of culinary pursuits?

Neither one of us says anything else while I prepare his coffee. When I put it in front of him, I watch while he sniffs it. His face contorts in such a way as to suggest he's not impressed. Then he takes a tentative sip before nearly spitting the contents across the room. "Gah!"

"Too hot?" I ask nervously.

His face wrinkles into a righteous scowl. "Too bitter. When did you brew this?"

So much for making a good impression. "Three hours ago," I tell him. "I made it extra strong so that I'd wake up faster." I hurry back to the coffee pot to start a new batch. While refilling the pitcher I ask, "Would you like a Toaster Strudel, or do you prefer frozen waffles?"

He releases a sound like I just offered him a choice between worm stroganoff or battery acid soup. "Why don't I make you breakfast while you go and get dressed?" he asks.

I should be grateful, but I'm not. Clearly, he thinks I'm a

subpar hostess who can't manage the smallest of tasks. *What's wrong with Toaster Strudel?* "I guess you can, if you want."

He stands up and shoos me out of the kitchen. "Come back in twenty minutes."

Walking out of the room I start to question why I spent so much of my life swooning after Luke Phillips. The man is rude. He should have drunk his coffee and eaten his Toaster Strudel like a normal person. After all, everyone knows that Toaster Strudel is the caviar of prepackaged breakfast treats.

As I climb the stairs, I remind myself that despite his surliness, Luke *is* the best eye candy I've seen in ages. I'm not sure that's enough to reinstate my childhood crush, but I suppose I'll make an effort to fix myself up just in case.

CHAPTER FOUR

LUKE

I haven't thought about Noah's little sister at all in the past decade. After reacquainting myself with her, I can see why that's the case. Not only is she quirky, but she's not super attractive. When she opened the front door, she looked like my great aunt Helen after she'd been on a bender for a week.

My mom's aunt has a penchant for making bathtub gin—and not to sell on the black market, either. She's too cheap to buy her own hooch, so she dug out an old family recipe that's been handed down since Prohibition. Being that she only has one bathroom, that means she only bathes after she's drained the tub for her martinis.

After Lorelai goes upstairs, I open the refrigerator door to check out the contents. It's full of takeout containers and little else. After some searching, I locate a stick of butter, four eggs that are stamped with an acceptable freshness date, and some cheddar cheese that looks like it's in decent enough shape. In the pantry, I grab olive oil, an onion, and a shaker of Herbs de Provence.

There's an empty skillet on the stove so I make quick work of heating up some oil and butter. I chop the onions and add them. As they crackle and pop, I crack the eggs into a bowl, and add a tablespoon of water, some salt, pepper, and the herbs. I whip everything into a froth before pouring the mixture over the onions. Then I finish making the fresh pot of coffee that Lorelai started.

Looking at the clock, I discover I'll have plenty of time to eat before visiting hours start at the hospital. I told my mom I'd meet her there at ten, which is probably why Noah thought I was arriving in Elk Lake at that time.

After checking to make sure the eggs are nearly done, I sprinkle on some shredded cheese before turning off the burner and flipping the omelet over on itself to finish cooking. Then I walk out of the room to call for Lorelai. Turning the corner, I practically run into her. At least I think it's her. She looks nothing like she did the last time I saw her.

"Lorelai?" Her hair is out of its confines and the auburn waves hang long and shiny down her back. She's also changed out of her granny gown and put on some slim cut jeans with an oversized men's flannel shirt. She looks adorable.

"Were you expecting someone else?" She's clearly annoyed and I guess I can see why after how I behaved earlier.

"No, nope. No one else," I say. "You just look very different than you did."

She does not take this as a compliment. "Well, if you'd come at ten like you were supposed to, you would have never seen me like that." Pushing past me, she walks into the kitchen and begrudgingly adds, "It smells great in here."

"I made an omelet."

Walking across the room, she pulls out a frozen pastry from the package she put on the counter earlier, and announces, "That should go nicely with my Toaster Strudel." Ignoring my look of distaste, she adds, "You don't know what you're missing."

"I guess I'll just have to suffer," I tell her. It will be a dark day when I put any preservative-laden, mass-produced baked good into my mouth.

I pull two plates down from the cabinet. After dishing up the omelets, I refill my mug with a fresh cup of coffee and offer to do the same for Lorelai. She shakes her head. "I'd better stop while I'm ahead. I'm already more caffeinated than I usually am."

She sits down at the table on the chair across from mine. Her demeanor seems to thaw after I serve her breakfast. "Do you eat like this every day?"

I shrug my shoulders. "It's just eggs."

"It's an *omelet*," she says in awe. Then she picks up her fork and digs in. The groan of pleasure she releases feels like a punch to the gut. Noah's little sister should not look like she does, and she certainly shouldn't be making sounds like that. "So good …"

I suddenly have no appetite for my own food, so I sit and watch her enjoy hers. She's finished in seconds. "Do you want some more?"

Her eyes light up. "*Is* there more? I would love that!" I pick up her plate and slide mine in front of her. Realization hits, and she says, "I can't eat your breakfast."

"Go ahead," I assure her. "You're enjoying it more than I ever could." But as I say this, my stomach grumbles loudly.

A delightful pink blush washes over Lorelai's cheeks as she pushes my breakfast back in front of me. "You, eat. But if you want to, I'll let you make me breakfast tomorrow."

I'm not sure why that sounds like a seductive offer, but it does. "I'll stop at the store on the way home from the hospital and get supplies."

"Or you can tell me what to get and I'll pick it up. It's my day off and I've got some free time."

I chew the bite I just put into my mouth before swallowing. "The least I can do is contribute groceries." As an afterthought, I add, "I'd be happy to pay you for letting me stay here, as well."

She waves her hand in front of her. "Nonsense. You're like family. I mean, you and Noah are like brothers."

"Which would make you, what, my sister?" I tease.

Her expression shifts from light and carefree to something a bit darker. "I guess so."

"Tell me about life in Elk Lake," I say. I know Noah said Lorelai just broke up with her boyfriend, but other than that and learning that she works at the Elk Lake Lodge, I don't know anything else about her.

She shrugs. "It's pretty much the same as it's always been. Busy in the summer with the tourist trade, slower in the winter. Although, that's changing now that the lodge has opened." She explains, "Heath and Trina have added a lot of fun attractions. We have a great tobogganing hill, and there's snowmobiling, and cross-country skiing …"

"It sounds like you enjoy working there." Her blue eyes sparkle enchantingly. *How did I ever think she was plain?*

"I do! I love my boss, and I really like meeting all the new people who come there to stay."

"Do you ever think of opening your own gift shop?" I ask her.

I'm not sure why but my question seems to annoy her. "I don't need to open my own shop to be happy."

I feel like I might've ruined our brief truce. "Good for you," I tell her. "I've found that owning my own restaurant has been harder than I thought it would be. I'm so busy doing all the stuff to keep everything going, I'm not in the kitchen as much as I'd like."

"You can cook for me anytime you want." Standing up, she walks across the room and opens a drawer. Then she pulls out a ring of keys. Bringing them over, she puts them on the counter. "There's one for the dead bolt and one for the doorknob. Feel free to come and go as you please."

"Thank you, Lorelai. I appreciate your hospitality.'

She stares at me for a long minute before finally opening her mouth. "Welcome home, Luke. It's nice to have you back." She walks out of the kitchen without saying another word.

Her welcoming me home feels good; it feels right. Even

though Elk Lake hasn't felt like it in the last several years, it *is* my home. All my best memories are from here.

When I finished high school, I went to the University of Wisconsin on a football scholarship. I majored in business. While there were conversations about what I would do with my degree, my parents didn't expect me to come back to Elk Lake.

After graduation, I worked in Chicago for a year, but I didn't love my job. Part of me thought fulfillment might come if I stuck it out, but a bigger part of me wanted to be excited about my career right away.

During that year, I worked sixty- and seventy-hour weeks, so I ate out a lot. That was when I learned to love food that was different from what I'd grown up with. I was always a fan of the stuff my dad made, but I learned to enjoy more high-end and exotic fare, and I was hooked.

One night I was invited to dine out with the president of my company. I was one of fifteen guests, so I wasn't responsible for holding up much of the conversation. As a result, I spent a lot of that meal looking around the restaurant. I began noticing the differences between my dad's diner and fine dining. That was the night I started to fantasize about going to culinary school.

For the next month I ate at every nice restaurant I could find, whether I could afford to or not. I decided that I was young enough that if I didn't like culinary school, I could always go back to finance. But if I did like it then I would be giving myself a fabulous opportunity. An opportunity to love my career.

My parents weren't quite sure how to react to the news that I was quitting my job and going back to school. They always wanted more for me than to be chained to a restaurant like they'd been. They wanted me to have normal hours and holidays that weren't filled with other people's celebrations while mine were put on hold. But then my dad got it into his head that I would come home and work with him after graduation, and he was all in.

I didn't tell him that I wanted to own my own place in the city.

I figured I'd let him enjoy the fantasy of what he envisioned. I just didn't realize that was the only outcome he was going to be okay with. As a result, we've lost a lot of years together. Even though I can't get that time back, I can certainly work toward not losing any more.

CHAPTER FIVE

LORELAI

My stomach feels like a herd of butterflies has invaded it. Scratch that. Whatever is going on in my gut is nothing as innocuous as butterflies. I'm hosting a vulture convention. Great big birds of prey are pecking at my insides. How am I going to share my house with Luke Phillips and still keep my sanity? The long and short of it is that I'm probably not.

I grab my car keys and head outside where I climb into my newer/old Volvo. Unlike my high school ride, which was twenty years old when it became mine, this one was only ten. After getting in, I blast the heat and sit there for five minutes while the frost melts off the windshield. I have no idea where I'm going, I just know that I can't be in the same house as Luke. Not without throwing myself at him and begging him to marry me and cook for me for the rest of my days. That was one crazy good omelet.

Pulling out of the driveway, I point the car in the direction of downtown. Most people I know are at work so there's no sense in calling anyone. The good news is that my best friend from high school works at Rosemary's on Main Street. Allie came home after her marriage ended. She also lives with her parents and is in the throes of trying to figure out what she's going to do next. She's only been back for a couple of months so I'm sure it's going to be awhile before she knows.

I park the car across the street from Elk Lake's oldest and best bakery. Even though I just ate a delicious breakfast, I immediately start to salivate for a blueberry scone. The bell rings as I walk through the front door and I spot Teddy Helms, movie star extraordinaire and husband to Faith Helms, the owner of the bakery.

Teddy raises a hand in the air when he sees me. "Lorelai, good morning!"

"Hey, Teddy. How's Faith? How are the twins?"

He smiles at my bringing up his favorite subject in the world. "They're at toddler ballet."

A smile spreads across my face. I remember hearing that Faith and Teddy were told they were going to have a boy and a girl, so they were surprised when they wound up with two daughters. "Are they even two yet?"

He shakes his head. "Not quite. I know what you're thinking. What could they be learning in ballet class at that age?" I don't bother to confirm that's exactly what I'm thinking because he continues, "I'm pretty sure Faith takes them to show off the dance wear she's bought for them. They're the most adorable things you've ever seen." His eyes twinkle like every father in love with his children.

"I'd love to see a picture sometime," I tell him. I want a family someday, too, but at the rate I'm going, I'm not sure that's going to happen. Elk Lake is not exactly overrun with eligible bachelors. Although, Teddy and Faith met right here in the bakery, so it's not unheard of that love can be found in a small Wisconsin town.

Teddy pulls out his phone and hands it across the counter. "Keep swiping until you run out of pictures."

I'm so enraptured by the images of Teddy and Faith's family that I hear my friend before I see her. "If she does that, she'll be here for a month."

Looking up, I smile at Allie. She's gorgeous as ever with her wavy brown hair and green eyes. Yet there's a quality about her that makes her seem like a skittish cat, which is not something she had when she was younger.

My friend hasn't gone into much detail regarding her ex, but I've gotten the impression he was not a nice man. I never met him because Allie and I lost touch during college. It wasn't until she moved home that we resumed our friendship.

Teddy reaches for his phone. "I won't bore you any more for now, but all you have to do is ask and I'll show you the latest." Smiling toward me and then Allie, he says, "Allie, I'm going to go meet Faith and the girls. Are you going to be okay here alone?"

She nods. "I'll be fine until the lunch rush. Abigail will be coming in to help around eleven."

I shake my head as Teddy walks out the front door. "Who would have ever thought we'd be talking to Teddy Helms like he was a normal guy?"

Allie laughs. "I know, right?"

"It gives me hope that some fabulous man will walk into town someday and sweep me off my feet." Luke Phillips' face immediately pops into my head. "Can you take a break?" I ask her. "I have something to tell you."

Allie looks around at the empty bakery and replies, "No problem. Can I get you something to eat first?"

"I'd love a blueberry scone if you have any left." While she goes to the counter to grab my order, I sit down at a nearby table.

Waving off the five I try to hand her, Allie places my scone in front of me. "What's up?" she asks.

I inhale deeply before saying, "Luke Phillips."

Her brow furrows slightly before recognition hits. "Your brother's best friend from high school?"

"He's back in Elk Lake."

"Why?" she asks, sounding like coming home is the worst thing she can imagine. Although I'm sure that in her case, it kind of feels that way—like she's going backward instead of moving forward.

"His dad fell off a roof."

"That's terrible! Is he okay?"

I tell my friend everything I know about Luke's dad before sharing more interesting personal news. "He's staying at my house."

"Ex-squeeze me?" I giggle at her usage of our old middle school vernacular.

"Yup. He and his dad are on the outs, so he doesn't want to stay with his parents. Noah asked if he could crash at our parents' with me."

Allie blushes when she hears my brother's name. As much as I used to crush on Luke, she felt similarly about Noah. But instead of asking about him, she wants to know, "Is Luke still single?"

"According to every article I've ever read about him, he rarely dates. Although Noah did say he just broke up with someone, which apparently never hit the papers." Because if it had, I would have most definitely seen it.

Allie's eyebrows arch so high they nearly reach her hairline. "Is he still as gorgeous as ever?"

I release a long, slow sigh as I answer, "Even though I haven't seen him in years, I practically jumped into his arms when he showed up this morning."

She looks from the right to the left like she's afraid someone is eavesdropping. When she sees that the coast is clear, she leans in conspiratorially and asks, "Did he seem interested?"

I laugh aloud. "I was wearing a purple bandana on my head and an old flannel night gown that practically buttoned to my chin. I looked like some kind of gangster nun."

Cringing, she accurately guesses, "So, no?"

"He seemed mildly less repulsed after I changed. He even made me breakfast," I tell her.

Her eyes brighten with interest. "A man who cooks breakfast … That's a novel thought." Once again, I assume Allie's husband was a real piece of work. Yet she's made it clear she doesn't want to talk about him, so I don't pry.

"He made me an omelet. It was amazing!"

"When are you going to see him again?"

"I don't know. He's here to spend time with his family." I almost tell her he's going to cook at Pop's, but I remember Noah's warning. "I told him to come and go like he would at his own house, but I am hoping to see him at least once a day." And if I know me, I will. But only because I'll sit by the front door if I have to so I can welcome him home.

"Girl, you have to keep me posted. In fact, you should invite me over some night so I can catch a glimpse of him for myself."

"Done," I tell her. "Now, what do you have going on other than work today?"

She rests her elbows on the table with her hands under her chin. "I'm here until three and then I've got nothing."

"You want to go to Pop's for dinner with me? I've been craving a cheeseburger lately." *And who knows, maybe we'll see Luke there.*

"That sounds great. My parents are leaving next week to go on a cruise and they're busy packing. They have stuff all over the house." She rolls her eyes. "They asked me to go with them."

"You totally should!" I say excitedly. "Get out of the cold and put on a bikini, girl. You'd have a blast!"

"It's from Quebec to Boston." Rolling her eyes, she adds, "It's a seniors' cruise."

I involuntarily shiver. "Why are they doing that? It's going to be cold." The only place anyone should cruise in March is the Mediterranean.

"The cruise line is hosting a pickleball tournament that my parents are all gung-ho about."

I swallow the last bite of scone before saying, "You can play pickleball at home. Why would you waste a cruise on that?"

Allie shakes her head. "If I knew why people made the choices they did, I'd have put my life savings into Beanie Babies back when that meant something. All I know is that I'm looking forward to ten days without anyone asking what my plans are for the future. Why can't people just let you figure things out for yourself?"

I push my chair back and cross my legs. "Family is the worst." I'm not talking about her parents, either. I'm talking about my brother and his impression that I'm wasting my life living in Elk Lake.

"We should have cocktails with dinner tonight," Allie decides.

"I'm in." On that note, I stand up and give my friend a tight hug. Then I tell her, "We're both young. We're going to figure everything out in our own time."

"Or not." She sounds like she couldn't care less either way.

"No matter what, we have each other, okay? We're not going to let the doubters doubt and we're not going to let our families push us. We're going to take life one day at a time."

"And we're going to drink lemon drops and eat cheeseburgers," she reminds me.

"Absolutely!"

As I walk out of Rosemary's, I wonder what would have happened had I moved back to Madison after Michael and I broke up. The reason I didn't is because most of our friends were his friends from work and I feared that I'd have to restart my life from scratch. If I was going to do that, why would I do it in a city that I only moved to because my boyfriend's job was there?

I'm home now, and I like being here. So what if there's a tiny failure to launch. I'll do that when I'm good and ready and no one is going to make me doubt myself. *You hear that Noah? I'm talking to you!*

CHAPTER SIX

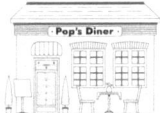

LUKE

Sitting in the hospital parking lot feels a lot like waiting to go into the dentist's office to have all my teeth pulled. I know that sounds extreme, but that's how unsettled I currently am. While my mom will be happy to see me, I have no idea how my dad is going to react.

I turn off the car as soon as the Hosier song I'm listening to ends. That guy is a genius when it comes to singing about everyday life. I wonder if he could write a hit about my situation. He could call it something poetic like, "Paternal Disappointment."

Getting out of my car, I walk determinedly into the hospital. I'm a thirty-two-year-old man for Pete's sake, not some uncertain kid with no life experience. I sternly order myself to pull it together while stopping at the information counter to get my dad's room number. I consider whether I should also go into the gift shop to get him some flowers, but ultimately decide he wouldn't care one way or another, so I don't bother.

I take the elevator to the third floor and then follow the signs to room 308. My heart is racing a million miles an hour. My mother came alone to my restaurant opening two years ago and I haven't seen her since. I haven't laid eyes on my dad in closer to four years. Growing up, there was no sign that anything could or would ever divide my family, which makes the whole situation hard to wrap my head around, especially when, oddly, I'm the one being blamed.

With a deep breath, I call on a supernatural force to push me through the door before I lose my courage and run in the other direction. It turns out that force isn't paranormal, it's human. "You must be John's son," I hear a voice over my shoulder say. "Your mother said you were on your way."

I turn and greet a man in his sixties. He's wearing a white coat with a stethoscope hanging around his neck. "Yes, hi," I tell him. "I'm Luke. You must be my dad's doctor."

He stretches his hand in my direction. "Mark Butler. It's nice to meet you." He gestures for me to precede him through the door. He follows close enough behind that I have no choice but to keep moving.

My dad is lying on the only bed in the room. One leg and one arm are attached to a pulley system hanging above the bed. He looks like he's in the throes of some medieval torture. Luckily he's sleeping, so I don't say anything.

My mom, who is sitting at his side, looks up and sees me. Tears flood her eyes as she stands up and walks into my arms. In the two years since I've seen her, she's obviously become older, but there's a new frailness about her that I don't remember noticing before.

"Luke." She exhales my name like it's been on the tip of her tongue for months.

"Hey, Mom." I hold her close while asking, "How are you doing?"

I look over to make sure my dad is still sleeping. "I've been better," she says. "I swear to God, watching your dad's body fall past the picture window in the living room took ten years off my life."

"That had to be scary."

Dr. Butler steps closer to my mom. In a low voice he tells her, "We'll keep him in traction for a few days to make sure he stays aligned." He adds, "Landing with as much force as he did is a real shock to the system."

"Jeez," I whisper under my breath before asking, "Are there any other injuries?"

"He has a mild concussion," the doctor tells me. "We just let him go to sleep after keeping him up for several hours which is probably why he didn't wake up when he heard your voice. He's exhausted and his body is desperate for rest."

Personally, I'm grateful he didn't wake up, but I don't say that. "He'll probably sleep for a while then." Turning to my mom, I tell her, "Why don't I stay with him while you go home and catch a nap?"

Her expression brightens. "Do you think that will be okay, Dr. Butler? I mean, is there anything you need me here for?"

He shakes his head and smiles kindly. "Taking care of yourself is the best thing you can do. We'll keep an eye on your husband." Gesturing toward me, he adds, "Your son can give you a call if there are any updates."

Walking my mom out to the hall, I tell her, "Take as long as you want."

She looks uncertain. "I kind of wanted to be here when your dad sees that you've come home."

Attempting a joke, I say, "It's good he's in the hospital. That way if he has a heart attack, he'll get immediate help."

"Ha, ha," she says in such a way that suggests she doesn't find my comment funny. "Be gentle with him," she warns.

I'm not sure what she thinks I'm planning. "Why would I be anything else?"

"Your dad has not always had an easy life, Luke."

I don't think anyone *always* has it easy so I'm not sure what trauma she's referencing. I simply nod my head and smile, then watch as she walks down the hallway. Once she gets on the elevator, I turn around and head back into my father's room.

Dr. Butler returns my dad's chart to a hook at the end of his bed before saying, "Let the nurses know if you need anything." Once he reaches the door, he adds, "Your dad is lucky to be alive." Then he's gone.

I know my dad is lucky to be alive, and honestly that's the only reason I'm here. The very real chance that he might have died before we patched things up has hit me hard. I've spent the last several years feeling like he's responsible for our rift, so it's his obligation to fix it. But knowing I'm right would be cold comfort if we never made things right between us.

I sit and stare at my dad for what feels like hours, but according to the clock is only forty-five minutes. He starts to stir, and groans loudly while trying to roll over—a feat he obviously can't perform.

Opening his eyes, my dad recognizes his predicament before calling out to my mom, "Brenda! Get the nurse, please."

Standing up, I walk over to his bed. When he sees that it's me and not my mom, I say, "Hi, Dad."

"Luke. What are you doing here?" He does not sound happy.

I feel like crying, but I opt to use humor to diffuse the tension that's started to build like a budding wildfire. "I figured I'd come see you before you did something really stupid like taking up skydiving without a parachute."

Instead of appreciating my attempt at levity, he says, "I didn't die, so there was no need for you to come."

"Are you serious?" *What is his problem with me?* "Did you really think I wouldn't come home unless you were dead?"

He tries to shrug but fails. The guy is in traction, after all. "You haven't been back in a long time. Seems to me you don't care about us one way or the other."

"Dad," I start to say, although I really don't have any idea where to go from here. He knows why I haven't been home, but there doesn't seem to be any point in rehashing all of that now.

"Where's your mom?"

"She went home to take a nap. It sounds like she's been awake all night with you."

Grumbling, he says, "I'm hungry. Can you please tell the nurse I want breakfast."

Nodding my head, I assure him, "I'll ask her to bring something. Anything special?"

"Toast is fine," he says. "Maybe a grapefruit."

Instead of ringing the call button, I walk out of the room. All kinds of emotions are running through me, and I need a minute away from my dad to start to process them.

Not only am I mad at him, but I'm also hurt and confused. During my whole childhood, he talked about how he wanted me to realize all my dreams and how he wanted to help me in any way that he could. Then my dream changed and so did his willingness to support my choices. It boggles the mind.

Stopping by the nurses' station, I find a bearded man about my age typing into the computer. "Hi there. My dad is in three-oh-eight and he was hoping to get some breakfast."

The man turns and looks up. Recognition hits immediately. "Tony Hill?"

"Luke Phillips!" he says excitedly before standing up and wrapping his arms around me. "How are you, man? I was hoping I might see you when I saw your dad came in." Tony and I were good friends from kindergarten until our junior year of high school when his family moved a couple of towns over. It was me, him, and Noah. We ran track together, played basketball, and still managed to chase after all the girls. Yet, once he left town, we hardly ever saw each other. It's amazing how twenty miles feels more like two thousand when you're young.

"So, you became a nurse, huh?" I tease him. "Hoping to score a lot of women, I bet."

"You know me," he snorts before explaining, "I really wanted to go to med school, but I didn't want to take on the debt."

"You probably get more dates this way." While I know my

comment might sound sexist, I'm guessing there are still more female nurses than male.

He's quiet for a moment before saying, "I met my husband in nursing school." The halting pattern of his speech makes me think he's worried about how I'll receive this information. But honestly, I could not care less. I work in the restaurant industry in Chicago; half of my staff is gay.

"Congratulations," I tell him. "Have you been married long?"

His smile indicates obvious relief over my lack of a negative reaction. "Three years. We moved to Elk Lake two years ago when we adopted our daughter. I wanted to raise Raven in the town where I was happiest."

"I love that," I tell him. "We had a really good upbringing here, didn't we?"

"It was idyllic. Tim and I want our daughter to have the same experience."

"I'd love to meet your family sometime," I tell him sincerely.

"That would be really nice, Luke." He turns to type something into his computer and adds, "I just ordered your dad his breakfast." Then he writes something down on a notepad before pulling the sheet off. Handing it to me, he says, "My number. Let me know when you're free and we'll set something up."

"Let's meet up at Pop's some night," I tell him. "Dinner is on me." Little does he know I'll probably be cooking it first, but I'm sure he'll keep my secret if I ask.

Walking back into my dad's room, I announce, "You'll never guess who I ran into."

My dad looks at me like he does not give a flying fig so instead of telling him, I say, "Your breakfast is on the way."

Several moments pass before he asks, "Who did you run into?"

"Tony Hill," I tell him.

"Your buddy from high school? I haven't heard that name in a long time."

"Tony came back to Elk Lake to raise his daughter." I'm not

sure if it's worth mentioning that Tony is married to a man. I don't think my dad would care, but it seems that I don't know the man as well as I once thought I did.

"It's nice that he came home." My dad's normally deep brown eyes narrow and appear to turn nearly black. "It's refreshing that someone your age thinks enough of Elk Lake to want to stay here."

I am not going to start fighting with him today. Hopefully not even tomorrow. I want my dad to get better and I don't think riling him up is the way to accomplish that. Sitting down, I tell him, "The doctor says you'll be here for a few days. Are you in any pain?"

He tips his graying head toward the IV next to the bed. "Not since they hooked me up. I don't even feel like I'm in my body anymore."

"Comfortably numb, then?" I reference my dad's favorite Pink Floyd song.

"You could say that." He lets his eyes close again and takes a cat nap. He doesn't open them until his breakfast arrives and then he keeps busy eating, so he doesn't have to carry on a conversation with me. When he's done with his food, he tells me, "You can go now. I'll be fine until your mom gets back."

I've been dismissed. Standing up, I tell him, "I'll see you later then."

"Why?"

"Because I want to see you later." *Don't fight me, old man, I am not in the mood.*

"Suit yourself," he says.

At this rate, I can't see the light at the end of the tunnel for us, but being that I'm already in the tunnel, I might as well keep the course.

CHAPTER SEVEN

LORELAI

After leaving Rosemary's, I drive over to the market to pick up a few things. I know Luke said he was going to stop as well, but I don't expect him to buy all the food for the house. In addition to loading up my cart with necessities, I add a few extras. I saw an enticing recipe on social media for cinnamon rolls that I want to try out on Luke. It's a definite step up from Toaster Strudel and it starts out with a tube of biscuit dough, so I'm pretty sure that even I can't screw it up.

My next stop is the Yarn Barn. I go through their clearance bin at least twice a week hoping to get enough matching yarn for my baby blankets. When I can't get all of one kind, I settle for a bunch of different skeins, and I donate those blankets to the Humane Society. Stray dogs are not picky, and they are extraordinarily grateful.

On my way into my house with my purchases, I notice that Luke's bags are still at the foot of the stairs. I'm tempted to carry them up to my room for him, but I don't want him to think I'm overstepping. Even though I would normally consider that being a good hostess, my feelings for Luke leave me a bit conflicted and I don't trust my instincts.

Going upstairs, I stop at my room to make sure everything is in order for my guest's stay. The queen-size bed is covered in a frilly white duvet and decorated with piles of girly throw pillows. I take off the heart shaped one, the flower-shaped one, and the big red lips, which leaves the solid-colored pink square ones. Even though they're pastel, the whole setting seems much more man-friendly this way.

After putting the pillows under the bed, I pull two of my homemade Afghans out of the cupboard in case he gets cold. Then I gather some towels from the linen closet and place them on my dresser. The bathroom is right across the hall, but I don't want Luke wondering if the towels in there are for his use. While I'm in the closet, I grab a couple of scented candles that are still in the box. They're pine, which ought to give the room more of a masculine vibe.

Once I'm done creating the best guest room I can, considering what I've started with, I go into my walk-in closet. Inside, I take a box down from the top shelf before placing it on the floor. Sitting next to it, I lift off the lid and start to go through the contents.

I pull out a photo album from my thirteenth birthday party. The cover says "My Teenage Years." I feel the same thrill I did when my mom gave it to me. I was finally a teenager, which in my head somehow meant the gap between Luke's and my age had narrowed. Even though thirteen and seventeen were still a big distance, it felt light years closer than twelve and sixteen. That's what I told myself, anyway.

Opening the album, I'm greeted with a five by seven photo that causes me to shiver. My awkward phase didn't end until twelfth grade. I blame that on the fact that my teeth refused to straighten, and I needed braces until the middle of my senior year. Add to that the very real problem that some redheads have finding the right color palette. I grew out of being carroty red, but my complexion was still so pale that any kind of bright color made my skin look almost translucent. Too pale a shade washed me out completely. This left me wearing a lot of black, which subsequently made me look vampirish. And not in a cool *Twilight* kind of way either.

It wasn't until I went to college that my hair started to darken to a deep auburn. With that change came the confidence I needed to experiment with my makeup and clothing. By the time I was nineteen, I was a different person entirely. And while the girl I was in my younger years wasn't malformed or anything, the new me was finally appealing to the opposite sex.

Flipping through the pages of my thirteenth birthday party makes me sad for the girl I used to be. I always thought I was the perfect "before" picture from a *Seventeen* magazine makeover. The truth is I wasn't horrible looking, I was just uncomfortable in my own skin.

On the third page of the album is the photo I was looking for. Allie and I are sitting at the dining room table with my birthday cake in front of me. I'm wearing a sweater I made for myself. I was so certain that sewing a bunch of potholders together would look great, that it never occurred to me that I could be mistaken for a Romanian refugee from another century.

Behind us in the living room are Luke and my brother. They're laughing at something, and the upturned expression on Luke's face profile makes him look like a movie star. If you added up all the time I spent staring at this picture during my teen years, it would probably account for an entire month of my life. Thirty-one days, seven hundred and forty-four hours, forty-four thousand, six hundred and forty minutes … I'd do the seconds but I'd need a calculator for that.

After putting the photo album down, I unearth my diary from the same year—the book I named "Luke" for obvious reasons.

Opening it to a random page, I read:

Dear Luke,
Today bit. Dillion McMillian (a stupid rhyming name

for a stupid boy) called me Big Red in class. Big Red. I'm
not even that tall! Then he asked me if I tasted like
cinnamon like the gum. My face burned so hot I thought
I was going to burst into flames. Of course, that made
things worse, because Dillion asked if I wanted him to
pour a bottle of water on me to put out the fire.

Boys suck monkey butts. I'm so sick of the immature
losers in the eighth grade I could spit. Why can't all boys
be like you?

I skip down a couple of entries and read:

Dear Luke,
You came over to our house today and stayed for
dinner! Mom made her tuna surprise and you and Noah
talked about your latest basketball game. You even looked
across the table at me and asked if I had a good day at
school. I didn't, but I told you it was fine. I didn't want
you to think I was a loser.

Then you and Noah started talking about some girl
in your class and I got so mad I wanted to kick her.
Why can't you see how much I like you? Why can't you
stop looking at other girls until I'm old enough for you?

My stomach twists into the all-too-familiar knot it was tied in
during my youth. I wish I could go back in time and be a different
person. I wish I could tell myself not to pine for a boy that far out
of my league. I wonder if I might have had a boyfriend in high
school had I not compared every guy to Luke and then found him
lacking. Having said that, I've mentioned my total absence of

fashion sense and lack of confidence, so the answer is probably still no. Whatever. I didn't want them anyway.

I wish someone would write a book for teenage girls that encourages them to believe in their own worth. But the sad truth is that even if such a manual existed, it would be hard getting young girls to accept their own power. *Why is that?*

I pick up my diary and move over to my bed. Climbing on top of the covers, I lay down and close my eyes. It's not so much that I need a nap as I'd like to discover the magic cure for adolescent angst. Instead of conjuring it, I fall into a deep sleep and don't wake up until nearly five.

On my second hard wakeup of the day, I wonder what I'm doing in my own bed. Then I remember unearthing my teenage memories. Luke Phillips, the heartthrob of my younger life, is staying in my house and once again wreaking havoc with my emotions.

I genuinely thought I was over this man years ago. And while I *have* cyber stalked him, I've chalked that more up to curiosity than any tangible interest. But now that he's here, I'm having second thoughts. It's not that I'm drawn to his personality—*who doesn't love Toaster Strudel?*—as much as I'm physically attracted to the guy. Tall, dark, and mega fine doesn't begin to cover his more subtle attributes. Those dimples! That butt!

Sitting up, I sternly tell myself to get a grip. Luke is a big-time chef with a big-time life in Chicago. I'm his best friend's little sister who still thinks knitting potholders is a great time. Not only are we in different leagues, but our lives are worlds apart. His is glamorous and mine is well—potholders.

I still want a Pop's cheeseburger, so I force myself to get up and get ready to meet Allie. As I brush my hair and change into a more stylish top, I think about my friend. I wish there were something I could do to make her happier. Allie's changed a lot since we were kids. She used to be vibrant and outgoing, funny and full of life. We weren't exactly part of the popular crowd, but everyone liked us—other than Dillion McMillian, that is. He was a turd through and through.

Allie got a scholarship to Michigan State which means she headed to a Big Ten school with all the opportunities that entailed. I was a B student, so I was going to the University of Wisconsin in Milwaukee. We stayed in touch the summer following our freshman year, but after that Allie remained at school and worked a summer job there instead of coming home.

I was thrilled when I ran into her at Rosemary's a couple of months ago. But I was also surprised by the change in her. Instead of being confident and daring, she's become introverted and borderline sad.

I vow that tonight I'm going to try to find out more about her story. I've been cautious up until now because she seems so jumpy anytime I ask a personal question. But we were once best friends which means that I have some rights. Tonight's mission not only includes hopefully seeing Luke again, but also finding out how I can help my friend.

CHAPTER EIGHT

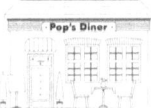

LUKE

After leaving the hospital, I drive around Elk Lake for a while. It's strange being home without it really feeling like home. It's like having someone else's memories, or like I've read a book and I'm relating to the main character without actually being him.

After thirty minutes or so, I've driven past the bait shop I used to supply worms for when I was in elementary school and made my way through downtown. As I pass Rosemary's, my mouth starts to water at the memory of their gingersnaps. When I was taking a pastry semester at culinary school, I based a recipe on them. I made a lemon tart with a gingersnap crust that has become a staple in every restaurant I've worked.

The old buildings along the brick streets look almost identical to how I remember them. I turn my car in the direction of the high school. Once I get there, I park in the senior parking lot before walking out onto the adjacent football field. School is in session but it's March so nobody is playing outdoor sports. I sit on the bleachers for an hour thinking about my past before my butt goes numb from the freezing cold metal.

Once I get back into my car, I sit for a few minutes to warm up.

Then I drive to my parents' house. I don't see my mom's car, so I'm guessing she's gone back to the hospital. I park in the driveway next to my dad's truck before getting out and sitting on a rocking chair at the far end of the front porch.

My family home looks like it always has—two stories with a wraparound porch and delightful dormer over the front door. The house is white, and the shutters are navy blue. The window boxes are bare, but in a few short months they will be overflowing with whatever flower catches my mom's fancy. If my memory serves, she'll probably use a variety of pink double impatiens. The whole scene will look like it could be featured in one of the calendars that highlight the most appealing domestic scenes.

Unfortunately, the family that once lived here so happily—mine—no longer fits that picture perfect image. Somehow, that's all thanks to me and the choices I've made in my life. Which is quite a burden, given that all I was doing was following my heart.

I stare out onto the front lawn and focus on the old oak tree. I used to climb that tree and swing from an old tire that hung from the largest branch. One summer I even tried to build a fort out there. I lost interest long before the project was complete, but I never stopped climbing that tree. Even in high school, I'd spend hours up there just thinking.

Sometimes I'd try to envision what I'd do when I grew up. Either that or I'd wonder where I was going to live. Would it be a big city or a smaller town like Elk Lake? I never saw myself in my hometown because I always dreamed of starting a brand-new chapter. I was drawn to a blank slate.

Living in Chicago has been great. I like being in a high rise right in the middle of all the action. I love having my favorite sports teams so close, and the food is incomparable. But even with all its pluses, I'm not a true Chicagoan. Natives of the Windy City are known for their love of a deep-dish pie and Chicago-style hotdogs. I'd take a good beer and fried cheese curds over both any day of the week.

With that thought in mind, I stand up and get back into my

car. Driving over to Pop's, I remember when my parents bought the place. Kelsey and I were both little. Up until that time, my dad worked the grill at another place in town. When Pop's location became available, my parents took out a second mortgage on our house so that they could buy it and make a go of owning their own place. It was the American dream through and through. It was also an insane amount of work. More days than not, Kels and I would go to the restaurant right after school and do our homework there while our parents fed the citizens of Elk Lake.

A myriad of sensations hit me as I was walking into Pop's, but the biggest one is a sense of coming home. It's the same traditional diner décor that I remember—red vinyl upholstered booths surrounding white Formica tabletops. The floor is a scarred pine. Nothing is in pristine condition, but that adds a sort of authenticity to the atmosphere. It says, "This is a great place to eat," without any of the pretense you find in restaurants where the owners feel like they have something to prove. Pop's has nothing to prove. It's withstood the test of time and as a result has earned its reputation as some of the best food in the area.

I don't know the girl standing at the hostess station, and I don't bother to introduce myself. Instead, I ask her, "Who's cooking today?"

She looks mildly affronted, in that teenage kind of way, before countering, "Who wants to know?"

"I'm a friend of the Phillips family." I don't know why I don't just tell her who I am, but if I were to guess, I'd say a small part of me is toying with the idea of running back to Chicago. My dad didn't welcome me with open arms, not that I really expected him to, but even so, I had hoped it would go better than it did.

"Have you heard about Mr. P?" I nod my head, so she says, "Jim is picking up the slack."

Jim Parnicky has been working at Pop's since it opened. He's as much a part of the landscape as my dad is. I'm halfway past her before asking, "Mind if I go back and talk to him?" I've got one foot inside the kitchen before I hear her say customers aren't allowed in the back.

Jim is standing at the grill cooking up a pile of onions in preparation for a busy night. He's as tall and thin as ever and his dark skin shines with beads of perspiration. Jim started as a dishwasher and has done every job that's needed doing here, even when that job wasn't his. Every restaurant needs at least one employee like him. Although he's always felt more like family than staff.

"Slim Jim!" I call out, which causes the man himself to turn around.

His eyes open widely in shock at seeing the prodigal son return. Dropping his spatula, he takes three long steps toward me, all the while opening his arms for me to make up the distance. "Luke, welcome home!" There's nothing but pure joy in his tone and it warms my heart. If only my dad could have greeted me the same way.

Stepping into his embrace, I tell him, "I'm here to help you out. You can't run this place single-handedly."

"Hallelujah!" he declares while patting my back. Then he steps back and stares at me. "Where have you been all this time?"

There's no sense in beating around the bush, so I tell him, "I've not exactly been welcome."

He grunts deeply. "Nonsense. Your daddy wants nothing more than for you to be here."

"Here, permanently," I clarify. "Not just to visit. And I've got a whole life waiting for me in Chicago."

Jim nods his chin up and down. "Things ain't always how they seem, boy."

"Maybe not, but I can't know how things are unless someone tells me. You want to do that?"

He shakes his head. "That's not my place, son. But I sure am glad to see you. I've been here since six this morning and I'd like to take a load off for a while."

"Why don't you take the night off?" I walk across the room and pick up an apron off the stack.

He shakes his head. "I'll just grab some lunch and then we can do the night together. You here for a while?"

"I'm planning to be," I reluctantly tell him. "At least until my dad is back on his feet. But I'd appreciate it if you didn't advertise my arrival. My mom thinks it's best if Dad doesn't know I'm working here." Rolling my eyes, I add, "She doesn't want him feeling indebted to me."

Jim's black eyes twinkle knowingly. "I'm guessing she doesn't want him to get his hopes up. Who are you gonna tell people you are?"

"Most people never give a second thought to the person who cooks their meals. If they ask, I'll just tell them my first name and let them know I'll only be here for a short time."

"What about the staff?"

"I didn't see anyone I recognized when I walked in, so I'll feed them the same story."

Jim flips a burger on the grill before slicing an entire beefsteak tomato and fanning it across a white dinner plate. "I'll get you up and running and then we can make a schedule between the two of us."

"You still eating all the tomatoes?" I tease him.

He simply smiles and drops the burger on his plate. "Check over the menu. We've added some new things and taken away some others. I don't imagine you'll have any trouble." Then he walks through the swinging door that leads to the dining room.

Being back in Pop's kitchen is a surreal experience. I worked here from the time I was in tenth grade through summers at college. I spent hundreds of hours right here chopping onions, washing dishes, and scrubbing down the stainless-steel counters. Those tasks led to me working the line and learning how to not only make an exceptional omelet, but the perfect burger, as well.

My history here is the reason I never wanted to work at Pop's as an adult. I interpreted my disinterest as thinking I had no interest in the restaurant business. But the truth is, I didn't want to churn out the same stuff day after day without change. Yet in retrospect, Pop's was the perfect start to becoming a world-class chef. In order to discover new flavor combinations, you have to be proficient in the basics.

My dad likes things to stay the same, but that's not who I am. Hopefully, I'll finally be able to get him to see that.

CHAPTER NINE

LORELAI

The dinner rush at Pop's is legendary, which is why Allie and I are meeting at five o'clock. It should pretty much just be us and whatever early bird seniors show up, which in Elk Lake could be a lot.

I changed into a pair of black pants and a fuzzy pink sweater before leaving the house. If I run into Luke, I don't want to look like I'm trying too hard, but I also want to make a nicer impression than I did the last two times he saw me today. The jeans and flannel were cute, but that nightgown sealed the deal that he'll never look at me with romantic interest.

Walking into the diner, I'm hit by a combination of delicious aromas. Seriously, if they could bottle this smell, people everywhere would stand in line for a month to buy it. No one can resist the sultry scent of french fries and beer batter, with underlying notes of hot fudge and toasted nuts. I preemptively wipe the corner of my mouth in case any slobber has escaped.

The girl standing by the hostess station looks at me with great disinterest. "Only one?"

"No," I tell her proudly. It's not like I don't ever eat by myself, but her tone suggests that's what she thinks. "I'm meeting a friend."

"Uh-huh." She picks up two menus and tries to sit me at a small table near the kitchen door. While I want to be close to Luke, if he's here, I'll have a better chance of seeing him from a more distant vantage point.

Gesturing toward the empty dining room, I tell her, "I would prefer to sit by the window."

She rolls her eyes and slows her speech like she's speaking to a foreign person with little grasp of the English language. "Those. Are. For. Four. People." Then she flashes the requisite number of fingers in case I didn't understand.

I look at her name tag before letting my tone state my displeasure. "There's no one in the restaurant, *Chloe*. I guarantee you that my friend and I will be gone before you need our table." I'm not generally nasty to people, but this girl is a real piece of work.

Her eyes narrow petulantly as she turns and walks in the direction I indicated. Then she slams the menus down. "Make sure of it," she says before walking back to the hostess stand.

I've got to wonder why Luke's dad hired a girl like that. There must be a hundred more pleasant teens looking for a job. For instance, when I was Chloe's age, I would have killed to have had a job at Pop's.

Sitting down, I flip over the menu until I find the thing I've been craving—a sirloin burger with sautéed mushrooms, onions, and swiss cheese. Yum!

A server about my age appears. The smile on her face more than makes up for the snotty hostess. "Hey, hon, can I get you a drink to start?" she asks.

"Two lemon drops, please. Straight up."

"You want that with sugar on the rim?"

"Absolutely." As she walks away, I warn myself to only have one drink. I'm not a big indulger of hard alcohol and I want to keep my wits about me in case Luke shows up.

I spot Allie as soon as she walks through the front door and immediately gesture for her to join me. The hostess doesn't even bother looking up from her cell phone. As my friend approaches, I notice that she has also changed clothes. "You look so cute!" I tell her while standing up and giving her a hug. She's wearing a red dress with a fitted bodice and a flared skirt.

When she pulls back, she does a small pirouette and declares, "I like dressing up. It's been a long time since I've worn any of my nicer clothes."

As soon as she takes her coat off and sits down, our server arrives with our drinks. Lifting my glass to my friend, I announce, "To us!"

Allie lifts her glass in return. "To finding the lives we were meant to have."

After we each take a small sip of our decadent cocktails, I decide this is the perfect entrée to what I want to talk to Allie about. "What life do you think you were meant to have?"

She seems caught off guard. Tipping her ear toward her shoulder like she's in deep thought, she finally says, "I guess I don't really know anymore."

"Are you happy?" I ask.

"There have been moments when I thought I was, but they didn't last."

After taking a substantial swig, I tell her, "Allie, you're skittish when it comes to talking about your ex-husband, so I haven't asked a lot of questions. I think it's time you tell me what happened."

Her eyebrows raise slightly. "I don't like talking about Brett."

"I still want to know about him." At this point, I start to worry she might stand up and walk out the door. In fact, for several moments she seems to be considering that very thing.

My friend finally picks up her drink and slams it back in one go before signaling the server for another. That's when I know she's planning on staying. She inhales deeply before announcing, "Brett and I met in business school. We both wanted the same things."

"Which were …" I prompt.

"We wanted a family and careers that would supply a significant income so that when our children arrived, I could take time off and stay home with them until they started school."

"You both had good jobs, right? I mean, I know you worked at a publishing house. That had to pay decent money. What did Brett do?"

"He was a day trader specializing in crypto currency."

"That sounds pretty profitable."

She nods her head. "We did fine financially."

"What was the problem then?"

The server arrives and delivers two more lemon drops. "Oh, I'm not …"

I'm about to tell her that I don't want another but Allie interrupts. "You're going to need it." Then she turns her attention to the server and asks for the beer batter fish with extra tartar sauce and coleslaw.

"I'd like the mushroom burger," I tell her. "With onion rings, please."

After our server leaves, I turn my attention back to Allie. "Why am I going to need another drink?"

She takes a moment to unroll her silverware from the confines of its paper napkin before laying it down in a proper setting. "Three years ago, Brett and I agreed to start trying for a family. It didn't go well."

"You couldn't get pregnant?" I ask.

She shakes her head. "Getting pregnant wasn't the problem. Keeping the baby was."

Oh, dear. I'm not quite sure what to say about that. I decide to go with, "How many times were you pregnant?"

"Three." *Poor Allie!*

"Do you know why you kept losing the pregnancies?"

"After the second, my doctor asked us to both get tested for any problems. I happily went in because I hoped they would find something we could fix. Brett did not."

"Because?"

"I thought it was because during that time we found out we were pregnant for the third time, and he thought there was no reason to. But then we miscarried again, and he told me he was sure he wasn't the problem."

"Because he's also a medical doctor?" I can't hide the disdain from my voice.

"More like because his precious ego couldn't handle thinking he might be responsible."

I finish my first drink with gusto, before starting my second. "So, what happened after the third time?"

"Brett declared that he wanted a family more than anything, and as much as he claimed to love me, he realized I wasn't up to the task." She practically growls the next part. "*Up to the task,* like I was some kind of paid employee."

My mouth hangs open like a mounted sea bass. I try to force myself to say something but really, what can I say? I ultimately go with, "He left you for that? What about adoption? What about fostering?"

"Brett would have never considered either of those things. He thought adoption made it look like there was something wrong with us. As far as fostering, there's no way he would have ever willingly helped raise a child who he considered from 'lesser' stock."

"Was he a Nazi?" I blurt this out a little louder than I'd planned to, but I'm seriously that horrified.

Allie smiles sadly. "He was just very particular."

"So, he walked out on you and left you to mourn the loss of three pregnancies by yourself?"

"That about sums it up."

As our food arrives, I take a minute to try to calm the red-hot anger pulsing through my veins. When the server leaves, I announce, "I'm not a violent person, but I'd be happy to donate if you want to hire a hit on him. Barring that, I know where to slip a knitting needle to take him off this planet."

Laughter erupts out of my friend, which is a wonderful sound, especially given the topic of our conversation. "You're a good friend, Lorelai. But I think our parting ways was for the best. I don't think Brett was the man for me. In fact, I'm pretty sure the universe was doing me a proper by getting rid of him."

I take a bite of onion ring, and chew it thoughtfully before asking, "If that's so, why are you always so sad? Like, seriously, Al, you've got no sparkle and that's the thing you've always been known for."

She smiles sorrowfully. "My doctor said that with every loss, my hormones went through the same shift as if I'd given birth. In addition, I'm mourning the loss of something I thought I really wanted to share with my husband." As though defending herself, she adds, "It's only been six months since my last miscarriage."

Shock does not begin to describe my reaction to hearing this. "He left you right after you lost your last pregnancy? What a dirt bag!"

"Three weeks after. He said it was better for both of us to just move on."

"Mother. Of. God. He was a monster!"

"Pretty much."

"What did you do? I mean, I know you came back to Elk Lake but that was three months ago. Where were you in the interim?"

"The day Brett walked out the door, I packed up all his things and donated them to a homeless shelter. Then I changed the locks, my phone number, and I quit my job."

"Amazing!" I marvel at her ability to think clearly enough to start sticking it to her loser ex.

"Then I took half the money out of our joint savings account, and I went to Europe."

"Seriously?"

"I took a first class vacation the likes of which only royalty go on." I take a giant bite of my burger and listen as she tells me, "I flew first class, I stayed in five-star hotels, and I ate solely at

Michelin-starred restaurants. I spent half of our nest egg in eight weeks."

"Allie, wow. I don't know what to say."

"I didn't want any of the money we'd saved together because the life we were planning wasn't going to happen. When I went back to Chicago, I found divorce papers that Brett had filed, so I signed them and moved out of our apartment. Luckily, we didn't own it, so there was no delay in walking away."

Morbid curiosity takes over. "Did you see him after that?"

She nods her head sharply. "I ran into him at our favorite restaurant. He was on a date."

"He'd started dating already?" How did Allie never see what a dirtbag this guy was?

My friend swallows the bite of fish in her mouth. "Apparently, he didn't wait until then. A woman from his office called me after he left and told me that I wasn't losing much. She said that she and Brett had been having an affair. He left her, too."

"She sounds like a piece of trash who got exactly what she deserved." I have no sympathy for women who fool around with married men. None.

Allie shifts in her seat. "I wasn't married to *her*. I was married to Brett. So, while I didn't condone what she did, he was the one I was mad at."

"I'm speechless."

We eat silently for several minutes. As much as I love the taste of my food, I find that I've lost my appetite. Meanwhile, Allie finishes her fish and orders two more drinks. It's a good thing I don't work tomorrow. Not only am I going to have to take an Uber home, but I'm sure I'll have a wicked headache in the morning.

When the server appears with our lemon drops, Allie orders a classic Pop's hot fudge sundae with two spoons. Then she asks me, "What happened with your breakup?"

"I think we just got bored with each other. Michael was kind of dry to begin with and one day I just looked at him and realized I didn't want a future with him. I wanted something else, I just didn't know what."

"Do you know now?"

I'm not sure I've ever put words to what I'm looking for, but suddenly I realize exactly what that is. "I want to feel an internal tornado when I'm with the man I love. I want him to surprise me and help me grow into a better person. I want passion."

"And you didn't have that with Michael?"

"Not really. We were only twenty-three when we started dating. He got a job offer in Madison when we were twenty-four. We probably should have broken up then, but I hoped things would get better." I continue to explain, "Once we moved, he kind of went his way and I stalled. I didn't have much of a social life outside of Michael's work friends. I just wasn't happy in any aspect of my life."

"Do you like being back in Elk Lake?" she asks in such a way that confirms she's not sold on this life.

"I love it," I tell her. "So many people are always in such a hurry to leave home, and if that's right for them, then good. But there are a lot of us who like living where we grew up. Don't get me wrong," I tell her. "I'm still not sure I'll stay here forever, but for now I'm happy."

At this point, it's possible she orders us a fourth martini. Either that or the first three really start to kick in. Every muscle in my body relaxes and my eyesight starts to blur around the edges. The bottom line is, I'm feeling no pain.

My gaze strays to the window behind the counter that leads into the kitchen, and I catch a glimpse of Luke. My stomach does a little flip.

I don't know him as an adult, but I figure there's no time like the present. I can't help but wonder if it's possible that our futures might be intertwined after all.

CHAPTER TEN

LUKE

Jim and I work in tandem like we've been doing this for years. He forms all the hamburger patties before sprinkling them with Worcestershire and steak sauce. I dust them with salt and garlic powder before putting them back in the refrigerator until we need them. Jim puts down the fry basket and I instinctually know when to lift it—which is never when the timer says it should be.

We hardly speak for the first two hours of service. We just move on automatic pilot. When things finally slow down, I tell him, "You need to get out of here and open your own place, Jim. You're too good to work for someone else."

He snort-laughs, "Son, I'm sixty-five years old. I have no desire to take on all the work needed to hang my own shingle."

"You should have done it years ago then. Why didn't you?"

He busies himself breaking apart wedges of iceberg lettuce. "I'm happy working for your dad. We don't all want to be the boss."

"What else do you have?" I belatedly realize my question might sound like I'm judging him, but he doesn't seem to notice or care.

"Luckily, my folks are both still around. I've got my garden and my dog."

"Did you ever want to get married?" I don't recall him ever being in a relationship, let alone a marriage.

Instead of answering, he tells me, "Get more onions on the grill. We're going to need them soon."

As I turn toward the island to start slicing, I glance out the opening between the kitchen and the dining room. That's when I make eye contact with Lorelai. By the number of empty martini glasses on her table, it looks like she and her friend are having a contest.

Lorelai's complexion turns pink, and I don't know if that's due to all the cocktails or her seeing me. I quickly avert my gaze and focus on getting the onions ready to sauté.

It's strange seeing my friend's sister after so many years. She's a grown woman now and nothing like the awkward girl I remember. When I went home this afternoon and saw her napping on her bed, I couldn't help myself from stopping and staring at her for a minute.

I remember people from my past at the age where they made the biggest impact on me. For instance, whenever I think about my grandparents, I remember them from when I was little. I knew them for years after that, but in my mind's eye, they are forever middle-aged.

Lorelai will always be in her early teens to me, and believe me when I say, that was a dicey stretch. She was constantly working on a new craft project that usually entailed yarn, or paint. Although there were also a lot of sequins there for a couple of years. I smile when an image of that pink and silver beret she bedazzled pops into my head. When the light hit it, it was positively blinding.

Looking at her across Pop's dining room, wearing a soft pink sweater and drinking martinis, really messes with how I've always thought about her—as an adolescent girl.

Turning around, I put the onions on the grill and get busy seasoning them. I've tossed them several times when the hostess from earlier today comes running into the kitchen. "Some lady just slipped and fell on her butt," she blurts out. "She says she's okay, but she sounds kind of drunk. What should I do?"

I untie my apron and put it on the counter. "I'll go check on her, Jim." Following the girl out to the dining room I find none other than Lorelai sitting on the floor by the front door. She's laughing like she just heard the best joke ever. What she's not doing is moving, and people are starting to step around her.

I extend a hand as I approach her. "How about some help up?"

She tips her head back and nearly shouts, "Come on down and join me!"

"I think you're drunk, Lorelai," I tell her, realizing what a cute drunk she is.

"I'm just happy."

She makes no move to take my hand, so I bend down and slide my arms under her before lifting her. She's dead weight. "Where's your friend?" I ask.

She eventually steadies on her feet. "Gone. She has work tomorrow. I stayed in case … you know …"

"You wanted to drink more?" I guess.

Her eyes narrow like she can't remember what she was going to say. "Absolutely not. I don't drink." *Uh-huh.*

"You can't drive like this," I tell her.

Pushing away from me, she says, "Of course I'm not going to drive like this. I called an Uber."

"We have Uber in Elk Lake?" For some reason, I'm surprised this little town has progressed that far.

"Psh, yeah." She sways slightly on her feet, so I take her by the elbow and lead her to the counter. Sitting her down on a round stool, I tell her, "You can wait here."

"I'm supposed to be outside," she says.

"That's not how Uber works. They text you when they arrive."

Her head lulls to the side. "It's not really Uber. It's just Kenny James driving people around town when they need a lift. He still has a flip phone, so he doesn't text."

That sounds more like Elk Lake. "I see. Well, then, why don't you call Kenny and tell him you have a ride. I'll take you home."

"But you're working!"

I hold up one finger to her before going back into the kitchen. "Jim, I'll be back in thirty. Noah's little sister tied one on and she needs a ride home."

I'm only gone for a minute or two, but by the time I get back to Lorelai, she's practically lying on the counter. Once again, I lift her like a rag doll. "Let's go, princess." I shuffle her out the front door toward my car that's parked a couple of buildings away.

After clicking the unlock button, I lean her against the back door while opening the passenger side for her. Then I help her inside. Getting behind the wheel, I can't help but think how embarrassed she's going to be tomorrow. We make the short drive in silence except for the occasional soft snores that come from the seat next to me.

When I get to Lorelai's house, I gently wake her. "Wake up sleepyhead."

Her eyes pop open and she looks at me with great concentration. "Did we just go to prom?"

Oh, boy, she's out of it. "We're coming home from Pop's," I tell her.

"Did we go there after prom?" She's so insistent on this prom thing, I realize the poor girl probably spent more time fantasizing about me than I knew.

"No prom," I tell her again. "You had one too many and you're drunk."

She sits up until her spine is rigid. "I rarely drink." She hurries to add, "A beer here and there, but that's all."

That certainly explains why she's such a lightweight and in the current state she's in. "You had more than beer tonight and it's gone to your head."

With a look of great confusion, Lorelai asks, "Are you home from college?"

"I'm home to help my dad in the restaurant," I tell her. "I'm out of college."

Ignoring my explanation, she closes her eyes and declares, "You took me to the prom. I always knew you would. My friends are going to be so jealous."

Getting out of the car, I walk over to the passenger side before opening the door and helping Noah's sister back onto her feet. I hope she doesn't remember any of this in the morning or she's never going to be able to look me in the eye again. Which could lead to a very uncomfortable stay at her house.

Lorelai leans against me as I walk her up the path. Taking my house key out of my pocket, I unlock the door and push it open. "Do you need help getting upstairs?"

She shoves her hands against my chest and playfully drawls, "I'm not gonna sleep with you." Then she puckers up her mouth and adds, "But I wouldn't mind a kiss. Maybe even a whole bunch of them."

Oh, brother. I lean in toward her and chastely give her a peck on her cheek, which causes her face to crunch up in consternation. "That's it? Huh. Kind of a letdown after dreaming about it since I was ten. Oh, well. You're still a very nice person."

Steering her toward the stairs, I gently push her from behind as she takes one step at a time. Once we reach the upstairs hall, I lead her to her bedroom door. "Do you need help getting into bed?"

Leaning against me, she says, "Wait until Allie hears that you tried to get me into bed." Then she slumps against me.

I carry Lorelai across the room before gently laying her on her duvet. Then I drape what I'm assuming is one of her homemade throws over her. I've got to say, she's certainly more talented in that department than I remember. Before I go, I find a bottle of Tylenol in the bathroom across the hall and leave it, along with a glass of water, on the nightstand next to her.

Lorelai is not going to feel well in the morning. Hopefully, she won't remember repeatedly propositioning me. She's a sweet kid. Scratch that, she's a nice woman, but I am here to fix things with my dad. I'm not here to complicate my life by getting involved with someone who lives two hours away from Chicago. And even if I were, it wouldn't be with my best friend's little sister.

CHAPTER ELEVEN

LORELAI

Rolling over in bed, I feel like I got hit by a truck. From the throbbing in my temples, I'm guessing it ran over my head. Looking at the clock, I discover it's only eleven p.m. As I sit up, a brutal wave of nausea overtakes me, so I throw the covers back and sprint across the hall. I get to the bathroom in the nick of time.

I feel a little bit better after throwing up but if I had to guess, I'm still pretty drunk. The last thing I remember is telling Allie that I absolutely do not need a third drink, especially as I only ate a couple bites of my burger. That's when I start to wonder how I got home. A flash of Luke and me in a car comes to mind, but I immediately know that must be a dream. I've been revisiting a recurring fantasy about him taking me to the prom. *OMG, Luke is back in Elk Lake and he's staying at my house!*

Staggering back to my room, I hurry to straighten the bedding so it's ready for him when he comes home. That's when I notice the glass of water and Tylenol at my bedside. Picking up the phone, I try to send a text to Allie, but I can't figure out where the send button is. Even though Allie got me drunk against my will, she's a good friend. Although, I suppose it wasn't really against my will as I took every sip of my own accord. Gentle reminder: no more lemon drops. *Ever.*

Grabbing the bottle of painkillers and the glass of water, I stagger down the hallway to my parents' room. Then I crawl into their bed. Even though I desperately want to remember what happened earlier, I need to sleep more.

I immediately fall back into the dream I was having about Luke and me going to prom. The theme is inexplicably *Jaws* and the school gym is decorated with posters of sharks with their mouths hanging open menacingly. The repetitive thumping of the theme song plays as it builds a tension that doesn't quite fit the setting.

Looking down, I see that my dress is made from the same rubber material they use for wetsuits, and I have a snorkel draped around my neck. This is so weird that I make a mental note to complain to the prom committee.

Looking around the gym, I spot Luke standing by the punch-bowl. He pulls a long straw out of his suit pocket and puts it into the bowl before taking a drink. I hope everyone doesn't do that. Talk about unhygienic. Yet, I don't mind that he does it because let's face it, if I have my way, I'm gonna suck the lips right off that boy later tonight.

Luke sees me and raises his hand in a wave before walking in my direction. I immediately throw my shoulders back, hoping this stupid dress shows off my curves to their best advantage. I didn't develop until late and hope against hope that I at least remembered to stuff my bra. That's when Luke reaches me, but instead of stopping, he walks right by.

I turn around and call out to him, but he just keeps going until he reaches a shark wearing a tiara and pink tutu. They dance to "Something from Nothing" by the Foo Fighters while I stare on, wondering what in the heck is happening.

That dream leads to one where I'm skydiving in a wedding dress. I don't realize until after I jump out of the plane that I'm not wearing a parachute. But dreams are crazy and for some reason that doesn't scare me. Instead, I start posing toward an invisible camera like I'm taking pictures for some extreme social media page.

I fall for what feels like hours before I finally hit the ground. But instead of the impact killing me, it feels like I land on another person. My target shouts, "What in the hell?" Then my body is thrown to the side.

Somewhere in the fog of this nightmare, I hear a voice yell, "What are you doing in my bed?" It sounds alarmingly like Luke. But it can't be his because he's sleeping in my room.

Cracking my eyes open the barest of slits, I see a shadowing figure sitting upright next to me. In response I let out a blood curdling scream.

The figure jumps out of bed and shouts back, "Why are you screaming? What are you doing in here?"

I lean over and turn on the bedside lamp which is when I discover Luke standing above me wearing only his boxer shorts. "What are *you* doing here?" I demand, while counting the indentations of his six-pack. Make that eight. *Nice.*

"I was trying to sleep."

"In *my* bed?" I'm not mad, just really confused.

"No, in your parents' bed. Noah's room kind of stunk, so I figured this is where you wanted me."

"*I* sleep in here while my parents are in Florida," I inform him.

Now he looks confused. "You were sleeping in your room earlier this afternoon."

He saw that, huh? "I was getting my room ready for you, and I must have dozed off." That sounds lame, even to my intoxicated ears.

"So, you sleep in here and not in your own room?" The poor guy is really agitated.

Nodding my head causes my eyeballs to throb, but I do it anyway.

Luke doesn't say anything else. He simply turns around and walks out the door. I'm too embarrassed to go after him. I'll apologize for the mix-up in the morning. Maybe I'll even make those canned biscuit cinnamon rolls for him.

Once my heart rate slows down from the shock of finding Luke in bed with me, I turn out the light and go back to sleep. Happily, I don't remember those dreams.

The next thing I know, there's sunlight peeking through the blinds. It's directly in my eyes so I turn on my other side. Looking at my phone I discover it's eight o'clock. That's when, slowly but surely, memories creep back into my consciousness. Holy crow, Luke and I were in bed together!

Mortification washes over me and heats up my face to what feels like a bad sunburn. Luke saw me sleeping in my old room which made him think my parents' room was his. This is bad. Really bad. The guy would have to be stupid not to remember my stalker-like ways from my early teen years. He probably thought I did this on purpose. Yet I was the first one in bed—at least I think I was— so this is really his fault. That realization makes me feel a lot better.

Getting out of bed, I see that I'm still in the clothes I wore last night. The stabbing pain in my temples helps me to discern that I had too much to drink.

Going into the bathroom, I take off my clothes and get into a hot shower. The pelting water on my head helps and hurts at the same time. While lathering my hair with my favorite apple scented shampoo, I try to put all the pieces of last night together.

I think about Allie and me eating at Pop's. I recall her telling me about her husband which causes my fists to clench. She is so much better without him. I recollect losing my appetite, and then I remember the lemon drops. *That's* why my head hurts so badly.

I try to figure out how I got home, but the only thing that comes to mind is the dream I had about Luke and me going to prom together. I make a mental note to call Allie later to see if she can fill in the gaps for me.

After getting out of the shower, I dry off before putting on a comfy pair of sweats and a hoodie. I have a choice to make. I can either go downstairs and act like nothing happened last night, or I can stay up here until I'm sure Luke has left for the day.

Walking to the bedroom door, I open it while staying hidden behind it. Then I listen for any sounds coming from my room. There's nothing, so I tiptoe down the hall. I discover my room is empty, so Luke must already be downstairs. Exhaling loudly in relief, I continue to stare at my bed. It's rumpled like it's been slept in, but the covers are pulled up as though an attempt has been made to make it.

Luke Phillips slept in my bed last night. As that image soaks into my consciousness, I feel teenage giddiness flow through me.

I hear a creaking noise behind me and immediately realize my mistake. Luke isn't in my room because he's in the bathroom across the hall. I turn to run back to my parents' room, but something in my brain decides that it's too far away, so I wind up dashing into my own room. I make a run for the closet and manage to cross the threshold in the nick of time.

From my secret vantage point, I watch Luke as he walks into the room. He's only wearing a towel. Holy heck! What do I do now? I can't stand here and watch him undress, *can I?* Well, maybe just for a second. I chastise myself not to act like a perve-o, but I take too long. Luke drops his towel which causes me to gasp, loudly.

"Lorelai?" I hear him call out. He doesn't sound pleased.

He knows I'm here. All he has to do is walk over for confirmation. "Oh, hey, Luke …" I sound like an idiot. "I just came in here to get a … a … a sweater."

He rustles around for a moment before I see his shadow creep toward the door frame. I turn to face my sweater collection, so I don't have to make eye contact with him. "Did you find one?" Oh yeah, he's mad.

Grabbing the first sweater I see, I take it off the stack and pull it over my head. Oh dear, it's tight so I know it's an old one. But the only way out of this situation is to keep going with the lie. Turning around, I force a smile to my face, and blurt out, "Good, you put some pants on." Great, now he knows I saw his towel fall off. Why can't I keep my mouth shut around him?

Embarrassment blooms across Luke's cheeks. "Lorelai, I think we need to talk."

Dear God, no! We can never speak of this, ever. "No need," I tell him. "I'll just move more of my clothes over to my parents' room, so this never happens again. But I'll do it later so you can keep getting ready."

I try to scurry past him, but he gently grabs my arm to stop me. "*This* is the sweater you came in here to get?"

"Yes, it is," I tell him emphatically. "It's my favorite." Belatedly, I look down and see that I'm wearing Mickey Mouse's face embroidered across a purple acrylic garment that's so small it's practically cropped. If that's not bad enough, there's a big hole in one of the armpits and a snag running through Mickey's face.

There's nothing I can do but brazen this out, so I disengage from Luke's hand and announce, "Mickey Mouse is my ideal man." Then I make a run for it.

CHAPTER TWELVE

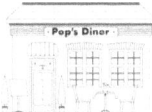

LUKE

I can't stay here with Lorelai any longer. It's obvious she still has feelings for me and that's going to make things very uncomfortable. I finish getting dressed before running my fingers through my damp hair to finger comb it. Then I head downstairs to the kitchen to confront my hostess.

Lorelai is standing in front of the refrigerator busily pulling things out. She's humming to herself, so I clear my throat to let her know she's not alone. Peeking out from behind the refrigerator door, she sees me and shrieks. "Luke! Hey there! Hi!"

As she crosses the room and drops the load she's carrying onto the counter, I tell her, "We need to talk."

"Why?" She's so flustered, I feel bad for her.

"I think I should find somewhere else to stay." The expression on her face makes me wish I didn't say that, but keeping things as they are is not an option.

"Look, Luke, I'm sorry about this morning. I forgot a few things in my room and when I saw you weren't there, I figured it was as good a time as ever to get them."

Indicating the ridiculous sweater she's wearing, I ask, "Things like your favorite sweater?"

Her face flushes prettily. "Exactly."

"What about last night?" I ask her.

"You climbed into bed with me, not the other way around!" She really was drunk if she thought that. The tube of biscuit dough drops onto the floor, but she doesn't bother to pick it up.

That wasn't what I was talking about, so I ask, "What about the prom?"

Panic etches across her features. "What prom? Neither one of us is in high school."

It occurs to me that she might not remember the ride home and what happened after. She appears to have no recollection that she fawned all over me like a starstruck teenager. If that's so, I might be able to stay here after all. I'll just have to make sure I see Lorelai as infrequently as possible.

Trying to make light of the prom comment, I tell her, "I thought you said something about a school dance last night."

Lorelai's posture becomes rigid. "I have no idea what you're talking about. Now, go sit down because I'm going to make you a world-class breakfast this morning. It's my turn."

She's not doing that with commercially bought biscuit dough, but the poor girl has really been through it, so I decide not to make things worse by telling her that. "Do you have any fresh coffee?" I ask.

She points to the coffee maker on the counter, "It's coming down now. It should be ready in a few minutes." She picks up the biscuits from the floor and pulls back the paper layer on the tube. Then she whacks it against the counter until it splits open.

I watch as Lorelai microwaves a stick of butter. She mixes it with cinnamon and brown sugar before pulling out a cookie sheet from a lower cabinet. She gets busy spacing the biscuits before flattening them with a drinking glass. Then she sprinkles the dough with the sugar mixture and folds them into what I'm guessing is meant to be some kind of cinnamon roll. I've never seen anything quite like it.

"What are your plans for today?" Lorelai asks.

"I'm going to go see my dad and then head over to the diner." I'm not sure she remembers seeing me there and I don't want to cause her anymore embarrassment, so I say, "I thought I might have spotted you there last night. Do you eat at Pop's often?"

"As often as I can," she responds without making eye contact.

"Well then, how about if in payment for letting me stay here, I open an account for you so you can eat there whenever you'd like. On the house." I rethink this almost immediately as I don't want to have to see my friend's sister more often than I already will, so I add, "You can get meals to-go."

"That's so nice." She seems genuinely pleased.

"Anything you want," I tell her. Although I hope she won't repeat her lemon drop indulgence.

As if reading my mind, she tells me, "I think I drank too much last night. I don't normally do that, but my friend was spilling some significant tea. It was pretty heavy stuff."

Not caring to know the details, I surmise, "I'm guessing you don't get drunk often."

She shakes her head slowly like she's feeling nauseous. "Not since that frat party in college." Before I can ask, she explains, "I got so hammered doing beer bongs, I spent the night in my dorm bathroom clinging to the toilet. It felt like I was hanging from the ceiling." With a sigh, she adds, "I vowed to never put myself through that again."

"Ah, college," I commiserate. "We've all been there. It sounds like you learned your lesson before most."

"I like being in control and I never want to do something that I'd regret."

Like asking your brother's best friend to kiss you and then proclaiming the chaste cheek kiss to be lackluster? But I don't say that. "That's very smart."

Lorelai pours a cup of fresh coffee and stirs in one spoonful of sugar. Then she hands it to me. After taking a sip, I tell her, "Thank you."

"It's better than yesterday's, right?"

I nod my head. Anything would be better than that sludge. Yet I still make a mental note to be the first one up so that I can make the coffee. Lorelai clearly didn't see the gourmet beans in the refrigerator. "What are you planning to do today?" I ask her.

"My parents texted that they needed to speak with me. I suppose I'll do some laundry after that."

"How long do they stay in Florida?" Noah mentioned that his folks had started to snowbird a couple of years ago. I wish my parents would do the same thing. It's time that they stopped working so hard and enjoyed some of the fruits of their labor.

"They leave right after Christmas and come back at the end of June."

"And you take care of everything while they're away?"

Lorelai's head bobs up and down. She finishes fixing her coffee before taking a long sip. "So good," she declares. Leaning back against the counter, she adds, "Noah doesn't think I should still live at home at twenty-eight."

"But you're providing a service to your family."

"That's what I said!" She looks pleased, until her nose scrunches. "My brother makes me out like one of those adult kids who needs to get a grip and move on with their lives." It's obvious she's trying to read my expression, and when she can't, she hurries to add, "I have a very full life."

I want to point out that she just broke up with her boyfriend so she shouldn't be so hard on herself. But Noah asked me not to mention it, so I don't. "You must be saving money," I tell her. "And with the price of real estate today, it's nearly impossible for people our age to buy a house. At least on one income."

"I guess so, but I'm only assistant manager at a gift shop. I'm not really making that much money." I can tell I've made her feel bad again.

Trying to dig my way out of a hole, I tell her, "Then it's nice to have a place to stay that you don't have to worry about paying for."

The timer on the oven rings and saves me from saying anything else. Lorelai puts on an oven mitt and pulls out her creation. The look on her face suggests it isn't quite what she expected. "Huh." She drops the tray on the stove top. "They looked better on the internet."

I stand up and walk over for a better view. She's right. In a word, they look *horrible*. She didn't roll the dough tightly enough, so instead of keeping their shape, they've all burst open. "Do you have any confectioners sugar?" I ask her.

"Is that powdered sugar?" she wants to know.

"Yes. And I'll need some vanilla extract and milk."

She turns around to collect the ingredients while I pull a cereal bowl down from the cabinet. When she comes back, I quickly pour in about a cup of sugar before mixing in a small amount of milk and a dash of vanilla. Then with a fork, I whip it until it's smooth. I drizzle a bit of the mixture onto each cinnamon bomb and announce, "They look great now. And they'll taste even better with a little icing." At least I hope they will.

Lorelai's eyes light up. "They look wonderful, thank you! But now I owe you breakfast again tomorrow because I was supposed to do this by myself."

"Nonsense. All I did was add the icing. You did everything else, and it looks fantastic." *Lies*, but there's no point in making her feel worse than she already does.

"Thank you, Luke. That's very sweet of you." She shyly confesses, "I was really looking forward to another omelet."

"How about crepes instead?" I ask her.

She beams like I just offered her a trip to Paris and a puppy. "Yes, please!"

I'm relieved things have smoothed out between us. I really didn't want to have to find another place to stay, and as long as Lorelai doesn't beg me to kiss her again, we should be okay.

Although, she looks so sweet this morning there's a tiny part of me that wonders what it would be like to kiss her properly. I wish she'd never put the idea in my head. I remind myself that she's my friend's little sister and no good can come from that. I will keep my hands to myself and when I go back to Chicago, I won't leave any messes behind.

CHAPTER THIRTEEN

LORELAI

The cinnamon rolls weren't great, but at least they were a step up from Toaster Strudel, especially with that icing.

After Luke leaves for the day, I go into the living room and plop down on the couch. Picking up my phone, I call my parents. It rings twice before I hear my mom's bubbly greeting. "Yellooooow!"

"Hey, Mom, it's me."

"Lorelai!" She sounds so excited you'd think she just won the lottery. "Hold on while I put you on speaker. William, your daughter is on the phone!" she shouts.

I hear my dad's voice as it gets closer to the phone. "Oh, goody!" A few beats later, he says, "How's my little girl?"

"Good, Dad. How are you? How's golf?"

"Your mother and I are great. Golf is good, but there's something else we wanted to talk to you about."

I don't know why but I suddenly feel nervous. "What's that?"

"Your mother and I were thinking it might be time for us to leave Elk Lake permanently. We've recently been given the opportunity to buy a condo in a golf community that we love. If we do that, we'd make it our only home."

"You'd leave Elk Lake for good?" Fear zaps through me like I've been hit by a bolt of lightning. If they move, what would I do? Where would I go? I guess I'd have to get that apartment in town. The problem is I'm not sure I make enough money at the lodge to be totally on my own.

"We've raised our family, which was our goal," my mom interjects. "There's really nothing keeping us in Wisconsin anymore."

"*I'm* here," I remind her.

She sounds like she's placating me when she says, "Of course you are, dear. But you're grown now. You're making your own decisions, and you don't need us anymore." I may not need them in the way she thinks, but I do need their house. At least until I can figure out what I'm going to do with my life.

"When are you making your decision?"

"We've already made it, Lorelai." This from my dad. "We're placing an offer on the condo today. We talked to a realtor, and she told us the best time to sell the Elk Lake house would be over the summer when the town is full of tourists looking for a vacation house."

Beads of sweat explode on my forehead. "That's not even three months from now!"

"That's plenty of time to get everything ready," my dad says.

"At the minimum, we want to have the house repainted and re-carpeted," my mom says. "And whatever else the realtor suggests. We'd like you to oversee that for us."

"I can't imagine going to work and leaving the house open for workers." While this *is* a slight concern, I'm really just trying to buy myself some time.

"We'll pay you, of course," my dad said. "You'll be our contractor."

"But I have a job."

"You make minimum wage, honey," my mom says hurtfully. "We'll pay you better than that."

"But it's my *job*!" I say this like I'm the only person in Wisconsin who knows how to sell toothbrushes—like I've contracted to stay there until I'm old and gray. Which, honestly, I might have done had everything remained the same "I can't just show up after taking three months off and expect them to take me back."

"Probably not, Lorelai." My dad sounds like he's talking to a mentally challenged child. "It's high time you got on with your life and started on a career path. Working in a gift shop isn't going to lead you anywhere." My parents are acting unusually mean. They've always been very encouraging of me and my endeavors, particularly my charitable works. But now, now it's like I've suddenly become some unwanted freeloader.

I start to wonder if I've been the topic of conversation between them and my brother. They all seem to think I'm a world-class loser. I attempt to clear the emotion out of my voice before saying, "I'm sorry I've been such a disappointment."

"Lorelai," my mother croons. "We're not disappointed. We're just concerned that you're in a bit of a rut."

My dad adds, "We want to encourage you to jump start your life. With your savings, and the money we'll pay you to oversee renovations, you should be able to find an apartment in Madison or Milwaukee ..." He highly overestimates the balance of my savings account. Even on sale, yarn is pretty spendy. Thank goodness for the donations I get from some of the ladies at the senior center. While their scraps can be pretty odd, they add up.

"You could live in Chicago!" my mom interjects. "You could get a studio there."

"And do what?" I want to know. I graduated college with an English degree, but I only majored in that because I wanted to put my love of reading to good use. Seriously, it was that or knitting and no one gets a college degree in the yarn arts.

"You could teach elementary school," my mom decides.

"I'd need to get certified for that."

"You could substitute teach during the day and go to school at night," my dad suggests.

An icy chill runs through my veins that causes goosebumps to pop up on my arms. They've made their decision. "Make a list of what you want done, and when you want it done by and I'll get started," I tell them. Even though I don't want them to sell, my blood starts to pump at the thought of finally getting my hands on this house and making the improvements I've dreamed about.

"Anna Tanaka from Elk Lake Realty is going to stop by tomorrow at three. She'll walk through the house and give her recommendations." My dad continues, "I've added your name to my Visa card and they're sending you a copy of your own. Put all the expenses on that."

If your dad putting your name on his Visa account isn't a dream come true, I don't know what is.

"Give notice at work," my mom adds. "Start making appointments."

Had I been paying attention, I might have guessed something like this was possible. My parents did mention they might only come home for a couple weeks this summer, but I thought they were kidding. *Who wants to spend the summer in Florida?* "What about all your things? When will you be coming back to pack them up?"

"We'd like you to pack for us," my dad says. "You can have all the dishes, pots, pans, and furniture that you'd like to start your new life." *They don't even want to come back to say goodbye?*

"You can keep the framed photographs, too," my mom adds. "Your dad and I bought one of those digital frames." *You mean like the one I already got you that you gave to charity?* I feel like I'm on the phone with strangers.

"You don't want Nana's roll-top desk?" I gasp. My mom cherishes that.

"Why don't you keep it, honey?" she says. "Our new condo won't have enough space for it."

"How big *is* your new condo?" I'm suddenly worried they won't have room for me to visit ... or God forbid *live* there if I can't get my crap together. Not that living in a seniors' golf community is my ideal, but in the beggars/choosers scenario, I would most definitely be classified as the former.

"It's one bed and one and a half baths," my dad informs me. "But that will be plenty because we plan on spending a lot of time out and about."

"Wait until you see the clubhouse!" my mom gushes. "There are three pools, and even a spa!"

"Sounds like there won't be room in your new condo for visitors." I know that sounds like sour apples, but I'm not feeling very wanted.

"Part of the condo fees includes the use of guest rooms," my dad says. "We can have one for two weeks every year. One week for you, and one for Noah." I guess that's it then. My parents are done with me.

Tears flood my eyes as my nose fills with snot. "I'd better get going," I tell them. "I have a lot to do."

My mom's tone takes a tender turn. "I know you love our house, honey, but it's time for all of us to see what life has in store for the future."

I'm tempted to say something sarcastic, like, "As long as *you're* happy ..." but I know that wouldn't be fair. My parents have given me refuge from life for the past three years. That's a huge gift that I shouldn't have expected to last forever.

"Email me lists of stuff you want to keep," I tell them. I hang up before they have a chance to say anything else.

My parents have a right to do whatever they want with their property, but I can't help but worry what's going to happen to me. Other than teaching, which I'd have to go back to school for, there's not going to be anything I can do in Elk Lake. Not only am I faced with being homeless, but I'm also going to be town-less.

Putting down my phone, I succumb to a big, fat cry. I know

I'm being pitiful, but I just can't seem to help myself. Not even Luke Phillips staying here is enough to make a dent in my sadness.

CHAPTER FOURTEEN

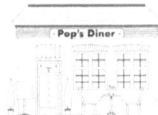

LUKE

I feel even less optimistic walking into the hospital today than I did yesterday. So much so, I'm tempted to turn around and go straight to the diner. I remind myself that the main reason for my being in Elk Lake is not work. I'm here to repair things with my dad. The problem is I don't know how to do that if he won't meet me halfway.

Stopping off in the gift shop, I buy my dad his favorite candy bar along with a spy novel. He always complains he doesn't have time to read. The way things stand now, he has nothing but time.

I take the elevator up to the third floor with as much excitement as if I were ascending to the hangman's platform. As soon as the doors open, I walk out and run into my old friend Tony.

"Luke, hi. You here to see your dad?"

"I'm sure not here for the fun of it," I tell him. Making a face, I ask, "How's he doing, anyway?"

Tony grimaces. "He's in a lot of pain and he's frustrated to be stuck in traction."

"So, delightful as always?" I predict.

"I remember your dad being a pretty cool guy," he says. "He's just in a bad place right now."

I'm not going to talk about my father's personality shift these last years, so I ask, "Is there anything else you can do for him?"

Tony shakes his head. "Unfortunately, he just has to get through it. I'm sure it helps having you and your mom here though."

I'm pretty sure he's wrong about my part in my dad's recovery. If nothing else, I'm probably raising his blood pressure to an alarming degree. "I guess I'll go see him."

I take a step forward as Tony says, "Let me know if you want me to order you a breakfast."

While I am hungry, neither Lorelai's attempt at cinnamon buns nor hospital food are what I consider enticing options. "Thanks, Tony, but I'm good." Then I walk toward my dad's room.

Peeking my head in, I confirm that my mom isn't there. I didn't think she would be, but I would have welcomed the buffer. "Hey, Dad," I say, trying to sound happier than I feel.

"Luke," he grumbles. "What are you doing here?"

Striding toward the bed, I tell him, "I'm here to see you. You did just fall off a roof."

"I thought you'd have gone back to Chicago by now." He's as friendly as an ax murderer.

"Nope," I tell him. "I'm planning to stay for a while."

"Why?" There is no pleasing this man.

"Even if you don't need me, Mom does. She's never going to leave your side if she doesn't have someone she trusts to sit with you."

He tips his head to the side and scans the room. "She's not here now."

"That's because she knew I was coming," I tell him. "I told her to sleep in."

My dad appears slightly chagrined like he hadn't been thinking of the toll his accident is taking on my mom. With a grunt, he says, "Fine. Sit down. We can watch the television."

I did not come all this way to sit and watch TV, but even so, it sounds like a decent diversion from having to keep up my end of this painful conversation. "What do you want to watch?" I ask while moving a chair closer to his bed so I can reach the remote attached to his side table.

"Whatever you want," he says. "I'm going to take a nap." He immediately closes his eyes and pretends to fall asleep.

Instead of turning on the TV, I sit down and open the spy novel I got for him. After reading the first paragraph six times, I come to the realization I'm not retaining any information. Closing the book, I look at my dad's still figure. I can tell he's asleep for real because his mouth is hanging half open as it always does once unconsciousness claims him.

He's starting to look old. Graying temples and laugh lines around his eyes aren't the only giveaway. Long wrinkles are forming on his cheeks that make him look almost gaunt. Scanning the rest of him, I notice that he weighs considerably less than he did a couple of years ago.

I have spent very little time thinking about my parents' age, but it occurs to me there are no guarantees in life, and every day is a gift. Standing up, I walk out the door and look for Tony. I find him typing away at his computer.

"Hey, man," I say. "Any chance I can get a cup of coffee?"

He looks up and points to the door closest to him. "That's the nurses' station. You can grab yourself a cup in there."

I walk in the direction he indicated and am happy to find a Keurig machine. Brewing myself a fresh cup, I consider ways I can connect with my dad. Once my coffee comes down, I add the sugar and then go back to his room. I'm surprised when his eyelids flutter open.

"I thought you left." Is it me or does he sound disappointed that I didn't?

"Nope, just got a cup of coffee." I extend my hand in offering. "You want one?"

He shakes his head. "Nah, I'm good."

I sit down on the chair next to him. "I was just thinking about the summer when I turned eight. Remember how we caught all those bullheads?"

His mouth turns up nearly imperceptibly. "They sure were delicious. Although, I started to get sick of them after five straight dinners."

I reminisce fondly, "We ate corn on the cob with each one and some kind of blueberry dessert that Mom made."

"You can't beat seasonal food," he says. For a moment it feels like we've declared a small truce and it's nice.

"You ever serve bullhead up at that restaurant of yours?" Now he sounds angry.

I don't take the bait to fight. Instead, I tell him, "We rely more on catfish or trout. Although, I have a butter-sautéed sole on the menu that melts in your mouth."

"You ever blacken that catfish?" he wants to know.

"Almost always," I tell him. "That's how you taught me, so that's how I serve it."

His head bobs slightly. "You serve it with coleslaw?"

"Mashed potatoes," I tell him.

"Why on earth would you do that?"

"It fits the vibe of Capon better."

"You mean it's fancier than coleslaw?" He sounds offended on coleslaw's behalf, which is ridiculous.

"Sometimes we serve it with fried green tomatoes," I tell him.

His eyebrows raise in surprise. "How do you make those fancy?"

"You don't. I make them with cornmeal, buttermilk, garlic and onion powder, just like you used to."

I can tell there's something he wants to ask me, but he doesn't. So, I add, "Remember how we ate those into the fall that one year? You even packed them in my school lunch."

He tries to shrug, but his suspended arm keeps him from succeeding. "What else are you supposed to do with a whole batch of tomatoes that don't ripen before the weather turns?"

I smile at the memories we're sharing. "From what I recall, you can make salsa and chutney, too."

He cringes. "That chutney wasn't the best, was it? Your mother pretended to accidentally knock the box off the root cellar shelf and break the jars."

In the spirit of our newly found camaraderie, I confess, "I helped her pour them down the garbage disposal."

My dad surprises me by releasing a loud bark of laughter. "I figured it was something like that. What about the salsa? You guys liked that well enough?"

"It was some of the best you ever made," I tell him honestly.

We sit silently for a couple of minutes, each of us seeming to relish the peace. Then my dad surprises me by saying, "I looked up that restaurant of yours on the internet."

I hold my breath waiting for him to elaborate. When he doesn't, I ask, "What do you think?"

"I think it's pretentious." So much for a ceasefire.

I'm not sure how to respond to him without sounding like I'm looking for a fight. "It fits the location and the clientele," I tell him.

"Everyone in Chicago can't be stuck up."

"I'm not stuck up, Dad. Which I'm sure you'd figure out for yourself if you'd ever bothered to visit me and let me cook for you." That clearly wasn't the right thing to say, but I have no idea what this man has against expensive restaurants.

"I know how you cook," he says. "Which is why I wanted you to come work with me."

That's probably as close to a compliment as he's going to give to me. "When I was in finance, you never complained about me not working at the diner."

"That's because you were in finance. It's what you went to school for."

"I also went to culinary school, Dad." My blood is nearly boiling at this point and it's all I can do not to get up and walk out on him.

"I taught you how to cook, Luke. *I* did that, not some fancy school."

It appears the crux of my dad's beef with me is that he thinks I hold myself above him, which is not the case. I just wanted to learn how to cook other things. "You did a great job, too, Dad. Such a good job that I wanted to learn more."

He lies there quietly, like he's deciding if this is a compliment or the gravest of insults. But instead of letting me off the hook and being gracious, he says, "Well then, you'd better get back to Chicago so you can do *more*."

"My life isn't all about my restaurant, Dad. I have a family, too."

"You wouldn't know that by how often we see you," he mutters.

His constant complaints are wearing thin. He cooks, and I cook. He taught me a lot, so you'd think he'd be proud, but he's so stuck on thinking that I look down on him he can't see that my career choice is a tribute to him. "The funny thing about roads, Dad, is that they go both ways." Standing up, I add, "You haven't come to see me either."

"I have a restaurant to run, Luke. I can't just take off and lollygag around Chicago."

"Who's running your restaurant while you're in the hospital?" I'm sorely tempted to tell him it's me, but I know that won't go well. Also, I promised my mom.

"I suppose Jim is."

"I'm sure Jim could have covered for you long enough for you to come to my grand opening." Gauntlet dropped. *Explain your way out of that*, I psychically challenge him.

Instead of making an excuse, he says, "I'm sure he could have." And just like that, my dad is telling me that my life is not a priority for him. At this point I can either yell at him and let him know how hurt I am, or I can simply walk away. I choose the latter.

Without so much as saying goodbye, I turn and walk out of

my dad's hospital room. I don't know how much longer I can take his anger. If he doesn't lighten up soon, I *will* go back to Chicago. Regardless of what I promised my mother, I can't handle being the target of his anger. Especially when I've done nothing to deserve it.

CHAPTER FIFTEEN

LORELAI

A strange sensation comes over me after hanging up with my parents. It's a cross between full-tilt boogie panic and blinding optimism. While this is still my home, at the same time, I can tell I've started to disconnect. I have no future here. The hourglass has turned, and the timer is on countdown to a new life that hopefully won't include me eating out of garbage cans.

I try to forcibly shake thoughts like that out of my head. I'm smart, talented, nicer than most, and I am not a loser. I'm tempted to pick up my phone to tell my brother that, but I decide not to waste my time.

I visualize a thousand memories from my life. This is the room where my family rehashed our daily adventures. We watched television here; we played charades and competed in Nintendo dance-offs. Our Christmas tree has been in the same corner since I was born. How can all that end? Am I supposed to go to Florida for Christmas now? Will we drink our eggnog poolside next to a Speedo-wearing Santa? I shudder at the thought.

I remind myself that I'm twenty-eight years old. I'm lucky to have had my family home for as long as I have. I repeat that sentiment three times like a mantra. Yet I can't help but think that family homes are supposed to remain in families. To make matters worse, I'm not even being given the option to create a new home with my parents, because they aren't going to have room for me in Florida.

I'm embarrassed to even be thinking like this. I'm a grown woman and I need to start acting like one. Not only do things not always stay the same, but I cannot control everything. Therefore, if I do not bend, I will break. *Grow. Up. Lorelai.* While that may not sound like the best peptalk, it's actually working a little bit. I have always liked a challenge and this one should be no different. Except now, I have a credit card that I won't be responsible for paying.

Pulling out my phone, I open my notes app and start typing.

- Call painters
- Pick out paint colors
- Call movers and get quotes to move my parents' things to Florida
- Look and see how much apartments cost in Elk Lake, Madison, and Chicago
- Try to figure out what job I can do to make more money
- Carpeting?

I suppose I'll have more clarity prioritizing tasks after talking to the realtor tomorrow. But no matter what, I'm going to be busy.

Even though I'm off today, I decide to go into the lodge and give my notice in person. I feel bad about deserting them, but it appears I have no choice. Hurrying upstairs, I change into something more presentable before tossing my Mickey Mouse sweater into the garbage can. Not only doesn't it fit, but I suppose it's high time I lighten my load as well.

Getting into my car, I sit and let it warm up while I stare at the front of my family home. I love this house. It's a classic two-story colonial with dove-grey siding and black shutters. The dormers on the second story windows give it an obvious charm. It will make some family a great summer house. I just wonder what they'll do with it when they're not there. That's when a thought hits me. Maybe they'll let me be their caretaker.

Even as I consider this, I know that's not an option. I could never live here with someone else's things. Without fully understanding why, I know that would ruin my memories.

By the time I pull into the lodge's parking lot, a trail of tears is making its way down my face. I don't know how to stop it, so I simply park my car and get out. The air is freezing cold—which strangely I didn't notice when I left my house. The shock of the windchill halts my tears and effectively keeps any new ones from falling. Today is an emotional rollercoaster I did not expect.

I experience my normal feeling of joy when I walk into the lodge. I really do love this place. Striding around the front desk, I wave to clerks on duty and keep going until I'm standing in front of my boss's door.

I give it a quick knock. When I hear Trina say, "Come in!" I follow instructions.

Trina used to host a television show called *The Midwestern Matchmaker*, which is why she came to Elk Lake in the first place. They filmed their last season here. When that ended, she rented a cottage on the lake for the summer. That's where she met her fiancé, billionaire Heath Fox. They opened the lodge together.

Trina smiles when she sees me. "What are you doing here, Lorelai?" She indicates a chair for me to sit on.

Once I'm situated, I tell her, "I have some bad news."

The look of concern on her face causes my eyes to once again fill. "No one died or anything," I say. "I just need to give my notice."

"No!" She sounds as devastated as I am, and honestly that gives me a boost. It's nice that someone sees me as valuable.

"My parents are selling their house."

"And?"

"I'm going to oversee all of the renovations for them to get it ready to sell," I tell her. "I live there so I'm really the obvious choice."

"I didn't realize you still lived at home." *Is that judgment in her voice?*

"My folks are in Florida most of the time, so I'm kind of their caretaker."

She nods her head. "Well, if they aren't here much, I suppose it makes sense to sell their house."

I feel a weight on my chest. It physically hurts when I tell her, "I don't know how much notice you need, but I'm here to give it."

Trina turns on the computer in front of her and clicks around for a bit before saying, "Josie just asked for more hours. I told her I wouldn't have them until the summer, but now I can give her your shifts. You can leave now if you want to." Now she looks like she's going to cry.

"I've really loved working here," I tell her while standing up.

She jumps up from her desk and wraps her arms around me. "We've loved having you!"

"Thank you. I can't tell you how much that means to me."

"I hope you'll consider coming back," Trina says. "You know, once your parents' house sells."

"Maybe," I tell her, although unless she's going to give me an insane raise, I don't see it happening.

Trina reluctantly releases me and walks back around her desk. Opening her top drawer, she hands me a plastic card. "Please take this with our gratitude. You've been a wonderful employee."

I look down and see that she's given me a gift card for the lodge's restaurant for two hundred dollars. I don't know how I'm ever going to use it because I'd feel so sad being here and not working here. "Thank you," I tell her. "That's very generous of you."

"It's nothing," she says. Then she opens her drawer again and pulls out another card. Handing it to me, she says, "This one will get you a complimentary weekend in one of our suites along with meals and a massage."

"Wow! That's really generous, Trina."

"We take care of our own," she tells me. "And you will always be part of the Elk Lake lodge family, even if you aren't working here."

I wonder if Trina would call my parents and brother and tell them what she just said. Seriously, this is the kind of appreciation I need. "Thank you for everything, Trina."

"You're still coming to our wedding, aren't you?"

"I wouldn't miss it," I tell her. "In fact, I still want to assemble your gift bags as my gift."

"You're the best!" She claps her hands together loudly which causes me to jump. "We love you!"

"I love you too," I tell her while giving her a wave. I walk out of her office and decide to stop by the gift shop one last time. I almost cry again when I see a little girl buying herself a candy bar. One of the things I loved about working here was being surrounded by people on vacation. I liked being part of their getaway story, even if it was just selling them some sunscreen.

Turning around, I walk out the front door. The next time I come back I'll be nothing more than a guest. Getting in my car, I drive over to Rosemary's, hoping Allie is there. Right now, I could really use a friend.

Allie isn't at the counter when I walk into the bakery. Instead, I see the owner, Faith. "Hey, Lorelai!" she calls out. "Teddy told me he bored you with pictures of our girls. Sorry about that."

"I wasn't bored at all," I tell her truthfully. "If I had kids as cute as yours, I'd have their pictures printed on sandwich boards that I'd wear around town."

She laughs. "Don't tell Teddy or he'll probably do the same."

"I don't suppose Allie is around," I say, wondering why I didn't just call my friend instead of stopping by.

"She just left. She was only scheduled for a couple of hours today."

"Did she say where she was going?" I ask, although I'm guessing she went back to her parents' house.

Faith shakes her head. "I'm sorry, she didn't." She holds up one finger before saying, "I'm glad you're here though. My grandmother brought in a bag full of old sheets that she wanted me to give to Allie for you." She walks into the back before returning with a giant Hefty bag. "What do you do with old sheets?" she wants to know.

"I cut them into strips and then knit them together to make rugs." I explain, "They love them down at the Humane Society." With a smile, I tell her, "Every dog that gets adopted comes with his own rug."

"That's about the sweetest thing I've ever heard," she says, and darn if it doesn't sound like she means it. "I don't suppose you'd like some help with that sometime?"

"I didn't know you knitted," I tell her.

"I'm not great but I don't imagine the dogs would mind. Plus, I really want to do something for the community. You always seem like you're in the middle of the action and I want a piece of that, too."

"I would love your help," I tell her sincerely. "I'll give you a call and we can set something up.

As I walk away, I can't help but think that Faith's life has turned out nicely. She grew up working in this bakery and now she owns it. Not only that, but she married a movie star and gave birth to their gorgeous twins. If things can work out so well for her, who's to say the same won't happen for me?

Once I'm outside, I take my phone out of my pocket and call Allie, but she doesn't answer. I briefly consider going over to Pop's to see if Luke is around, but we're not really friends and I'm sure he doesn't want to hear about my troubles. So instead, I get back into my car and call my brother.

The phone rings three times before he finally answers, "Lorelai, hi."

Not bothering with niceties, because let's face it, I'm not overly pleased with my brother right now, I demand, "I don't suppose you've talked to Mom and Dad."

He sighs loudly. "They finally told you, huh?"

"So, you *did* know."

"We talked about it last month."

"And you didn't tell me!" Not only am I mad, but I feel betrayed.

"Look, Lorelai, Mom and Dad love you. We all do. They told me first because they didn't know how to break the news to you."

I turn the heater up to high. "They said I only have three months to get out."

"I'm sure they didn't phrase it like that."

"No," I tell him. "They told me they wanted me to get every-thing ready for sale, and then they told me to get out." I'm making this harsher for dramatic effect. I just can't believe that Noah and my parents have been keeping news like this from me. Did they think I'd fall apart?

"You knew you couldn't stay there forever."

"It's not like I thought I was a character in a Jane Austen novel that could spend her spinster years living at home polishing the silver while waiting for an early death from consumption," I snap at him.

"Of course not, Lorelai."

Now that he feels bad, I tentatively say, "I don't suppose you're looking for a roommate in Chicago."

"I like living alone." So much for sympathy.

When he doesn't say anything else, I know it's time to cut the call short. "Let me know if you want to visit and see the place before it doesn't belong to us anymore."

"I'll be back," he says. "I just don't know when."

"Okay. Bye." I hang up before he can respond.

Sitting in my car, I feel like I'm in an episode of my grandfa-ther's favorite television show. He used to watch *The Twilight Zone* which was essentially a science fiction program about how nothing is the way you think it is. Which is exactly how my life currently seems. I wouldn't be too shocked if a portal opened in front of me and I drove into a parallel universe.

I wonder what my life would look like there. Wouldn't it be nice if I was hugely successful and owned my own home? Maybe even the one I'm currently being evicted from? I might even have an adorable family like Faith and Teddy have. Maybe even a great husband. And once again, my mind creates an image of me and Luke together. But instead of being a couple at the senior prom, we're adults.

I remind myself that I shouldn't believe in pipe dreams. I've lost my home, my job, and my town, all in one day. And as much as I know I can overcome all of that, I cannot allow hope as big as me and Luke into my life without opening myself up to total devastation.

CHAPTER SIXTEEN

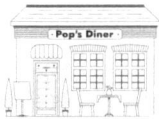

LUKE

Even though I told my mom to sleep in, I still drive by the house before going into the diner. She'll probably be cleaning or doing laundry. She has never been the kind of person who can relax in a crisis.

Standing by the front door, I wonder if I should knock or just walk in. I've always just walked in, but it's been so long since I've been back, I don't want to give her a heart attack. Making a fist, I bang on the door three times before taking a step back.

My mom opens the door immediately like she was waiting for someone. "Luke?" She seems surprised it's me. "Why did you knock?"

"I didn't want to scare you."

"Why would I be scared if you walked into your own home?" Her eyebrows furrow like she's trying to cut me in half with an invisible laser coming from her corneas. Stepping aside, she gestures for me to enter.

"I haven't been here in a long time," I tell her. "It almost doesn't even feel like my home anymore."

"Whose fault is that?" she asks harshly.

"Dad's."

Shaking her head, my mom walks down the hallway and leads the way into the family room. She sits down on the sofa before telling me, "It's your dad's fault that he hasn't visited you in Chicago. It's your fault that you haven't come home."

How can she see it that way? "Why would I visit someone who's made it clear they don't want to see me?" I give her a "talk your way out of that one" look.

My mom shakes her head with enough vigor to cause her graying bob to sway back and forth. "You're two peas in a pod," she says.

Excuse me? "I'm nothing like Dad," I say while sitting on the La-Z-Boy recliner directly across from her.

My mom laughs mirthlessly. "That's what your dad says. The truth is, you're both so pig-headed and stubborn you can't see your own culpability."

"I'm not responsible for the rift between us," I tell her. "All I did was follow my dreams, which if I recall correctly is what you and Dad taught me to do."

"You could have told your dad when you started culinary school that you had no intention of coming back to Elk Lake to work with him."

She's not wrong about that. But instead of agreeing with her, I say, "I didn't tell him because I didn't know what I wanted to do yet."

"Lucas Adam Phillips."

The usage of my full name indicates the amount of trouble I'm in. "How could I have known?"

"You didn't need culinary school to work with your dad in Elk Lake. You'd already learned everything you needed to know about running Pop's. You clearly went because you didn't want to be at Pop's."

"If you knew that," I say, "How is it that Dad didn't?"

She rolls her eyes like I'm too stupid to continue drawing breath. "Your father thought you would bring the benefits of your education home and give Pop's customers more of a selection."

"Then why didn't he say that?" I never considered my dad was open to changing his restaurant. And even if I knew, I don't think that knowledge would have made any difference. Yet, how can I know for sure if he never shared that information with me? At least if he'd said something, it would have opened the door for civilized conversation between us.

"See what I mean?" My mom is clearly exasperated. "Two peas in a pod. Your dad wants to retire at sixty-five, which is only two years from now."

"What does that have to do with me?"

"Are you really as thick as you're pretending to be?" she demands.

"If Dad wants to retire at sixty-five, then he should retire." Once again, I don't know how I figure in.

"Your dad has owned Pop's for thirty years, Luke. You spent your whole childhood there. What do you think he planned to do with the place when he retired?"

"Sell it?"

"Are you serious?" My mom is getting extremely annoyed with me now.

"Why not? I mean, unless he wants to hire a general manager to run it for him. But why would he bother? He should just sell it and be done with it."

"Your father has always wanted to leave Pop's to his children. When Kelsey moved out to LA to work in publicity, Dad knew she didn't have any interest. But then you went to culinary school, Luke. That told him loud and clear that you loved the food industry, making you the obvious choice to inherit Pop's."

"But I don't want Pop's," I tell her honestly.

My mom shifts in her seat before grabbing a throw pillow off the couch. She flings it across the coffee table at me with force. "I know! And your dad knows!" In a quieter tone, she adds, "And it breaks his heart."

I guess I was too wrapped up in my own dreams to even consider that my dad wanted me to take over for him. I feel kind of stupid for not putting that together. But to be fair, he never said as much.

My mom watches me closely. She's clearly wondering where she went wrong with me. "Luke, your dad's childhood was nothing like yours. Nana and Grandpa doted on you kids. They always encouraged you, like they did me. You never knew your dad's parents and there's a reason for that."

"Dad never wanted to talk about them, so I eventually took the hint and quit asking," I tell her. "I'm not a mind reader, Mom."

"No, honey, you're not. But you are an adult. You're grown up enough to know your parents don't know everything. We're not perfect. We're just people with our own journeys doing the best we can."

"And?"

"Maybe it's time you talk to your dad and get to know about his childhood."

I exhale loudly. "He doesn't want to talk to me, Mom."

"Don't give him a chance not to, Luke. The man is in traction for Pete's sake, he can't exactly run away from you."

"I can't make him talk if he doesn't want to."

She grabs another pillow like she's going to wing that one at me too. But instead of doing so, she holds it close to her chest. "It's time for you to act like the adult, Luke. Treat your dad like you would a child. Show him that you aren't the enemy. That's the only way he'll open up to you."

The very thought causes the little hairs all over my body to stand at attention. I really don't want to do what she's asking of me. I already feel like I've let my dad down so badly that he'll never forgive me. But before I can articulate my thoughts, my mom asks, "What do you have to lose?"

"The tiny shred of pride I have left?" I realize how melodramatic that sounds but I'm feeling a touch overemotional.

"You could have lost your dad when he fell off the roof, Luke.

Ask yourself if your precious pride is worth risking your relationship."

"I'm not the one risking it!" I practically yell. I immediately feel bad for raising my voice to her. It's not like our feud is her doing and I know it's taken a toll on her.

"You're as much responsible as he is. And until one of you makes the first move, you will never find your way back to each other. And if you don't, you will regret it for the rest of your life."

"I hope you tell Dad that, too," I challenge.

My mom stares at me quietly for so long I start to shift nervously in my seat. "You grew up with a great father, Luke. He was always there for you; he taught you how to do so many things. Not everyone is so lucky."

"You're talking about Dad's parents?"

"I'm talking about what *you* had. You were given love and stability, and as such, it may fall to you to be the bigger man in this situation."

"By forcing my company on a man while he's stuck in a hospital bed?"

"I can't think of a better place," she says. "Help your dad understand how you feel. Help him to see your vision."

"And if he doesn't?" I want to know.

"Don't take no for an answer, Luke."

"You're giving me too much credit, Mom. I can't move a mountain all by myself."

"How do you know?" she demands. "Have you ever tried?"

Standing up, I turn around to leave, but I suddenly stop when she asks, "Do you love your dad, Luke?"

What kind of question is that? "Of course, I do."

"Then accept him for who he is and help him find a way to do the same with you."

For the life of me, I can't see this working. My dad is going to throw a fit if I go and visit him and refuse to leave when he gets angry with me. But I know my mom is right. If something happens to him before we can fix things between us, I will mourn his loss forever.

I'm going to need to think long and hard about the best way to reach him. I've done all I can do today, but tomorrow I vow to try again. Tomorrow, I will start to find a way to penetrate his armor and help him to see how much I love and respect him. But for now, I need a break from everything, and the best way for me to center myself is to cook.

Turning back toward my mom, I tell her, "I'll do my best. But I can't make any promises."

CHAPTER SEVENTEEN

LORELAI

I decide to stop at the grocery store on my way home. I was just there yesterday so I don't need anything. But I'm in the market for comfort, and I'm thinking pudding is the way to go. When I get to the proper aisle, I scope out the flavors, but I can't decide what I want. This is how I come to buy all four kinds. Six boxes of each because this feels like it's going to be an ongoing need.

Once I've nearly wiped the shelves clean of pudding, I walk around the aisles and look for something else to impulse buy. I add a bag of chocolate chips, a bag of pretzels and a box of Golden Grahams to my cart. *That's right, cheater s'mores are calling my name!*

After paying for my purchases, I drive home. Getting out of the car, I grab my grocery bag before slogging through a particularly wet slush that leads to the front door. The snow is melting and spring is nearly here, which is the seasonal start of new beginnings. *You and me both, spring. Let's do this!*

I open the front door before taking off my coat and letting it drop at my feet. Then I make my way to the kitchen where I pull a gallon of milk out of the refrigerator. I pour the contents of a box of chocolate pudding into a mixing bowl and add the required amount of liquid. I whisk the mixture until it starts to thicken, all the while wondering at the magic of instant pudding. How did pioneer women ever survive without it?

I don't bother refrigerating my creation for optimal thickness. Instead, I take the bowl, along with a can of whipped cream spray, to the couch. I sit down and don't move until I've consumed all four servings. Even though my stomach is full to bursting, I still feel oddly empty.

Rolling off the sofa, I crawl to the built-in bookcase across the room. I stare at the titles and ponder which ones, if any, my parents will want to keep. I'm guessing the complete series of Danielle Steel novels can go, but what about all my dad's books on aliens? He's convinced that any time now the truth about our standing in the universe is going to be revealed. He vacillates between mentally trying to prepare for planetary takeover and wondering what kind of clothes he'll need on Mars.

For now, I leave his books on the shelf and start to make a pile of my mom's. She's big into women's fiction that focusses heavily on generational sagas. You know, a mother, daughter, and grand-daughter all raising their families in the same ancestral home. I guess she didn't like them enough to create the same kind of story for our lives. *Bitter, party of one.*

Once half the shelves are empty, I lay on the floor and close my eyes. When Noah and I were little, our mom used to crawl around the carpet with us and we'd pretend to be cats. This was always around nap time, and inevitably we snoozed where we fell. It's a nice memory that I decide to reenact.

I'm not sure how long I sleep before the doorbell interrupts my rest. Rolling over, I wipe a trail of saliva and carpet fibers off my mouth before getting up to see who it is.

Pulling the door open, I exclaim, "Allie!"

She pushes past me. "You called, which is weird. Is something wrong?"

It's true that most people our age text instead of actually

talking to each other, but needs must. If today isn't an emergency, I don't know what is. Leading the way to the living room, I tell her, "My parents are selling our house."

"Okay." She doesn't seem concerned.

"They're buying a place in Florida." When her expression doesn't shift, I add, "They're leaving Elk Lake."

Sitting down on the couch, she looks around the room. "I see you've already started packing. When are they selling?"

"As soon as I can get the place repainted, re-carpeted, and emptied."

"Good for them." She still doesn't appear to be worried on my behalf.

"I'm a little concerned about me."

"What about you?"

"I've been home for a few years now. I'm worried about how I'll make it on the outside.

"Lorelai." She scoots over to console me. "You're going to be okay."

I shake my head. "I hope so."

"People move all the time."

I stand up and start to pace back and forth across the room. "People do move all the time. But I don't. I'm not sure I know how."

"You moved to Madison," she reminds me. "You haven't always lived at home."

"That's true," I tell her. "But that was my decision. This isn't."

"Just take the next step," my friend says. "You don't have to know what comes after that. Not yet."

"What do you think my next step is?" Because pudding was my first thought and that's currently laying in my stomach like a lead weight.

Stating the obvious, she says, "You'll need to find an apartment."

"I'm not sure I make enough money." She shrugs. "We'll find

you something you can afford. You don't need a lot of space," she says. "You're only one person."

Allie has had a much harder road than I have, and she's still managed to hold her own. I try to let that console me, while saying, "I can't imagine my parents not living in Elk Lake."

"They're only here for part of the year. So, I suppose it will be a lot like it is now, except that you'll be living somewhere else."

"I guess I'm feeling sorry for myself."

"No one gets that like I do," she says. "Heck, I'm still there. But if my parents decided to move, I'd have to go, too."

"It's just that …" I don't really know what I'm going to say, so it's a good thing she interrupts me.

"You've been on your own before, Lorelai. You can do it again. You just need to put one foot in front of the other until you see where your path is leading you."

My head bobs up and down. "You're right."

"Life is shocking at times. And it's hard. Things happen that you never, in a million years, thought would happen. But even so," she says, "I have to believe the struggles are worth the journey."

"Do you want to get an apartment with me?" That would make this a lot less difficult on me both financially, as well as emotionally.

Instead of coming to my rescue, Allie shakes her head "I've only been home a few months. I'm not ready to commit to staying in Elk Lake."

"Let me know if you change your mind," I say hopefully

She smiles kindly. "You've got this. You don't need your parents. You're a remarkable woman."

She's wrong. I need all my people, but I still appreciate the props. "You feel like going to the box store with me?"

"You don't have to pack right now," she says. "Why don't we go see a movie or something. Get your mind off things."

That actually sounds like a great idea. "What's showing?"

"A Sandra Bullock marathon. *The Proposal* first, then *Miss*

Congeniality, followed by *The Lost City*. If six hours of romcoms can't take your mind off things, nothing can."

"I'm in!" I tell her enthusiastically. And while I'm currently full of pudding, I'm sure I can fit some buttered popcorn in there, too. I lead the way to the front door and pick my coat up off the floor. Grabbing my purse, I say, "Thanks for being my friend, Allie."

"Thanks for being my friend, Lor." Taking my hand, she adds, "We're both going to find our way."

"One day at a time."

"One step at a time."

And even though I'm currently facing what feels like the biggest challenge of my life, I suddenly have hope that there might be some light at the end of the tunnel. So long as it isn't a train …

CHAPTER EIGHTEEN

LUKE

Walking into the kitchen at Pop's, I find Jim flipping a burger. He's whistling along to an old song on the radio. "Don't worry, be happy, huh?"

"It's the only way, son," he says with a big smile on his face.

"You're in a good mood today."

"No point being in a bad mood."

Putting an apron over my head, I ask him, "Is my dad usually happy?"

He seems to ponder the question for a moment before answering, "He's not unhappy."

"But is he in a *good* mood?" I want to know.

"Hard to say," Jim decides. "Your dad is his own man. You know, kind of complicated and stoic."

"Have you always thought that?" I'm wondering how much my decision to stay in Chicago has transformed his disposition. Because before that time, I always thought my dad was pretty chill.

Jim shrugs. "People ebb and flow. They change along with the world."

"That's pretty cryptic, Jim."

"I know what you're asking me, Luke, and I know why. So, I'll tell you what I told you yesterday. Your dad's life is his to share. It's none of my business."

"You know something," I accuse, while pulling a pile of ground meat out of the refrigerator.

He flips a burger in the air with expertise. "I know all kinds of things, son. *All* kinds of things." It feels like he's insinuating he knows something about me, which is enough to get me to change the subject.

"You got big plans tonight?" I ask him.

With a smile on his face, he tells me, "Not a one."

"That's sounds like the perfect night. Enjoy yourself."

"You know I will." Jim assembles the burger he's been working on before ringing the bell to alert the servers there's an order up. Then he takes off his apron and tells me, "Life isn't nearly as hard as you're making it." With that, he walks out the back door.

Life shouldn't be hard at all, and I don't normally think it is, but that's changing now that I'm back in Elk Lake.

The kitchen door opens and a middle-aged woman with bright red hair walks in. "Luke Phillips! Jim said you were back, but I didn't believe him." She strides toward me with her bony arms outstretched and doesn't stop until she nearly has me in a bear hug. She's a lot stronger than she looks.

"Tanya," I say fondly. "I didn't know you were still here." Tanya has been working for my dad nearly as long as Jim has. It says something about a person who can instill that kind of loyalty in his staff. Even though we're having troubles, my dad has always been steadfast. He stands by people, and treats them with respect. Most would find him the ideal employer.

"Where else would I be? I love Pop's." Then she asks, "How long are you going to be here?"

"Until we know more about how Dad is healing." I add, "Don't tell him I'm working here, okay?"

She waves her hand in front of herself. "I know you're a big secret," she says, not seeming to think this is an odd thing.

"Are you working the night shift with me?"

"I'm closing." She pulls a pad of paper out of her apron and asks, "You running any specials tonight?"

Her question catches me off guard. "Since when has Pop's offered anything that's not on the menu?"

"Couple years now," she says. "Your dad has been shaking things up a bit."

"Really?" My dad has never been one to shake things up. "Like what?"

"Ohhh, let me see." She taps her head with the end of her pen before saying, "He did this great blackened catfish a while back and served it with garlic mashed potatoes. Folks loved it!"

"He did what?" I told my dad this morning that I served the same thing at my restaurant, and he practically choked on the fact that I served fish with mashed potatoes instead of coleslaw.

"He says folks like a change occasionally. So far he knows what he's talking about."

I can't help but wonder what other specials he's served and make a mental note to look through the desk in his office. Until then, I turn toward the walk-in to see what I can offer tonight. "Come back in five, Tanya," I tell her. "I'll have something for you by then."

Walking into the refrigerator, I discover a number of unexpected things, including pea clams and zebra mussels. I serve both at Capon. As far as I know, my dad has never offered them. They weren't in the refrigerator last night, so I can only assume he ordered them ahead of time, like he plans his specials in advance.

I check the pantry and make sure we have plenty of linguini, before ringing the bell to call Tanya back in. When she returns, I tell her, "Tonight's special is steamed clams and mussels in a white wine garlic sauce with a side of linguini. I can probably throw together some garlic bread to serve with it."

"Folks love that one!" she says enthusiastically.

"You've served it before?"

"Several times. It's a big hit."

I'm totally confounded by this. When did my dad step outside of his comfort zone? But instead of asking, I want to know, "Is there a line cook on the schedule for tonight?"

"You need a line cook?" Tanya teases. "Your daddy does this all on his own."

There's pride in her voice and I like it. My father has always been a hard worker. That's one of the biggest things he taught me. That, along with never ask someone to do something for you that you wouldn't do yourself.

"I guess I'm just used to a bigger restaurant," I tell Tanya. "I'm sure I'll be fine."

She winks at me. "I'm sure you'll be fine, too. You learned from the best."

The rest of the night is a blur of activity. It feels good to be cooking. It takes my mind off wondering how I'm going to get my dad to open up to me.

At eight o'clock, Tanya leans her head through the window. "Last order just came in."

My last order at Capon isn't usually until after eleven. I reluctantly realize that it's nice to do what I like to do without having it eat up my whole night. I should be cleaned up and out of here in an hour which is four full hours earlier than if I were cooking at home.

I wonder what would happen if I changed the hours of Capon so I could knock off early? I'm guessing the first thing would be a slew of bad press. Nobody closes early in the city. Not only do people organically eat later there, but there's the whole post-theater crowd that needs to be catered to.

Ah, well, I love my job, so there's no use complaining. I guess I'll just enjoy the earlier hours while I can. The downside is that now I have plenty of time to worry about seeing my dad tomorrow.

CHAPTER NINETEEN

LORELAI

It turns out Sandra Bullock movies are just what the doctor ordered. It doesn't matter if that woman is twenty-six or fifty-six, she's the perfect romcom star. I spent the whole night dreaming I was playing the heroine in one of her movies. And while I don't remember the plot, I do remember the happy ending—me and Luke together.

Rolling over in bed, I catch a whiff of something delicious in the air. Is that sausage? After sitting up, I scoot off the mattress and follow my nose down the stairs. Luke is standing in front of the stove stirring a pot. Before I can stop myself, I tell him, "If whatever that is tastes as good as it smells, I'm going to drop to one knee and propose to you." The horror of speaking my mind so plainly leaves my face hot with embarrassment.

Before I can run out of the room and hide, Luke laughs. "I've gotten more than one proposal because of my sausage and mushroom crepes."

Walking past him, I take a mug out of the cabinet and pour myself a cup of coffee. Even the coffee smells better than normal. I take a sip, and groan, "Did you go to Starbucks to fill the pot?"

He points to a bag sitting on the counter. "Arabica dark roast."

"Even your coffee is gourmet, huh?"

"It takes the same amount of time to brew as the more commercial kind. It just tastes better."

He's not wrong about that. Taking another sip, I realize that I'd better not develop a taste for expensive coffee now that I'm going to have to pay rent somewhere. "My parents are moving," I blurt out.

"To Florida?" Even he doesn't sound surprised. *Am I the only one who didn't see this coming?*

"Yeah." I probably shouldn't complain to him, but I can't seem to help myself. "I'm not sure what that means for me."

Luke flips a crepe in the omelet pan he's holding. "I suppose it means you're going to move too."

"To where though?"

"Where were you before?"

"Madison," I tell him. "But I don't want to go back there."

"Bad breakup?" he asks before hurrying to add, "I didn't mean to ask that. Noah said I shouldn't mention it."

"Noah said not to mention what?"

"That you and your boyfriend just broke up. I'm sorry." He pulls two plates down from the cabinet and puts them in the microwave.

"That was over two years ago," I tell him. "And it wasn't a particularly bad break up. I just realized Michael wasn't the guy for me."

"Really? Noah said it just happened." He's back to looking nervous.

What is my brother up to? But then it hits me. "You didn't happen to just break up with your girlfriend, too?" I ask him.

"What girlfriend?"

"The girlfriend Noah said you recently parted ways with."

Luke raises an eyebrow. "Your brother has some explaining to do."

Picking up my phone, I push the button beside Noah's picture, then I put the call on speaker. It rings three times before I hear him say, "Lorelai, what's up? You feeling any better about Mom and Dad's move?"

"No, I'm not," I tell him plainly. "But that's not why I'm calling. I'm wondering why you told Luke that Michael and I just broke up."

"What?" He sounds guilty. "Luke must have misheard me. I didn't say …"

Luke joins the conversation. "What exactly did I mishear?"

"Oh, hey, Luke." Noah's caught now and I half expect him to make up an excuse that he has to go.

Before he can, I volunteer, "Luke says he didn't break up with anyone, either."

"Fine, you've caught me." My brother confesses, "The truth is that now that we're all grown up, I got to thinking that you two might be a good match. You know, you're both so creative and all."

"So, my staying here wasn't for my benefit?" Luke sounds angry. "It was to set me up with your *sister*?" He says sister like it's a synonym for vampire, or slug. Either way, it's not very flattering.

I'm insulted that he's taking it so hard. If he weren't standing here, I'd probably thank my brother for his intervention. Yet I feel pressured to sound as offended as Luke does, so, I tell Noah, "I can find my own dates, thank you very much."

"Can you though?" he demands. "You've had the biggest crush on Luke ever since you first met him. I thought I was doing you a favor." It's my turn to blush.

Glancing up nervously, I attempt to smile at my guest. Though, I'm certain it comes out more as a grimace. "I did have a crush on you, but I don't anymore. I mean, obviously." The image of me playing peeping Tom yesterday pops into my mind and I lower my head in shame.

"Noah," Luke tells my brother, "I'm too busy to date. Not to mention, Lorelai and I don't even live in the same town." Happily, he doesn't mention my childhood infatuation, or my voyeuristic tendencies. I'm not sure I could handle that.

"Lorelai might be leaving Elk Lake," Noah says, which once again makes me angry that he learned of my fate before I did.

"I *may* have to move," I tell him, "But I have no plans on moving to Chicago." If I did, I'd probably only be able to afford to rent a stoop in front of a seedy liquor store.

"You could move to Chicago if you wanted," Noah says. "I'd even let you stay with me for a month while you got settled." Apparently, the word is out in my family. *Don't let Lorelai stay for long or she'll never leave.*

"How magnanimous of you." The sarcasm is heavy. "But I'll find some way to make it on my own, and that won't be in Chicago."

"You're both missing the point," Noah says.

"Which is?" Luke sounds perturbed, which of course ruffles me.

"You're both single and reasonably good-looking ..." Luke is straight up hot, so I suppose I'm the one being damned by this dim compliment. Noah continues, "And I love you both. I think you'd be great together."

The tension is suddenly so thick you'd think the room was about to explode like an atomic bomb being detonated. "I don't have time to think about dating anyone," I tell my brother.

"Luke isn't just anyone," he says. "He's your childhood heart-throb." I want to slink under the table and hide. I so badly want to look at Luke but I'm afraid I'll see an expression of disgust etched across his features.

The object of my fantasies interjects, "I'm in Elk Lake to patch things up with my dad, Noah. And while I appreciate your helping me find a place to stay, I'd be grateful if you'd stay out of the rest of my business."

I am mortified.

Inhaling deeply, I somehow manage to add, "That goes double for me. My biggest problem isn't my single status. It's that my whole life is about to change."

"In three months."

"If you're going to pity me, Noah, pity my housing situation, not my lack of a social life."

"There's no pity at play here," he tells me. "I'm just trying to help two people who mean the world to me."

I have never been this embarrassed in my life and that includes the time my shorts fell off while riding the centrifugal force ride at the county fair when I was a sophomore in high school. There's no humiliation quite like having a good chunk of the town know you prefer granny panties to something more age appropriate. I can't think of anything else to say, so I tell my brother, "Goodbye, Noah. Mind your own business." Then I hang up on him.

Luke turns around and walks back to the stove. He serves up two plates and brings them back to the table. Sitting across from me, he says, "I know you used to like me, Lorelai, but I'm really not looking right now."

Oh no, he didn't. "I *did* have a crush on you, Luke, but I assure you that I no longer do. I'm an adult now. I've moved on." I don't make eye contact while I say this because I'm sure if I did, he'd be able to tell that I'm lying.

"Good," he says. "It's not that you're not a nice kid . . woman … but like I told Noah, I'm not looking to get involved with anyone."

Oh, My. God. Why can't he let this go? "Neither am I," I assure him.

"Good," he repeats.

"Yes, it is."

I pick up my fork with the intention of not saying another word to him. Then I take a bite of the crepe. I groan out oud like I'm experiencing some form of ecstasy, which I am. My taste buds have never been this happy. "Thank you for making breakfast," I tell him. "It's delicious."

"You're welcome." We eat the rest of our meal in excruciating silence. Not only do I have to leave my home soon, but my brother has made my dream turn into a nightmare. What else can go wrong?

CHAPTER TWENTY

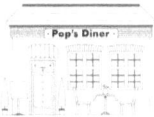

LUKE

I would have to be blind not to have noticed that Lorelai has turned into a beautiful woman. Her tangerine hair is now a gorgeous auburn, which sets off her blue eyes beautifully. She's tallish and quite graceful. But it's not just physical attractiveness. I've noticed stacks of baby blankets strewn about which I'm sure she's donating somewhere, which makes her super kind. She's got a quirkiness about her that I find intriguing. And every once in a while, the thought of kissing her lands right in the middle of my mind. But none of that matters. She's Noah's little sister, and she lives in Elk Lake. There's no way she and I are ever going to be a couple. No. Way.

Having said that, I do suddenly wonder what Lorelai is like on a date. I have to suppress a laugh at the image of her offering her romantic interest a Toaster Strudel for breakfast. If I'm honest, she's endearingly unpredictable and that realization is not exactly welcome.

Trying to get us back on more comfortable footing, I tell her, "Noah said that you wanted to own a bed and breakfast someday."

"I thought it could be fun, but that won't be in my near future. I'm not even sure I can afford rent, let alone a house."

"Maybe you could find work in a hotel or something. You know, to further your education of what owning a bed and breakfast would entail."

"I did work at the Elk Lake Lodge," she says. "But I quit so I can get this place ready for sale."

"Noah mentioned that. I was hoping to check out their restaurant some time."

"You totally should. It's great." It's obvious she's still annoyed. I just don't know if it's directed toward me or Noah.

As soon as she's done eating, Lorelai stands up and takes her plate to the kitchen sink. "I'm sorry about my brother," she offers. "I'm horrified by what he did."

"Don't be." I try to soften the blow of my earlier reaction by adding, "I mean, it's not like it would have been totally out of the question had he tried to set us up another time. It's just that … you know … there's a lot going on in my life right now."

I can't tell if Lorelai is about to run across the room and throw herself into my arms or if she's going to flee the kitchen. Either way, a sprint seems imminent. But before she can do either thing, the doorbell rings. *Saved by the bell.*

Lorelai looks as relieved as I am. "I'd better get that."

Once she leaves the room, I stand up and make quick work of cleaning up after breakfast. I find a plastic container in the pantry and wrap some of the food to take to my dad. I figure if I share my creations with him, he might start to understand me better.

After packing a plastic grocery sack, I walk into the living room to get my coat. Lorelai is talking to a woman I recognize from high school. She was a senior when I was a freshman. "Anna?"

Our guest turns toward me wearing a radiant smile. "Luke Phillips?"

"That's me." I walk over to her and give her a quick hug. "How have you been? You're still living in Elk Lake, huh?"

"I was in Chicago, but my husband and I came back when we found out we were pregnant. This really is the perfect town to raise a family." Lorelai is working hard not to look at me. So much so that she stares at the floor, the ceiling, and even her own hands, but she won't make eye contact with me.

"I heard about your dad's accident," Anna says. "Please give him and your mom my best."

"Will do," I tell her. "It was nice running into you."

I'm not sure why she's visiting Lorelai, but I don't stick around to ask. I just wave to both women and say, "Have a nice day."

The drive to the hospital is quick. I wish I were more excited to see my dad, but the truth is that I'm dreading it. There's only so much small talk we can make with each other. Getting out of my car, I grab the sausage crepes and then lock the door before walking into the hospital.

My goal today is to stay long enough to see my mom as we switch shifts. Looking at the clock, that means that I'll need to be here for three hours. That might as well be three days for how smoothly I anticipate things going.

I don't see Tony upstairs, so I'm guessing it's his day off. Taking a deep breath, I walk into my dad's room. I'm surprised to find an empty bed. Panic floods my nervous system. Did something happen to him? Dear God, please let him not have had a stroke or heart attack. I force myself to breathe deeply and try to calm down. Surely, if there had been an emergency the hospital would have called my mom, and she in turn would have called me. Unless, of course, it just happened, and she hasn't had a chance.

A short, middle-aged woman wearing green scrubs walks into the room. "Where's my dad?" I don't mean to sound as forceful as I do, but I'm ridiculously anxious.

Taking the chart off the hook at the end of the bed, she says, "He's having another MRI. It shouldn't take more than another thirty minutes or so."

"Why does he need another MRI?"

"The doctor wanted to make sure he wasn't forming any blood clots." She explains, "They're sometimes a result of forced immobility."

"So, he's all right?"

"As all right as he was before." She marks something on the chart before putting it back and walking out of the room.

Slumping down in the chair next to the bed, it suddenly hits me how very lucky it was that my dad didn't break his neck when he fell, or worse. He could have died. I close my eyes while I wait for his return and try to formulate a course of action. My brain tells me to be calm and pleasant, but my heart is saying something much different. Which is why when my dad is wheeled back into the room, I practically shout, "Thank goodness you're okay!"

He's lying face-up on a gurney, so I can see his expression clearly. Confusion is written across his features. "I wouldn't call being in traction okay."

"Of course not." I stand up and move to his side while his attendants start to transfer him to his bed. They're very careful to go slowly so as not to cause him more discomfort. As they reattach the pulleys to his arm and leg, I explain, "I just panicked when I got here, and you were gone."

"Thought I bit the big one, huh?"

So much for being touched by my concern.

"The thought had crossed my mind," I tell him truthfully.

He remains quiet while the nurse puts a blood pressure cuff on his arm. She fusses around for a bit longer before telling him, "Call if you need anything, Mr. Phillips." Then she walks out of the room.

"Did you have breakfast?" I ask my dad.

"They brought me some oatmeal a while ago, but I couldn't eat it. It was awful."

"How can you screw up oatmeal?"

He rolls his eyes before explaining, "You can overcook it, under-season it, and serve it soupy. They did all the above."

I reach for the grocery bag that I brought with me. "How do sausage and mushroom crepes sound?"

"You'd better not be joking around, Luke." My dad's warning nearly makes me laugh.

"I would never joke about crepes." Walking toward the door, I add, "I'll just go heat this up for you at the nurses' station."

It takes me a grand total of two minutes to transfer my dad's food to a paper plate and give it a quick zap in the microwave. When I get back to his room, he says, "I hope you brought a lot. I'm starving."

I put the plate down on the rolling tabletop next to his bed before cutting the crepes into bite-sized pieces. "You want me to feed you?" I ask him.

He lifts his good arm. "I got it."

Sitting down on the chair next to him, I watch while he picks up a plastic fork. Stabbing it into a piece of crepe, he moves it around the plate to pick up the sauce, then he puts it into his mouth. Closing his eyes, he chews it and swallows before saying, "So much better than soupy oatmeal."

"I'd like to take that as a compliment," I joke. "But there really isn't anything much worse than soupy oatmeal."

A small smile begins to form, but he hurries to suppress it. "It's good, Luke. Really good."

His praise makes me feel like a little kid who just hit a home run in the ninth inning of a Little League championship game. "Thanks, Dad."

"You serve this at your restaurant?" I detect a note of irritation.

"Not at Capon," I tell him. "But I served it at the last place I worked."

"I like the rosemary and thyme," he says. "Very earthy tasting."

We don't say anything else while he finishes the food on his plate. Once he's done, I ask, "Can I get you some coffee?"

"Nah, I'm good."

"Dad …" I want to ask him a million questions, but I don't want to make him angry.

"What, Luke?"

I want to ask him about the specials at Pop's but I don't want him to think I'm checking up on him. "I'm really glad you're doing okay."

His head bobs up and down slowly. "You know what I'd really like?"

"I don't."

"I'd love a burger for lunch. I don't suppose you'd be willing to stop by Pop's and ask Jim to make one for me."

"I'd be happy to, Dad." Keeping up the pretense that I haven't been into the diner yet, I tell him, "I'd like to see Jim again. How's he doing?"

"He's Jim. Always on time, always smiling …"

"He's a great guy," I say.

His only response is a grunt. Then he wants to know, "When's your mom coming by?"

"She'll be here at lunch time." I suddenly wonder how we're going to pass the time. We clearly don't have anything to say to each other.

My dad surprises me by demanding, "Tell me about your restaurant."

"What do you want to know?"

"Everything."

I can't read the expression on his face, so I don't know if I'm walking into a land mine or not. I simply start talking. "It's down by the river …"

CHAPTER TWENTY-ONE

LORELAI

While showing Anna around the house, I ask her, "How do you know Luke Phillips?"

"He was three years younger than me, but you know how high school-aged kids are. They don't usually bother with anyone even a year younger."

"Tell me about it." I don't know why, but I feel comfortable enough with Anna that I admit, "I used to have a huge crush on Luke when I was a kid, but I was four years younger, so he didn't know I existed."

She laughs before nudging me with her arm. "Looks like you've remedied that situation, huh?"

"Oh, no. He's not … We're not …" I'm suddenly overwhelmingly flustered that she thinks we're an item. "Luke is my brother's friend. He's only staying here. In a different bedroom," I feel the need to explain.

She tips her head to the side until her box braids are nearly sitting on her shoulder. "Why isn't he staying with his parents?"

"It's complicated," I tell her.

Her face suddenly brightens. "Is your brother Noah Riley?"

"Yeah."

"He played basketball with my high school boyfriend. Small world, huh?"

"I guess so." Then I ask, "You don't by any chance do rentals at your agency, do you?"

"Vacation rentals," she says.

"I might be looking for an apartment in town," I tell her. "Do you know of anything that's nice but cheap?"

"Not off the top of my head, but I'll keep my ears open." As I lead her into the kitchen, she says, "Your parents asked for a list of things that will help this house sell faster." Looking around, she says, "I definitely think the kitchen needs to be repainted, and as much as it's a pain, you should lay some vinyl planking in here to replace this old tile." She gestures toward the cracked flooring. "It's kind of dated."

"Planking would definitely look more modern," I tell her thinking about how I've been advocating this very thing for years. "Any idea what color we should paint?"

"Just make everything as neutral as you can. Not all white, but blank enough of a slate that people can see their own furnishings here."

An idea hits me. "If this house is going to be used as a vacation house, do you think we might sell it furnished?"

"That's a possibility," she says. "But you'd want to get some neutral slipcovers in the living room." I knew giant faded cabbage roses were a thing of the past, but my mom disagreed.

Anna and I spend the next hour walking around the house. She seems to think we'll get a lot more money for the place once I fulfill everything on her list. She also thinks new appliances would add a lot of value. Apparently, people aren't super excited about a twenty-year-old washer and dryer.

"My parents want to put the house on the market at the beginning of the season. They're hoping for a quick sell."

"If you do everything we talked about, you should get one." Reaching into her purse, Anna hands me a piece of paper. "Here are some numbers for painters and handymen. The first thing you need to do is to empty the closets and bookshelves of personal items. Then paint and carpet, lay other flooring, and finally replace the appliances."

Walking down the stairs to the front door, I tell her, "It's going to take me some time to get everything packed."

"It's best if you move whatever you don't want to sell with the house to a storage unit. The less clutter, the bigger everything looks."

My head nods like a bobble head on the dashboard of a speeding car. "It sounds like I have a lot to do."

"It'll go faster than you think," she says. "In the meantime, I'll look at comps and recommend a listing price."

"Thanks, Anna," I tell her as I open the door.

After she leaves, I move over to the stairs where I sit down and try to evaluate my next step. I need to start packing. If we're able to make more money by selling the place furnished, I wonder if my parents will throw a little extra cash my way. I don't want to be greedy, but every little bit will help me get reestablished.

My first task of the day needs to be acquiring packing supplies. I pick up my phone and call my parents.

My dad answers using my childhood nickname. "Hey there, Lorie Loo." If I had to guess, I'd say he's trying to get on my good side.

"Dad." I'm all business. "I need you and Mom to send me that list of things you want to keep so I can figure out how many boxes to buy."

"We've been talking about that," he says. "We think it would be easier if you just take pictures of everything. That way we can see what we're talking about."

If they're looking for easier, they should come home and go through everything themselves. Although if they did that, I'd be homeless much sooner. "Sounds good," I tell him. "What do you want to do with all your alien books? You ready to let those go?"

"No!" he practically shouts. "They're coming this year for sure and I want to be ready."

"Ready, how? Are you going to roll out the red carpet and welcome them?"

"Depends on which kind show up," he says. "If it's the Nordics or the Arcturians, I'm all in for a party, but if it's the Draco Reptilians, we're screwed." Most people would have no idea what he's talking about, but I grew up on this kind of talk, so I'm fluent. The reptilians could possibly eat us. Either that or return us to the slave race we apparently started as. Regardless, it won't be much fun.

"So, I'm packing the books?"

"Yes. And I want the alien garden gnomes, too."

"Why? You'll be in a condo. You won't have a garden of your own."

"Your mom says I can keep them on our patio." *Hurray.*

"What about all your winter clothes?" I ask.

"Take pictures. We're going to want to do some traveling, so we'll need some basics."

"Are you planning on coming back to Wisconsin in the winter?" Because if so, they might reconsider selling.

"We're not coming back to the Midwest. We're thinking about going to Switzerland or Austria next winter." I want to go to Switzerland. Maybe they'll hire me to carry their bags.

"I've gotta go, Dad. Lots for me to do here." *Like figure out what my future holds.* Maybe the reptilians will take over by then and I won't have to decide for myself.

"Love you, honey!" He hangs up before I have a chance to say anything else.

Grabbing my car keys, I leave the house. My first stop is packing supplies. I figure I'll get enough for my stuff, too. That way, while I wait to hear what my parents want to keep, I can start getting my things ready.

My second stop is the paint store where I pick up color samples. Anna suggests giving the bedrooms each their own color but to make them light and refreshing. The rest of the house can be one basic shade of beige. I didn't tell her but I'm considering having the upper kitchen cabinets painted navy blue. I've always loved that classical nautical look and the way I'm going I may never have the chance to do that in my own house. I might as well enjoy this process as much as I can.

I wind up spending most of the afternoon out. After getting all the supplies I went for, I drive around town looking for rental places. According to the Elk Lake website, there are a couple apartments available above shops in town. The one that caught my eye is above the Yarn Barn, which seems fortuitous. According to the pictures online, it small but cute and feminine looking.

While I'm not going to rent something today, I'd like to check out the locations of what's available. As in, I prefer not to be located behind a gas station or convenience store. I've seen way too many true crime shows to know that never turns out well. But life above a yarn shop feels like a sweet romcom, so I put it on the top of my list to go see.

When I'm finally on my way home, I realize that I missed lunch and it's almost supper time. I could either go home and microwave a frozen meal, or I could stop at Pop's and take Luke up on his offer to order meals as compensation for letting him stay with me. Of course, if he keeps feeding me breakfast, there's really no need to supply my suppers as well. But now that I'm soon to be on my own, I decide to get all the freebies I can.

After parking in front of Pop's, I walk inside and find the mean hostess from the other day. She glares at me. "Let me guess, you're meeting someone, and you want to sit by the window." She looks as pleased as she sounds.

I force a smile, wondering what has turned such a young girl so bitter. "I'm alone but I still want to sit by the window."

She snorts so loudly I'm sure she's about to tell me that won't be possible, but then Luke walks up behind her. "Lorelai! I'm glad you came in." He sounds happy to see me, which means he's likely trying to compensate for this morning's conversation. The one where he made it clear he doesn't want to date me.

"Luke, hi." I wave in such a way that it might be misconstrued as a seizure.

"I'll seat Lorelai," Luke tells the hostess. Chloe rolls her eyes in response.

I hurry to catch up with him as he leads the way to a booth by the window. When we get there, he asks, "Mind if I eat with you? I've got a forty-minute break and I'm starving."

He wants to eat with me? I'm not quite sure how I feel about that. If he'd asked me yesterday, I would have been all for it. But now that I know there's no chance for us, I'm not sure. Although maybe now that there's no pressure, I can relax and be myself. I finally decide, "That would be nice."

Luke looks relieved. "I'm going to get myself a soda. You want one?"

I ask for a Sprite. As he walks away, I realize that it's too bad our timing isn't better. But what's the point of falling for him all over again only to have him go back to Chicago?

Luke comes back with two glasses. He puts them on the table before taking the seat across from me. "You know what you want?" he asks.

"Cheeseburger," I tell him. "With onion rings."

He gets up again and walks across the room. When he gets to the counter, he fills out a ticket and passes it through the window leading to the kitchen. When he returns, he says, "I ate cheeseburgers here at least three times a week when I was growing up."

"I don't know what the secret is," I tell him, "but I've never had them as good as your dad makes them."

He puts his pointer finger up to his lips before telling me, "We slip an ice cube into the patty before cooking it. That ensures the burger stays juicy."

"Your secret's safe with me," I tell him.

Mrs. Harry, an older volunteer from the Humane Society, walks through the front door with a goldendoodle on a leash. The dog spots me immediately and breaks free of her walker's grip. She runs right up to me and jumps into the seat next to me.

"Penelope!" I say excitedly while scratching behind her ears. "Looks like you're on a field trip."

"Who's this?" Luke asks, laughing.

Mrs. Harry hurries over. "I'm sorry about Penelope, Lorelai, but you know how much she likes you."

I turn to Luke and explain, "Penelope is one of the dogs from the pound. Her owner died two months ago and she's looking for her forever home." He raises his eyebrows in question, so I add, "I go in and walk her a couple of times a week so she can remember what life on the outside looks like."

Luke's face crumples. "That's so nice and so sad."

Shrugging, I tell him, "It's life, right?" I add, "I would love to have a sweet girl like this, but I won't be able to keep her in an apartment."

"Are you moving?" Mrs. Harry wants to know.

"My parents are selling their house," I tell her. "So, I'll be moving into an apartment soon."

"That's too bad, dear. We all thought that you and Penelope were meant to be."

So did I but I'll start crying again if I think about it. "I'm sure she'll go to a nice home with little kids she can grow up with."

Mrs. Harry takes Penelope's leash and gently disengages her from my side. "We'll see you soon, dear. Come on, Penny, let's go get my order and we can share a burger in the park together."

This is an obvious routine of theirs because Penny smiles in that derpy doodle way of hers and jumps down to leave with Mrs. Harry.

Once they're gone, Luke says, "I could see you with a dog like that. I bet you'd knit her sweaters."

"I've already made her two," I tell him, surprised that he'd have that kind of insight about me.

After a short lull in conversation, I worry we might have just exhausted everything we have to say to each other. Which is why

I unexpectedly decide to tell him, "Michael hated cheeseburgers. That should have tipped me off long before it did that we weren't going to make it."

He laughs in response. "I once dated a vegan. That was rough."

"Even if I could live without meat," I tell him, "I'd never be able to cut cheese from my diet."

I know he feels my pain when he adds, "No ice cream, no whipped cream, no cream sauces!"

"It's got to be a miserable kind of life."

I take a sip of my soda right as Luke asks, "Have you dated anyone else since Michael?"

I snort, causing bubbles of carbonation to enter my brain. "It's Elk Lake. Who would I date?"

Is it me or is Luke having a hard time making eye contact with me? I wish I knew what he was thinking, but I suppose it might be in my best interest if I don't.

CHAPTER TWENTY-TWO

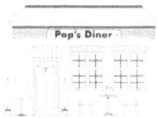

LUKE

I feel bad about how things went down with Lorelai this morning. She's been very accommodating, if not a bit awkward. Although, my mood did lighten when I saw her walk into Pop's. Hopefully, having dinner together will give us a chance to put any uncomfortableness behind us. After I place our order, I ask her, "How was your day?"

She shifts in her seat like she's nervous. "Busy. Anna gave me a long list of things that need to get done to the house before we list it."

It suddenly hits me. "Anna's a realtor!"

She nods her head. "A lot of people who grew up here like living here as adults." She looks at me accusingly like there's something wrong with me that I don't feel the same way.

Staring at Lorelai across the booth, it occurs to me that if I did live here, I might ask her out on a date. She's beautiful, funny, easy to talk to, very community minded, and she's a meat eater. All wins in my book. She's also nothing like the women I meet in Chicago.

Everyone in the city seems determined to achieve a big life

with all that entails. Being that my schedule is diametrically opposite to most of theirs—as in, I work nights—that leaves precious
little time to get to know each other.

"What's your restaurant like?" Lorelai wants to know.

I explain it the same way I did with my dad earlier today. "It's
bigger than I wanted starting out, but once I saw the space, I knew
I had to open it there." I tell her, "It's in Marina City, right next to
the matching round towers."

"I totally know that place!" she exclaims excitedly. "It's in all
the movies filmed in Chicago."

Nodding my head, "I explain, "Capon faces the river. We even
have outdoor seating for warmer weather."

"That sounds amazing," she says longingly.

"Have you ever wanted to live in Chicago?"

Lorelai shakes her head. "It's not that I don't like to visit. I'm
just fundamentally a small-town girl. Even Madison was larger
than I like."

She and I couldn't be more different. "I love the hum of city
living," I tell her. "I like being able to order food at two in the
morning if I want to. I like not knowing everyone that lives in my
building."

"Why wouldn't you want to know all your neighbors?" She
makes it sound like anonymity is the craziest idea she's ever
heard of.

"It keeps life interesting," I tell her. "People come and go all
the time, so there are always new ones to meet."

She ponders that for a minute before saying, "I like meeting
people at the lodge. But that's all the new I need. I want to know
everyone in my town."

"And there a lot of people still here from high school?"

"Enough. There's Faith, who owns the bakery. She and Anna
are best friends. Then there's Melissa, Paige, and Tim. Tim's
family owns the country club."

"I know them all," I tell her. "We were all in the same gradu-
ating class." I'm actually surprised so many of my classmates still

live here. I would have thought they'd have all gone on to bigger and better things.

"My friend Allie, who I went through all of school with, just moved back. She and her husband got divorced."

I can see coming back after experiencing a trauma like that, so I say, "Home is a good place to regroup."

"Just not to live permanently, huh?" She sounds slightly defensive.

"I guess we all have a different idea of what feels like home."

A young waitress that I haven't met yet stops by with our food. Once she leaves, Lorelai says, "I figured you'd be one of those people like Faith who took over the family business."

"That's what my dad thought, too." I'm not sure why I tell her that other than I feel very comfortable with Lorelai. Also, her life seems to currently be in as much turmoil as mine, so I assume she'll be sympathetic.

"Can't you do both?" she asks. "You know, have a restaurant in the city and keep Pop's once your dad retires."

"I've truthfully never considered it. I like fine dining, and while diner food is great to eat, it's not that creative to make."

She takes a bite of her burger, chews it, and swallows before saying, "Bobby Flay must have a hundred restaurants. He can't be at all of them all the time, and I'm sure they serve different kinds of food."

"I suppose that's true," I tell her. "But I'm not Bobby Flay. I just want to make a hit out of my one place."

"You're the one with big ideas." She says this like she's challenging me. "I'd think you'd already have your eye on your next project."

It's not that I haven't thought about opening a second restaurant, but I've always assumed that it would be years down the line. "Maybe someday," I tell her. "But right now, I just want to be successful where I'm at."

"I read about Capon in *Chicago* magazine. It looks like you've already made it." She picks up an onion ring and dunks it into a side of ranch.

"We're doing pretty well," I tell her. We're actually doing great. It's just such a big dream come true that I don't want to spread myself too thin by taking on more than I can handle.

"I'd love to eat there sometime," Lorelai says. Her face turns bright red, and she adds, "You know, if I'm ever in Chicago."

"Chicago is only two hours away," I tell her. "I assume that even if you don't want to live there, you will visit. When you do, give me a call. I'd love to host you at Capon." She smiles adorably and I start to wonder how I ever thought this lovely woman was annoying.

"I'll let you know if I ever visit Noah," she says. "He's probably the only person I'd go there for." She lowers her eyes bashfully.

"You're always welcome to visit me, too," I tell her. "After all, we're almost like family, right?"

She glances at me briefly, but her expression quickly falls. I wonder if Lorelai's crush on me isn't as over as she claims it is. "Lucky me," she says. "The only thing better than one big brother is two."

I'm not currently feeling very big brotherly toward Lorelai. In fact, the more I see of her and her life—I mean walking dogs at the pound?—I'm wondering what it would be like to pull her into my arms and give her a real kiss? In an attempt to change the subject to something safer, I tell her, "I don't see as much of Noah as I'd like to."

Lorelai rolls her eyes. "He's probably too busy trying to make his basketball team hate him."

"He must be doing something right. I hear they're in the top five in the state."

"They're third," Lorelai says. "But Noah has his eye on taking first place this year. I'm pretty sure if he manages it, his team will be ready to kill him."

Throwing out one of my dad's favorite platitudes, I tell her, "You've got to work hard if you want to get ahead."

"There's more to life than winning," she retaliates. I suddenly wonder if she's talking about basketball, or something else. Like cooking, for instance.

"What did you do when you lived in Madison?" I ask.

"I worked the desk at the spa at Water's Edge."

"Swanky." I've always wanted to stay at that hotel, but I really have no reason to be in Madison.

"It was fine." She doesn't sound too excited.

"What did your boyfriend do?"

"Michael was in banking." She adds, "I think his friends looked down on me for doing what they considered a blue-collar kind of job."

"There's nothing blue collar about Water's Edge," I tell her. I can't help but wonder if Michael also thought she wasn't meeting her potential. Maybe he was embarrassed by her. While I don't know this for sure, I feel disgust brewing in me.

"Their girlfriends and wives were the kind of people who went to the spa. They would never work at one."

"Some professional people look down on restaurant workers, too," I tell her.

"It's funny, isn't it? I mean, if people are filling a demand, you'd think you'd appreciate them." She adds, "Michael wasn't that fancy, but he liked to hold himself up above others. Almost like other people's lack of success made him feel better about himself."

"Did he do that with you?"

She considers my question closely before answering, "He didn't say as much, but I still knew he would have preferred if I did something else. The thing is that I want to work to live, not the other way around. There's so much more to life than your job. Michael never seemed to think that."

My fists clench in anger. If the guy was sitting here, I might not be able to keep myself from punching him. "Why were you ever with someone like that?"

She lowers her eyes to her plate. "Maybe I felt like there was something wrong with me that I wasn't driven to rise in the ranks of some hot shot job. Being with Michael made it feel like I was successful by default."

"That doesn't seem like you at all," I tell her truthfully. "You're clearly more put together than that."

"Thank you?" I can tell she's not sure if that's a compliment or not.

"You're better off without him."

"I obviously think so, too," she agrees. "I did leave him."

I remind myself that while I like Lorelai, I cannot allow myself to get distracted by her. I'm here to make things right with my dad and as soon as I do that I'm going back to Chicago. I hurry to finish my burger before saying, "I'd better get going."

She forces a smile. "Thanks for dinner, Luke. I'll see you at home later."

A warm rush of contentment fills me. She'll see me at *home*. I like how that sounds. Better yet, I like how it makes me feel. It's too bad Lorelai never wants to live in Chicago, because I'm starting to think that I'd like to see her there.

CHAPTER TWENTY-THREE

LORELAI

Time is starting to blend together, and I'm no longer sure what day it is. My life has become all about sorting, packing, and schlepping. It turns out my parents want even less from their lives here than I thought they did and the trips to Goodwill have increased. *Am I the only one who has fond memories of this house?*

After consulting the calendar, I discover it's only been three days since I found out about my mom and dad's relocation plans. I decide to take a break from boxing up their seasonal clothes to call Noah. I'm still piqued that he knew about my parents wanting to sell before I did, so I tell him, "I am not packing up your room for you."

"Um, okay. Hi, by the way."

"If you want to keep anything, you'd better come home and pack it yourself. Then get rid of whatever you don't want." I'm usually way nicer than this, but my family is currently on my list.

"You're in a mood," he grumbles.

"I've been packing for three straight days and I'm getting tired of it."

He shouts, "Get back onto that court and walk it off!"

I hear a poor soul, who I'm guessing is one of his basketball players, say, "But Coach, it's starting to swell."

"Is it broken? Can you see bone?" He can't be serious, but then he hurries to add, "Fine, sit down and put it up, but only for five minutes. No more."

"Noah," I say, hoping to remind my brother that he's on the phone.

"What?" he practically yells before lowering his voice. "If you're packing up everyone else's stuff, why can't you pack mine, too? How long could it possibly take?"

"Mom and Dad are paying me," I remind him. "You're not."

"Would you do it if I paid you?" He sounds desperate and for a moment I feel bad about my surly attitude. The moment passes quickly.

"I would not. Listen, Noah, I know you don't think I do much of anything, but my life is busy. I'm serious. If you don't come home within the next two weeks, I'm going to call a charity to come in and clean out your room. The painters need to get in there and so do the guys laying carpet."

"I've got practice every day this week and next …"

I cut him off. "Not my problem. Get here or it all goes." To punctuate my sincerity, I hang up. A hum of power flows through me and I like it.

Staring at the closet shelves in my parents' room, I realize I haven't laid eyes on Luke since our supper together at Pop's. I wonder if I said something to scare him off. Although, I suppose it's possible he's just super busy. Allie mentioned something about the town's seniors meeting at Pop's every night this week before their bingo tournament at St. Mary's. Word is that Faith's grandmother is up three hundred dollars. She's using the proceeds to buy more cards so she can take home the thousand-dollar grand prize. She's promised to use some of her winnings to keep me in yarn.

Thinking about Faith's grandmother makes me smile. I hope my golden years are spent right here in Elk Lake like Miss Rosemary's. Yet, if that's ever going to happen, I'm going to need to figure out a revenue stream to support that dream. Elk Lake is a resort location in summer, and quickly becoming something of a winter destination as well. As such, rents are not as cheap as you'd think they'd be in a small Wisconsin town.

Walking down the stairs, I look at all the paint chips I've taped up on the walls. I've been checking them at different times of day to see what they look like in various lighting. Today, I'm going to buy some samples and cover larger areas before I commit to the final shades.

I'm surprised to see Luke when I walk into the kitchen. He's been leaving the house before I get up, and it's already past nine. He's sitting at the table staring across the room like he's in a trance. "Hey," I say.

He seems startled by the sound of my voice. "Hey, yourself. It looks like you're going full steam ahead getting everything packed up."

"There's so much to do," I moan, while pouring myself a cup of coffee and joining him. Instead of asking him where he's been, I say, "I haven't seen you in a while."

"Life has been busy."

"Is your dad okay?"

"I haven't seen him a lot, but my mom said he's been doing so well that he's being released today."

"Are you spending all of your time at Pop's?"

"When I'm not at the diner, I've been at my parents' house getting things ready for Dad's return." He explains, "Stairs will be tough for him to climb for a while, so we're setting up his bedroom in the living room. I've rented him a hospital bed, a wheelchair, a walker, and all kinds of aids for the bathroom. It's a lot."

"I bet your mom is happy you're home."

He looks pained as he answers, "She thinks it's up to me to get my dad to see the light and forgive me for living in Chicago."

"Have you tried?"

Luke gives me a sarcastic look. "No, Lorelai, I haven't. I like being the target of his anger." He offers a big sigh before looking straight at my face and adding, "Of course, I've tried, but the man is not interested."

I have no idea what to say to that, so I stand up and walk across the kitchen to see if Luke made anything for breakfast. There's a pot of oatmeal on the stove. "Is there enough for two?" I take his grunt to mean yes, so I fill a bowl before coming back to the table.

Luke says, "I tried cooking for him, hoping that would give us something to bond over, but after the third time, he told me to stop. He said he didn't want fancy stuff."

"Did you try talking to him about your restaurant? Maybe the way to his heart is to tell him what you're doing."

"I told him on the second day," he practically spits. "I don't know what else to do. I've talked about our memories from my childhood like how we used to cook the fish we caught right on the beach. I've waxed poetic about all the fun times we had, but he just turns off."

"And your mom doesn't know how you can reach him?"

He shakes his head. "I know she's upset. She seems as frustrated as I am, but she's mostly unhappy with me for not making it right with him."

"What does your dad like to do when he's not at Pop's?" I ask in hopes of helping Luke find common ground with his father.

"He likes to fish in the summer. He skis in the winter. I'm not sure what he does in the spring."

Taking a bite of oatmeal, I release a sound of pleasure. "Yum! Is there ginger in here?"

"Candied ginger, peanut butter, cinnamon, and frozen blueberries."

"It's a weird and wonderful combination," I tell him. "Seriously good."

"Thanks." My praise doesn't seem to affect him.

"Look, Luke," I finally say, "even if you tied your dad up and forced him to talk, you can't make him see your side of things. You can only do your best."

"That's what I have been doing, but I'm not making any headway."

"Have you thought about telling him that you're cooking at Pop's?"

His eyes widen with anxiety. "He might never speak to me again if he knew that."

I haven't been into Pop's since the supper we shared the other day, so I tell him, "I was thinking about eating there tonight. Any chance you'll be around?"

"I'll be there," he says. "Why don't you come by around seven. I'm off early tonight."

"Sounds like a date." I quickly realize my mistake and amend that to, "Sounds like a plan."

Luke stands up and puts his coffee cup into the sink. "Thanks for listening, Lorelai. Sorry I'm so grumpy. I'm just frustrated."

"I know the feeling," I tell him. "Life doesn't always turn out the way we think it should and that can be quite a shock."

"You mean like you having to leave your house?"

"That's certainly one of the things." It's more like the main thing. Other than having to move, I really like my life.

"I've always been of the mind that we make our own opportunities," he tells me.

For as simple a statement as that is, something about it really hits home. I guess I've always just gone with the flow and hoped for the best. Tucking his words into the back of my mind, I tell him, "I'm here if you ever need to talk." The truth is that I really like talking to Luke. I feel like he is becoming a lot more than just a past crush. He's a really decent guy in his own right.

The expression in his eyes softens. "Thank you. I really enjoy talking to you." Walking toward the door, he says, "I'll see you tonight."

As Luke leaves, I realize that I cannot let myself keep pining after him like I have been. I'm just not sure how to stop my feelings. While my original crush on him was one hundred percent motivated by teenage hormones—and there's still a large percentage of raw attraction going on—I'm also getting to know him. And darn if I don't like what I see. Luke is a good person. He's hard-working and driven, but he's also determined to make things right with his dad. That says a lot about the caliber of man he is.

After finishing my breakfast, I put my bowl into the sink and head into the living room. My parents have collected a weird array of stuff over the years, from bookends shaped like giant noses to animal statues carved from compressed walnut shells. There's nothing here I would fight my brother for possession of, yet I can't imagine relegating it all to the shelves at the charity shop. I send pictures to Noah, hoping he'll take custody of some of it.

My dad's alien books take up three boxes. Then I pack a drawer full of candles, thinking I might take those with me. If things don't go well in the hunt for the perfect apartment, I might need a little mood lighting to keep me from noticing the water stains on the walls and the rats running across the floor of my living room. Not to mention keeping things bright after dark should my electricity be shut off for non-payment. Hypothetically speaking, of course.

I'm not sure why I think I'll be lowered to living in some Dickensian slum, but honestly, that's all that comes to mind at the moment.

I close my eyes and advise myself, "Buckle up, buttercup. You. Have. Got. This. Failure is not an option."

CHAPTER TWENTY-FOUR

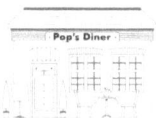

LUKE

After leaving Lorelai's, I head straight to my parents' house where I discover my mom has already left for the hospital. My dad is going to be discharged today, which means my mom, in her typical drill sergeant way, is ready to take command. She texted me earlier to let me know they should be arriving home somewhere between eleven and one. She's also left me a list of things to do.

Once I get everything in order, I'll get to work and make my dad a special welcome home lunch. He might not want it, but there really isn't much else I can offer him.

After letting myself through the front door, I realize how depressing it looks. The hospital bed in the living room reminds me what it was like at my grandparents' house when my grandfather started hospice. He could no longer take the stairs, so he spent his remaining days in the living room. Thank goodness my dad will only be downstairs until he heals. Yet, it's still an unpleasant reminder that there are no guarantees in life.

After hanging my coat up, I go into the kitchen to make a pot of coffee. That's where I find another note from my mom. It's sitting on top of an old photo album that I've never seen before. It says:

Luke,

Look at this and then return it to my room when you're done. I'll put it away from there.

Mom

I'm interested enough in the contents of the book that I forgo making coffee. Instead, I pick up the album and take it to the family room.

After sitting on the couch, I open the cover. I feel a sharp pang in my heart when I see an image of a small boy. Based on the shape of his face and familiar lopsided grin, I assume it's my father. The first few pages are pictures of him with a couple I'm guessing are his parents. No one is smiling, including my dad. The whole feel is like that old *American Gothic* painting. Misery seems to be the main emotion.

Yet, in a couple of the pictures, my dad is playing with a boy a year or two older than him, and in those shots, he looks very happy. The resemblance between the two leads me to believe they're brothers. My dad has never mentioned having any siblings, but the proof seems to be right in front of me.

It appears that my mom has decided the only way to get me and my dad back on track is to give me some information about his early years. So far, it doesn't look like it was full of great memories.

Several pages in, the photographs stop, and the letters start.

The first one reads:

Dear Johnny,

I hate my new family so much. They don't talk and laugh like we used to when Mom and Dad were alive. They just tell me what to do. Make your bed, Bob. Clean your room, Bob. Mow the lawn, Bob. It's like they don't even want to know me.

I hope things are going better for you. Remember, I love you and we'll find some way to be together again someday. I promise.

Bobby

The notes from Bobby continue in the same vein for about a year. They're all so sad, I can understand why my dad never wanted to talk about them. Turning another page, I find a memorial pamphlet from a church service. Opening it up, I discover a funeral card for Bobby. *Oh my God, his brother died, too?* This is beyond heart wrenching.

I finish looking through the album, but I don't learn anything more about the people who raised my dad. All I discover is that he grew up in a small town in South Dakota. I'd always thought he was from Wisconsin, but how was I to think differently when he never told me anything?

Toward the end of the book, I find my dad's high school diploma along with a card of congratulations. The inscription reads:

John,

Congratulations on your graduation. We wish you the best in life.

Your adoptive parents,
Joshua and Liv

Who wishes their child, adopted or not good luck on the rest of their life? It's like they're telling him they're done with him and he's on his own. It makes my blood run cold.

I continue to flip through the photo album and find a certificate that says my dad completed his associate's degree in restaurant management. The degree came from a school in Milwaukee, which is where he met my mom. I have no idea how he came to leave South Dakota and move to Wisconsin. Although, I'm guessing his lack of a warm relationship with his adoptive parents had something to do with it.

I suddenly see why my mom said it was time for me to be an adult and treat my father like a child who needs to be shown the way. There must be a big part of his emotional growth that was stunted when he lost his parents and then his brother. The lack of nurturing he received from Joshua and Liv is sobering.

I think about how my whole life, my dad used to say, "Food heals." He said this if we were sick, and he spoon-fed us home-made chicken noodle soup. He said this if we fell off our bikes and skinned a knee when he handed us a cookie. I always thought he meant that food was nourishing and good for us. I'm starting to think he meant it less literally. Like food heals your heart. That must be why he started cooking. He had a hole in his heart that he was trying to repair, and food brought him comfort.

My poor dad. A tear slides down my cheek as I think about how much he's had to endure. I would never have imagined he started his life with such a significant deficit of care. I mean, I knew things couldn't have been great being that he never wanted to talk about his younger years, but still, nothing like this was ever on my radar.

Closing the book, I take it upstairs and leave it on my mom's dresser. I take a minute to look around my parents' bedroom. Every surface is covered with pictures of me and Kelsey. They range from the time we were babies and progress until very recently. Walking over to my

dad's dresser, I spot a framed picture of me and my mom that was taken at the opening of Capon. Why would he display that if he's so mad at me?

I'm left more confused than ever about my father's attitude toward me. Yet at the same time, I feel a reservoir of determination build. I don't know how, but I'm going to make things right between us once and for all.

I go back downstairs and put sheets on the hospital bed. Then I leave the house to grocery shop. I'm not going to make him my food, I'm going to make my dad the food he served to me when I was a child. Food that he wanted to "heal" me with.

In the baking aisle, I pick up a container of marshmallow fluff and laugh. I'm not a marshmallow fluff kind of guy, but my dad is. He used to eat the stuff right out of the jar. I put three containers into the cart before searching the store for the needed ingredients to make his chicken noodle soup. In the peanut butter aisle, I buy his favorite brand of extra chunky, and in the produce aisle, I add a bunch of bananas.

On my way to the cashier, I pick up five bouquets of flowers that I'll put in vases around the house. They're for my mom. She's been through a lot, and she deserves a dose of joy, too.

As soon as I get back to my parents' house, I put the pot of soup on. Not only will the aroma be comforting as it cooks, but it will make a nice dinner for them. I triple the recipe so there will be leftovers for a couple of days.

After cleaning up my mess, I put a batch of my dad's favorite chocolate chip cookies into the oven. Then I get busy assembling a plate of peanut butter, jelly, marshmallow, and banana sand-wiches. Truth be told, I still make them for myself occasionally. Not only does it bring back great memories, but I really do think the combination is somehow medicinal.

At eleven o'clock, my mom texts that they're about to leave the hospital. I run around making quick work of placing flowers throughout the first floor. I even build a fire in the living room fireplace so that my dad can watch it while he's in bed.

I know I can't make my father talk to me about his younger years, but I can change the way I treat our relationship. Forcing him to accept responsibility for our divide isn't going to get us on track. Instead, I'll be kind to him, and show love. I'll try to be more understanding of his wounds that I know nothing about.

CHAPTER TWENTY-FIVE

LORELAI

Luke's comment from this morning runs through my head on a loop. *We make our own opportunities. We make our own opportunities. We make our own opportunities.* And darn if he isn't right!

I didn't love my first job out of college, but I took it because I didn't know what I wanted to do with my life. Then I followed my boyfriend to a city I didn't want to live in and got another job that didn't excite me. I didn't make my own opportunities. I settled, and I'm going to call a do-over.

I know I want to live in Elk Lake, which means I have to figure out how to make that happen. The only problem is that I like so many things, I'm not sure what to focus on. Having said that, I need to pick something that will pay the bills so I suppose that limits my options a bit.

I think about it while picking up paint samples. I toss around several ideas while brushing different shades on the walls. I ultimately conclude that nothing I enjoy has anything to do with my English degree. Unless someone is willing to pay me to read romcoms. *Why can't that be a thing?*

As much as I don't want to leave this house, I love the thought of renovating it. I'm having the time of my life picking out colors and planning how to update and rearrange the furniture once the walls are painted and the new carpet is laid. I even look into how much it will cost to convert the wood-burning fireplace to gas. I make a note to call Anna and see if that upgrade will add enough value to make it worth doing.

I hate the thought of leaving my childhood home, but I adore turning it into my own vision. I don't know if anyone would hire me as an interior designer, but if this place turns out like I think it will, I'm going to have some great before and after pictures to show clients. Luckily, the day my parents told me they wanted to sell, I took a bunch of pictures so I could always remember how it was when my family lived here.

Now that something has clicked in my brain, I'm experiencing an invigorating new sensation. I *can* make my own opportunities. And I *will*. I don't know all the nitty and gritty details yet, but I'm determined to keep moving forward.

After washing down the built-in bookcase, I dab a small amount of Oyster White on the first shelf. I enjoy watching the dingy old paint get covered up by something brighter, shinier, and newer. Before I know it, I've covered half the shelves, and I've run out of paint. It's like painting has become a metaphor for my life. I can make change by simply making a change. It really is that easy.

I go back to the hardware store before the day is over, and I stop by the carpet store to get samples there, as well. When I get home, I spend the rest of the day on Pinterest looking for inspiration. The thing about old houses is that they're full of so many little details that newer construction never tries to replicate. So that's a win. The hard part comes with trying to create an open concept that everyone seems to expect these days.

On a whim, I call Allie. I know her parents are on a cruise for a few more days, but her dad's a contractor and I want to pick his brain about an idea I have. After explaining my vision to my friend, she demands, "You want to do what?"

"I want to see if the wall between the living room and dining room is load bearing. If it's not, I want to take it down."

"What do your parents think about that?"

"I'm not going to tell them."

"Lorelai, have you lost your mind? I know you're creative and all, but you can't knock a wall down and not tell your folks. It's their house! Not to mention, how are you going to pay for it?"

With a smile on my face, I tell her, "My dad added me to his credit card. I just got my copy in the mail yesterday."

"You'd knock a wall down and charge it to your parents without telling them first?"

"Why not? They put me in charge, so I'm taking charge." The more I think about this idea, the more I like it.

"Okay, Lor, but I think you're crazy."

Borrowing one of my mom's favorite sayings, I tell her, "Crazy like a fox." I'm not even a little concerned about what my parents are going to say when they find out. They want me to be a boss, so that's what I'm going to do. I'm certainly not going to let one little wall get in my way. And if I've learned anything from my HGTV addiction over the years it's this—knock that wall down!

I just have to keep them from finding out until after the deed is done. And the only way to keep them in the dark is to make sure my brother doesn't come home. He's just the kind of blabber-mouth that would tell them everything. "I need to go, Al," I tell my friend. "Let me know when your dad gets back so I can make an appointment to talk to him."

Once she hangs up, I call Noah. "Hey, bro."

"Lorelai." His tone and lack of verbiage make it clear he's still upset about our last conversation.

"I got to thinking about how busy you are."

"And?"

In a burst, I tell him, "I can't expect you to come home and pack your room without much notice. I've decided to do it for you."

"How much?" he wants to know.

"You don't have to pay me," I say magnanimously.

"Why?" *Why is he questioning my motives?*

Lying through my teeth, I tell him, "It's as unfair to you as it is to me that Mom and Dad are selling our family home out from under us. I'm here, so it wouldn't take me more than a day to pack your stuff for you."

"Lorelai, what are you up to?"

Scoffing a little too loudly, I answer, "Nothing. I mean, what could I be up to other than getting our house ready to sell?" Which *is* the truth, although somewhat of a convoluted version of it.

Noah inhales deeply before exhaling loudly in my ear. "Fine. Thank you. I mean it. You're doing me a big favor and I won't forget it."

He's doing me a big favor too, but of course I don't tell him that. "Maybe you'll let me visit you in Chicago. Luke has invited me to come to his restaurant sometime."

"You'd come all the way to Chicago to eat at Capon, but you don't want to date Luke? Something isn't adding up here, Lor."

Oh, I'm interested in Luke, but not if he's going to live somewhere other than Elk Lake. So I tell him, "It was nice of you to think about setting us up, Noah, but Luke really loves living in the city and he has no intention of leaving."

"Why can't you move to Chicago?"

I pull a throw off the back of my couch and snuggle under it. "I've never wanted to live there."

"Yet you moved to Madison because Michael got a job there."

"Yeah, and look how that turned out."

"But you've loved Luke your whole life," he reminds me.

I suddenly experience my second epiphany of the day. At this rate I'm going to have the issue of world peace locked down by tomorrow. "I'm done making choices based on other people's dreams," I tell my brother. "I'm going to make choices based on making my own dreams come true."

"Not to be rude, but *what* dreams?"

How could he have meant that any other way than rudely? "I *have* dreams," I assure him. "And the biggest one is to keep living in Elk Lake. I love it here."

"Even if it means nothing can ever happen between you and Luke?"

"Even then." Somewhere between this morning and now, I've become the champion of my own life. I know what I want and I'm not going to put any man's desires above my own. Not ever again. I know a lot of women who have met their husbands right here in Elk Lake, so it's possible. I might not fall in love with a movie star like Faith did, but who knows, maybe Teddy will have a friend visit, and I might!

"Well, good for you, little sister. I'm proud of you."

I'm proud of myself, too. "Thanks, Noah," I tell him. "I've got to go. I'm meeting a friend for dinner."

"Okay, sis. And thanks, again. Just put all my stuff in the garage and I'll come and get it before you put the house on the market."

After we hang up, I run upstairs and get ready for my dinner with Luke. I know I just said I wasn't going to date the guy but that doesn't mean I don't want to look good for him. And if I'm being honest, I don't have to date him to want to kiss him. One kiss as payment for years of devotion doesn't seem too much to ask, does it?

CHAPTER TWENTY-SIX

LUKE

I meet my parents in the driveway so I can help my dad get out of the car. His first words upon seeing me are, "You're *still* in Elk Lake?"

"I'm still here, Dad," I assure him.

"Are you staying at our house?" Even though I'm not, I wonder why he would think I'd stay anywhere else. My mom rolls her eyes. While sympathetic to my dad, it's obvious his attitude is wearing thin with her, as well.

"I'm staying at Noah's parents'," I tell him. "They're in Florida. But I'm happy to move home if you think you'll need me."

The look of terror on his face is almost laughable. "I'll be fine." He turns to my mom. "We'll be fine, won't we, Brenda?"

She doesn't seem as sold. "We'll see how well you can move in and out of bed."

Taking her cue, I tell him, "You might *need* my help."

"The nurses showed me how to do everything." He points to the wheelchair. "As long as I have that, I'll be fine."

Even though I finally know more about my dad's earlier life

than I did, I can't help feeling irritated by his attitude. I gently help him out of the passenger side of the car and into the wheelchair before turning him around so he's facing the front door. Pointing to the joystick on the right side, I tell him, "It's self-explanatory."

He pushes the mechanism forward as my mom leads the way. Once we're in the house, my mom exclaims, "It smells so good in here!" Turning to me, she adds, "You've been busy."

I give her a knowing look. "I've been cooking the healing foods."

"You made my chicken noodle soup?" My dad's voice quivers with emotion.

"And chocolate chip cookies. I also whipped up a plate of peanut butter, jelly, marshmallow, and banana sandwiches." He looks like he's about to cry.

My dad clears his throat before saying, "That's very nice of you, son. Thank you." And darn if he doesn't sound sincere.

Noticing the setup in the living room, he says, "You built a fire, too."

"I thought it made the room look a little more welcoming "

From the other room, I hear my mom exclaim, "You bought flowers! Thank you, Luke!"

My mom walks over to the hospital bed and pats the mattress before telling my dad, "Time to show us how you can do this by yourself."

My father maneuvers his wheelchair with precision, positioning himself expertly next to the hospital bed. Then he pushes out of it with his good arm and his good leg before swiveling to the side. Once he's on the mattress, he's able to reach the remote and raise the top of the mattress until he can finagle himself into a sitting position.

"Nice work," I tell him sincerely.

He grunts. "I'm so dang relieved to be out of traction, I feel like I could sprint down a soccer field."

"No more talk like that," my mom mutters. "Your x-rays may look great, but you're on strict bedrest for at least another week."

My dad closes his eyes as he pushes the button to recline the bed. "I'm tired," he says. "I think I'll take a nap."

Things have taken such a nice turn I don't want to leave to go into Pop's, but Jim is waiting for a break. Reaching over, I squeeze the hand on my dad's good arm, "I'll check in with you tomorrow."

His breathing changes almost immediately, making it clear he's worn out. I gesture to my mom to follow me to the kitchen. Once we get there, I tell her, "I can't believe I didn't know anything about Dad's childhood."

She shrugs. "What good would it have done if you had?"

"It's not that it would have changed anything, but it would have been nice to know. I feel like I don't know Dad at all."

The tension around my mom's mouth relaxes slightly before she says, "There are some burdens only the person living with them can understand. Your dad never wanted you and Kelsey to know how hard life can be. He wanted to protect you from that."

"It's like he's a stranger though."

"You know all the best parts of him, Luke. Unfortunately, in the last couple of years, you've gotten to know some of the tough parts. He's still a person with struggles."

"Yes, but he's made me feel like his challenges are my fault, which is frustrating." Even though I'm happy to have learned more about my dad's life, I'm the one who still needs to figure out how to reach him.

"Maybe so," my mom says while pointing to the plate of sandwiches on the counter. "But it seems to me like you've figured some things out for yourself."

"Maybe."

She smiles before reaching out to take me in her arms. Giving me a firm hug she says, "You can't win a race if you don't take the first step."

"I love you, Mom," I tell her. "Thank you for finally giving me a clue about how to get us through this."

"I'm pretty sure you would have eventually gotten on the right path." Then she teases, "I just didn't want to have to wait another twenty years before you did."

"Ha, ha." Stepping out of her embrace, I tell her, "I'll be at Pop's until about eight. Call me if you need anything and I'll be right over."

"I think we'll be fine," she says. "I'm going to sleep on the roll out couch next to your dad, so I'll be there if he needs me. But we'll look forward to seeing you in the morning."

"Anything special you want for breakfast?"

"Whatever your dad made for you when you were little," she says. "Exactly how he made it."

"Yes, ma'am." I make a mental note to pick up all the fixings for french toast on my way over.

As my mom walks me to the front door, I stop and turn back to look at my dad. "I'm so glad he's going to be okay. I'm going to do everything in my power to heal our relationship."

"Everything?" she wants to know.

"I'm going to work my butt off," I tell her without giving her the real assurance she's looking for. I love my dad, but my life is still in Chicago. And shouldn't I be given the same right to choose where I live just like my parents did?

My afternoon at Pop's flies by. Cooking here is something I can do on automatic pilot, and as much as I claim to want more than that, I'm currently enjoying the robotic motions of serving up diner food to the citizens of Elk Lake. I particularly like it when the old folks come in before bingo. They're very animated and sociable even if there's a startling number of requests for no salt in their food.

I can see why so many people think retiring here is a good idea. There's got to be comfort heading into your senior years surrounded by people you've known your whole life. Having said that, I'm nowhere near retirement, so I don't currently feel that lure.

Jim comes off break at five, which is peak early bird time. We work in tandem for an hour before we finally get a lull. That's when I ask him, "What do you know about my dad's childhood?"

His hand stalls mid burger flip. "I know some."

"Did you know that he was an orphan?"

"I did," Jim says.

"Did you know he used to have a brother?"

Jim nods. "Yup."

"What I can't help but wonder," I tell him, "is why my dad told you this stuff and not me and Kelsey?"

Jim finishes cooking the burger. "He didn't have to tell me. I was there."

"Excuse me?"

With a shrug, he says, "I was best friends with your dad's older brother, Bobby." He explains, "After their parents died, Bobby got adopted by our neighbors."

"How did he die?" There was no indication in my dad's memory book.

Jim picks up a napkin and wipes his brow. "We were playing basketball out in the street. Some drunken fool came down the road and plowed right into Bobby. It was plain awful."

"I'm so sorry, Jim." I wait a beat before asking, "How did you get to know my dad?"

"He lived with his new family in the town next to ours. I waited awhile, then I sent him a letter and told him that if he ever needed anything I was there for him."

"Had you met him before?" I want to know.

"Nah, but I knew his story and I loved his brother like he was my own. You take care of your own."

"How did you take care of my dad?"

Jim snatches a ticket out of the window and gets busy putting a chicken breast on the grill. "My parents and I moved to Milwaukee after I graduated from high school. When your dad graduated the next year, he reached out and asked if he could stay with us while he looked for a job."

"And you took him in?" This is certainly a part of my dad's history I would have liked to have known. It's no wonder Jim has always felt like family. He's the closest thing my dad has to it.

"My folks told your dad he could live with them for free so long as he kept up with his education. I was going to junior college, so it made sense for your dad to go to the same school."

I don't really know what to say, so I finally ask, "How did you end up moving to Elk Lake?"

A slow smile creeps across his face. "That's when your daddy returned the favor. I had been working at a restaurant in Milwaukee and the place burned down. My folks lost the lease on their house at the same time. That's when I started to think it might be time for us to make a move. So, I called your dad and asked what he thought about us living here."

"He obviously liked the idea," I prompt him for more information.

"He loved it. And so have we."

This is a lot to take in. "Didn't you ever wonder why my dad never talked about his childhood with us?"

He shakes his head. "Not my business."

"Yeah, but …"

"No, son," he says. "It's not my business and it's not yours. When you survive something as bad as your daddy did, you earn the right to keep your peace if that's what you want to do."

I can't seem to leave well enough alone. "I just can't imagine my kids not knowing all about me."

"That's because you've had a great life," he tells me. "Your dad's road wasn't as easy."

This has been a big day for me. So many secrets revealed that I never saw coming. I have a lot to think about and for some reason, I feel like Lorelai is the person I want to share it all with.

I don't know when she became important to me, but as I think back to our many conversations, even the mundane ones, I realize it's easy to open up to her and I enjoy her company. She obviously cares about people. I mean, who makes blankets for babies they've never met? She loves animals and if Penelope's reaction to her is to be believed, they love her back. If that doesn't speak to the quality of person that Lorelai is, I don't know what does.

CHAPTER TWENTY-SEVEN

LORELAI

I know it's silly to dress up just to go to Pop's, but if I want to get Luke to kiss me before he goes back to Chicago, I'm going to have to up my game. I'm afraid the image of my flannel night gown might be seared into his brain.

Slipping into a black pencil skirt, I pair it with a blue cashmere sweater that's almost a perfect match for my eyes. I would never have worn this color when I was a kid, but happily, I'm a lot more confident now.

Once I'm dressed, I apply a coat of mascara and then swipe on my favorite red lipstick. Looking in the mirror, I confirm that I look highly kissable. A quick spray of perfume and I'm ready to roll.

I vow to avoid eating another burger tonight and go for something a little more delicate. I don't currently possess the kind of money needed for dry cleaning, and ketchup on cashmere would most certainly require professional help. If past experience is anything to go on, my sheer effort to avoid making a mess of myself will guarantee that I do the exact opposite.

After slipping into rubber boots—dressed up or not, I do not want to step ankle deep into a puddle—I grab my black fake fur coat and set off.

I jack up the heat in my Volvo and sit for five minutes to give the warmth an opportunity to circulate. Also, sitting gives me a chance to think. I don't know what happened to me today, but when Luke said that we create our own opportunity, my brain finally turned on.

I do not have to wait for the things I want to come to me, like I've always thought they would. *Why did I think that?* I need to go after what I want and simply make it mine. Sadly, that does not include Luke because he's going to make choices that will break my heart and I'm not in the market for any more of that. That kiss I'm determined to get had better be great because it's all I'm going to get.

After pulling out of my driveway, it takes fewer than five minutes to get to Pop's. I park right out front and scurry across the pavement to the front door. The hostess that I detest is standing up front, and for the first time she doesn't glare at me. Instead, she looks like she's about to burst into tears.

I'm not sure why, but I suddenly feel protective. Jogging up to her, I demand, "What happened? Why are you so upset?"

Her top lip quivers as she blinks her eyes rapidly to keep tears from falling.

"Go to the bathroom and splash your face with cold water," I order. "I'll cover for you while you're gone."

"Are you sure?"

I give her a little push in response. I may not have a big important career, but I feel confident I can manage to seat people and hand them menus.

As soon as the girl is gone, the fun starts. A boatload of teenagers stroll in, almost like a bus just dropped them off. Oddly, they're all dressed up like they're going to a dance.

I check out the calendar lying on the hostess stand and discover that it's Saturday night. I really have lost track of time. I thought it might be Wednesday or Thursday.

What kind of dance is in early March on a Saturday night? It can't be homecoming or winter formal. Those have both come and gone. Other dances like black light and old school are generally on Friday nights. That's when it hits me. The only formal dance in spring is prom. Little lightning bolts of electricity shoot through my nervous system. I'm having supper with Luke on prom night. That must be a good omen.

Speak of the devil, Luke himself comes out of the kitchen. He stops dead in his tracks when he sees me picking up menus and seating people. After watching me take four groups to their table, he asks, "Did you get a job here?"

"In your dreams," I tease him. Then I explain, "The hostess was in a bad way, so I sent her to the bathroom to get ahold of herself."

"That was nice of you," he says. "She's not exactly a ray of sunshine, is she?"

"Teenage girls are not always the nicest, take it from me." Several more couples come in and Luke and I take turns leading them to their tables.

We meet back at the front of the restaurant at the same time the hostess returns from the bathroom. She doesn't look much better for her trip. "I'm Lorelai," I tell her.

"Chloe," she says quietly before adding, "Thank you for covering for me."

"I would have thought you'd be going to prom yourself," I tell her.

That was clearly the wrong thing to say because now she does burst into tears. Turning her back against the dining room, she says, "I wanted to go, but the guy I like didn't ask me."

"I'm sorry." I put my arm around her shoulder and give her a brief side hug. Trying my darndest to avoid Luke's gaze, I whisper, "The guy I liked didn't ask me either."

"How did you spend prom night?" she wants to know.

"I planned a girls' night with some of my friends who were in the same boat. Do you have any friends who aren't going?"

"There are a few," she mumbles.

"What time are you off tonight?"

She affirms she's off at eight, so I step away from her and ask Luke, "How do you feel about buying dinner for Chloe and her friends? I'll cover the rest of her shift."

He cocks one eyebrow. "What about *our* dinner?"

"I'm sure you can wait another hour," I tell him. "I feel sorry for the poor girl. I've been in her shoes."

A slow smile forms on his face. "If you can wait, then so can I."

I turn back to Chloe. "Call your friends and have them meet you here. You can celebrate prom night together."

Luke interjects, "Dinner's on me."

Chloe manages to look sad, elated, and worried all at the same time. "What will all these other kids think if we eat out without dates."

"They'll probably think you're having more fun than they are." Glancing around the dining room, I tell her, "There are a lot of awkward looking couples out there."

Chloe's eyes pop open as she gasps, "The guy I like is at table thirteen."

I turn around and look. "Is he the one with the mohawk or the crutch?"

"Crutch. He hurt himself in the last basketball game."

Looking at her crush makes me realize why I always liked Luke instead of boys my age. A seventeen-year-old boy and girl are miles apart in maturity. "Go call your friends," I tell her.

She pulls her phone out of her pocket and walks away. Luke leans in and tells me, "That was very nice of you."

"You're the one buying them dinner."

"Then it's very nice of *us*."

"I can live with that."

He points to the one free booth by the window. "I was saving that one for us, but what do you say we let Chloe and her friends have it?"

The thought that he had reserved the best table in the house for our meal makes goosebumps appear on my arms. "That would be perfect," I tell him.

Within twenty minutes, a group of young girls pours into Pop's. Chloe greets them with a squeal of excitement and leads the way to their table. I continue to seat people as they come in. The older folks appear a little upset when they have to wait for a table, but when they see all the kids dressed up, they take it in stride.

I hear one woman tell her friend, "Remember when that was us, Barb? It's hard to believe we ever looked that good."

"I *still* look that good," Barb retorts. When her friend locks at her incredulously, she says, "When I don't have my glasses on, I'm gorgeous!"

I stifle a giggle. I wonder if that's what Allie and I will be like some day. I sure hope she stays in Elk Lake so we can find out.

Luke and I keep busy for the next hour and a half. I seat customers and get them water and he helps bus and reset tables when people leave. When Chloe and her friends get up, she comes over to us and says, "Thank you both so much. I know I haven't been very nice to either of you and I'm sorry."

"It's stressful being a teenager," I tell her. "I'm glad you got to make a nice memory with your friends."

"After my shift, we're meeting over at Meghan's house to hang out. I don't know why we didn't think of this on our own."

"Sometimes we need the help of our elders." I cannot believe I'm referring to myself in such a way, but there it is. Chloe probably already thinks I'm forty years old.

I catch Luke's eye from across the room and motion to a free table by the window. He grabs two sodas and meets me there. "I'm starving."

"I'm a little hungry, too," I tell him. As soon as we're seated, I confess, "I wasn't going to have a burger because I didn't want to drip anything on my sweater, but I've changed my mind."

"Why would you wear something to supper that you couldn't

get dirty?" *Ah, the sweet naïveté of a man who doesn't know he's being stalked with romantic intent.*

"I don't get to dress up very often, and I like to," I tell him plainly.

"There aren't many places to dress up in Elk Lake," he agrees. "Unless you're a member of the country club."

"I'm not," I assure him. "Which is why I put some effort into tonight."

"Prom night." He says this in such a way that I can't help but wonder if he's recalling some of my drunken ramblings from his first night here. I wish I could remember exactly what happened, but maybe I'm better off not knowing.

I put my napkin in my lap before picking up my menu. "I thought prom happened later in the month."

"They move it around based on how well the basketball season is going. If we're in the playoffs, it's later in the month."

"So I'm guessing we don't have a great team this year," I deduce.

He laughs. "That would appear to be the case."

Luke writes down our dinner order and puts it in the window before coming back to the table. I don't know where he got them but he's carrying a bottle of champagne and two glasses. "What do you say we celebrate prom night in style?"

My stomach flutters with excitement.

"You can tell me all about your proms," he says.

"That'll be a short conversation," I tell him. "I didn't go to either."

"I'm sorry." It sounds like he's pitying me.

"Don't be. I had my dreams and sometimes that's enough."

"Does the boy you wanted to go with know what he missed out on?" Darn if that doesn't sound flirty.

"I'm guessing he doesn't," I tell him while shifting nervously in my seat. I can't seem to make eye contact, while adding, "I wasn't even on his radar back then."

"Who knows, maybe he still lives in town and is hoping to run into you?"

I slowly raise my gaze to his. He looks too innocent to have any idea what he's just said so I tell him, "I've heard through the grapevine that he lives in a big city now. I don't expect he'll ever be back."

"I'm sure stranger things have happened." He'd never say that if he knew I was talking about him.

CHAPTER TWENTY-EIGHT

LUKE

I knew Lorelai was nice, I just never knew how nice. The teenage hostess who works here is nothing short of a brat and yet, Lorelai immediately came to her aid when she sensed her distress. Babies, dogs, and now teenagers? Talk about the trifecta of endorsements.

Opening the bottle of champagne, I pour a little for both of us then raise my glass, "To prom. May it mend more hearts than it breaks."

Lorelai laughs. "It was strange seeing all those kids from an adult perspective. They don't look nearly as put together as we gave them credit for when we were their age."

"That's the truth." I take a sip of my drink before saying, "Junior year I went with Ashleigh Ryan, and with Tallia Smith senior year. I have no idea what's happened to either of them."

"Did you date either for very long?" she asks.

"A couple months, I think. How about you? Who did you date in high school?"

She nearly chokes on her champagne. "Do you remember what I looked like in high school?"

"Not well," I lie. The truth is I remember just fine. She was cute enough, but she was much younger than me. There was no chance that I was ever going to look at her the way she wanted me to. More importantly, she was my best friend's little sister and looking at her in that way would break all kinds of bro codes.

"Well, let me refresh your memory. My hair was orange. Neon orange."

He laughs loudly. "I don't quite remember it like that. Do you dye it now?"

She shakes her hair. "No. It just started changing on its own."

"It's very pretty," I tell her, which causes a blush to cover her cheeks.

Ignoring my compliment, she says, "And I was really skinny, and I wore braces. Also," she hurries to add, "I was a late developer." Her face reddens again.

"I grew two more inches while I was in college. It's funny how some kids peak early, and it takes others more time."

She grimaces. "Yeah, it's a laugh riot."

"What about college? What did you major in?"

She rolls her eyes. "English. Which is crazy because what in the world do you do with an English degree other than teach?"

Shaking my head, I answer, "No idea. Don't you want to teach?"

Her mouth contorts into something of a scowl. "Not particularly. I mean, I suppose I could but it's not where my heart is. I think the reason I chose that major is because of my love of reading.

"That's how it was with me. I thought I wanted to be in finance, but after a year I decided to go back to culinary school."

"Your dad must have been proud." Her smile is so sweet I can't help but take a moment to catch my breath. Being with Lorelai is like standing in the sunshine after months of rain.

"Has Noah told you anything about what's going on between me and my dad?" I ask.

She shrugs. "Not much. Only that you're having some troubles. At least, I assume that's why you're staying with me and not your parents."

I pour more champagne into our glasses before explaining, "My dad has taken offense that I went to culinary school and didn't come home to work at Pop's with him."

"I could see how that might have upset him."

"But it's my life," I tell her. "Don't I get to make the decisions for my own life?"

"Of course you do, but you can't tell someone else how to feel. People have the right to their own emotions, even if it breaks their hearts."

It sounds like she's talking about something else here, but I don't delve into it. "I just found out today that my dad was an orphan who was separated from his brother when their parents died."

The look of shock on her face could only be equaled by my own. "How did you just find that out? Isn't that something your dad would have told you before now?"

"You'd think, but he didn't. My mom left an old photo album out for me so I could get some insight." I take a breath before adding, "His brother was killed when they were both little boys, too."

"Oh, my gosh, Luke! That's horrible! Your poor dad."

"If I'd known this before I would have seen him differently."

"Maybe that's why he didn't tell you."

The server arrives with our food, and Lorelai gushes, "Thank you so much!" She's nice to everyone. I don't care if you're the king of England, if you don't treat service people with respect, you're nothing in my book. I'd better watch out because if I don't, Lorelai could become everything to me.

We take a minute to enjoy a few bites without talking. Lorelai is the first to speak. "It makes sense why your dad was so hurt that you didn't come home and work with him."

"How do you figure that?"

She wipes her mouth carefully on a napkin before saying, "He must have felt abandoned when his parents died, and even more so when his brother died."

I probably should have put that together on my own. "Go on …"

"For you to follow in his footsteps but not want to work with him in the business he spent his adult life building, well, you can see how that could seem harsh."

"You're suggesting that my dad thinks I abandoned him too?" Now I feel like a real heel.

"I can see how he might. I mean, I'm sure there's a big part of him that's still trying to prove himself to the parents that never got to see him grow up."

So much for getting Lorelai to take my side, although I know this isn't really an issue of sides. "He never told me and Kelsey anything about this. Not a thing."

"He was probably focusing on building a better life for you both." She takes a sip of water before adding, "They say people heal early childhood trauma through raising kids of their own. Your dad was probably just trying to rewrite the past."

"By pretending it never happened?"

"Maybe," she says. "How old was your dad when his parents died?"

"I don't know."

"If he was old enough to really remember them then the trauma would have been greater."

"He and his brother were adopted by different families," I tell her.

She looks as horrified as I was when I discovered this. "That's had to have compounded his issues."

"He had it rough. I just wish he could have trusted us with the truth so that we could have known this side of him."

"I don't think he was keeping anything from you, Luke. I think he was just protecting himself." She exhales loudly. "Life can be really tough, can't it?"

"Yeah." We finish the rest of our meal in companionable

silence. There aren't too many people you can sit with quietly without feeling a nervous need to fill the air with chatter. It's not like that with Lorelai. Sitting with her feels good. It feels right. It's not just that she's familiar, but she's so darn loving to everyone. She's seriously the best person I've ever met.

After our dishes are cleared, I leave a ten-dollar bill on the table for the server, and ask Lorelai, "Do you feel like walking down the street to the ice cream parlor?"

If the smile on her face is any indication, she likes the idea. "I love their Bordeaux cherry."

"Add a scoop of pistachio and you've got my favorite combination." Standing up, I tell her, "I just need to get my stuff out of the kitchen."

When I come out, Lorelai is already wearing her coat and standing by the front door. She looks endearingly sweet, and not for the first time since being back in Elk Lake, I wonder what it would be like if something were to happen between us.

Opening the door, I tell her, "I used to ask my dad why he didn't carry cherry and pistachio at the diner for me." She looks up questioningly. "He said he didn't want to take the business away from a fellow shop keeper."

"That was nice of him," she says.

"My dad has always had a strong sense of fair play. He's always been honorable that way."

Lorelai shivers and pulls her coat tighter around her. "I should have brought mittens, but it feels ridiculous to still be wearing them in March. You know in some parts of the country they don't even have to wear coats in March?" She sounds so annoyed, it causes me to smile.

"I do know this. Did you know that in Hawaii they're even wearing their swimsuits now?"

She flicks my ear with her fingers. "You don't have to rub it in." I reach up and touch her hand before she can move it away and it really is cold. Capturing it in mine, I bring it down and keep holding onto it. She doesn't pull it away, so I tell her, "I'll keep you warm." I don't realize until afterwards that sounded like some kind of a romantic pledge.

As we walk down the street, it starts to rain, and Lorelai groans, "Now we can be cold *and* wet. In case you're wondering this is not the kind of thing I like about living here."

"You could move to Florida," I tease.

"I would rather live at the South Pole," she says. "Midwestern humidity is one thing, but Florida humidity is godawful."

"I used to think I'd like to live in Costa Rica," I tell her. "I always felt I was best suited for a tropical climate."

"Maybe you'll open a restaurant there someday," she says. She keeps her eyes straight ahead.

"Maybe so," I tell her. "But if I did that then I'd be spending a lot of my life traveling."

"I would have thought that would appeal to you. You seem like an adventurer."

"I like to travel on vacation," I tell her. "But if I started opening restaurants all over the world, I'd never be able to stay put long enough to do the other things I want to do."

She slows down as we reach the ice cream parlor and asks, "Like what?"

This probably isn't the thing to say while holding her hand, but I do anyway. "I want to have a family some day and I don't want to be on the road all the time and miss out on spending time with them."

Lorelai's posture tenses. "You want to raise kids in Chicago?"

"I hadn't really thought about it," I tell her. "I mean, it might not be ideal, but that's where Capon is."

"I want to raise a family in Elk Lake," she says. "I know exactly what it's like to grow up here and I couldn't imagine there being a better place."

I open the door to the ice cream parlor for her before following her in. The old-fashioned décor is how I have always remembered it. White, cast-iron chairs surrounding glass tabletops. Pink and white striped wallpaper as the backdrop to pictures of different ice cream creations.

"You should try my favorite," I tell her.

She smiles sweetly. "I'm game."

I point to a table by the window. "Go sit down and I'll be right back." I watch as she walks away, and I realize my heart is starting to beat in double time whenever I'm around her.

CHAPTER TWENTY-NINE

LORELAI

My stomach is doing flips of joy. Not only did Luke and I have supper together *on* prom night, but he's taking me out for ice cream, *and* he held my hand the entire way here. *Dear younger self, all your dreams are coming true!*

After a couple of minutes, Luke walks across the ice cream parlor carrying identical sundaes served in sugar cone cups. He announces, "As per our earlier conversation, one scoop of Bordeaux cherry and one scoop of pistachio with homemade hot fudge."

"Yum!"

Instead of sitting across from me, Luke positions himself right next to me. The little hairs all over my body respond by standing at attention. Handing me a spoon, he says, "I got you your own because I'm pretty competitive when it comes to this flavor combination."

The thought that he even considered sharing makes me wonder what the heck is going on here. Luke has made it clear that nothing is going to happen between us, and yet he held my hand for three blocks and now he's making reference to our sharing dessert? Even though I'm sure this doesn't mean anything, it still feels pretty romantic.

I take a spoonful of Bordeaux cherry first and nearly swoon from pleasure. "A boy from school asked me out for ice cream once," I tell him. *Why did I say that?*

He shrugs his eyebrows up and down. "And? How did that go?"

"Poorly," I tell him. "It was two weeks before prom so I was hopeful he was going to ask me, but instead he wanted to talk about Allie. He asked if she had any plans to go."

His face contorts into a grimace. "Ouch."

I hurry to explain, "It's not like I was hung up on him or anything, but it was senior year, so it was my last chance to go to a high school prom." I internally scream at myself to stop oversharing, but of course, I don't. I feel compelled to add, "I never wanted to have to tell my daughter that no boy ever asked me to a high school dance."

The expression on Luke's face makes it clear he feels bad for me. But instead of commenting, he puts his spoon down and stands up. Then he walks across the room to the juke box and pulls coins out of his pocket. He inserts them into the machine before making a couple of selections. Moments later, he walks back and reaches out to take my hand again. "Lorelai, will you do me the honor of going to prom with me?"

"What?" Giddiness fills every corner of me. "You can't be serious, Luke."

"Why not?" he asks. "It *is* prom night. So, all you have to do is say yes and we'll have our own little dance right here. That way if your daughter asks you how your prom was you can tell her you had a great time."

"A great time, huh?" A nearly ancient tune starts to play, and I giggle. "Frank Sinatra?"

He rolls his eyes comically. "I don't think they've updated the juke box since our grandparents were kids."

I let Luke take my hand and help me to my feet. He puts one

arm around my waist and pulls me close before putting the other around my shoulder. "Does this mean you'll go to the prom with me?"

I feel like I'm living a dream. "Yes, Luke. I'll go to prom with you."

We start to sway back and forth to "The Way You Look Tonight." We're dancing so closely I can smell remnants of Luke's cologne mixed with the more prominent aroma of fried food from the diner. Good thing I love the smell of onion rings above all else.

Even though this isn't a real high school dance, the fact that Luke is acting out such a charade for my benefit speaks volumes about what a considerate man he is. Leaning down, he whispers in my ear, "This is actually more fun than the real prom."

I know he can't possibly be talking about his choice of date, so I tease, "It's the cherry ice cream, isn't it?"

"Among other things." His answer makes my heart skip a beat. Why can't Luke want to live in Elk Lake like I do? It's not just because he's every bit as attractive as I remember. He's such a thoughtful and caring son; he's funny—except for when he's poking fun at me; and that man can cook! If not for the location issue, I think we might just be perfect together.

Once the song ends, "Crocodile Rock" by Elton John comes on. Luke breaks apart from me and starts some weird interpretive dance routine that both enchants me and makes me want to jump into his arms. "Ready for a fast number?" he asks.

Shaking my head slowly, I tell him, "I'm ready for the pistachio ice cream."

As soon as we sit down, Luke says, "My dad should get a juke box for the diner."

"That would be amazing," I tell him.

"But he won't because my dad is a creature of habit who doesn't like change."

"Some people might say the same thing about me," I tell him before explaining, "Change is scary."

"It's exciting though!" His eyes start to shine in such a way that, compared to me, it's clear Luke is an adrenaline junkie.

"What's the most exciting thing you've ever done?" I ask.

He thinks for a beat before saying, "Cliff jumping. Kahekili's Leap in Hawaii is a seventy-five-foot straight jump right into the Pacific." The animated expression on his face makes his enthusiasm clear. "How about you? What's the most exciting thing you've ever done?"

There's no way to answer his question without him learning what a true dud I am. "I shoplifted a tube of ChapStick once when I was seven."

"Excuse me?" Luke barks with amusement.

"It's true," I tell him. "I really wanted a grape Chapstick, but my mom said no because she'd just bought me a cherry one the week before."

"Did you get caught?" I shake my head, so he asks, "Why was it so exciting then?"

"I *could* have gotten caught. I was terrified I would." I take another bite of my ice cream.

"Did anyone ever find out?"

Nodding my head slowly, I tell him, "Yeah. I turned myself in."

"What?" Now he really is laughing.

"I turned myself in when my mom was paying for her prescription."

His eyes are twinkling with downright merriment. "What happened?"

"My mom tried to make me give the Chapstick back."

"So, you didn't really shoplift it," he concludes.

"Oh, I took it all right. I opened it up right in front of my mom and the clerk and put it on my lips so they couldn't make me give it back." I explain, "My mom paid for it, but she grounded me, *and* she took my Chapstick away."

"You're a renegade," Luke teases.

"I like my Chapstick," I assure him smugly before going back to my ice cream. This time I combine the pistachio and cherry. The result is sublime.

"I don't remember much of your childhood," Luke says, "But I do have one very clear memory."

"My unfortunate looks?" I guess.

He shakes his head, so I ask, "The eight years of braces?"

"No. I remember when Noah and I were in the eighth grade, and you knocked on his bedroom door one night. When he told you to go away, you flung the door open and staggered in on a pair of high heels. You were wearing bright red lipstick and ..."

A flash of that night pops into my mind and compels me to interrupt him. "Please don't finish that sentence."

"Ah, you remember then?" He looks enormously happy with himself for bringing this up.

"I remember," I tell him. My face burns hot with embarrassment for my younger self.

"What *were* those things?" he wants to know.

"I thought we were done talking about this." I sound angrier than I am. I just want to move on.

"We can be done once you answer my question."

I inhale deeply before exhaling with even more force. "My mom used to wear panty hose that came in a plastic egg. I used to ... you know ..." I gesture toward my chest to finish the thought.

"You put plastic eggs down your shirt to make it look like you had boobs!" I swear to God, he practically yells that.

"Yes, Luke, that's what I did. I was nine."

He starts laughing so hard I'm tempted to get up and leave. "I'm so glad you're enjoying yourself," I drawl.

He valiantly tries to compose himself but is not successful because he apparently feels the need to add, "And those shoes! We thought you were going to kill yourself!"

I don't know what comes over me, but I decide to confess, "I did that for you, Luke. I was trying to show you that I wasn't the little girl you thought I was."

His expression turns to sympathy. "I know that, Lorelai. You weren't very subtle."

"Maybe not, but my feelings were real. I wanted you to see me as a big girl, and I don't appreciate you making fun of me now."

"Oh Lorelai." He reaches up and takes one of my hands. "I'm not making fun. It was really sweet."

I put my spoon down. I've totally lost my appetite. "Well, this is a terrible ending to what has so far been a very nice evening."

"Why is this a terrible ending?" he wants to know.

"You're laughing at me," I point out.

"I was in the eighth grade, Lorelai. It was funny."

"While that may be, you are no longer in the eighth grade, and I find this to be a very embarrassing topic of conversation."

"There has been no other girl, or woman for that matter, who has ever gone to the lengths you did to get my attention," he tells me. "It was very sweet."

"More like mortifying," I tell him.

"I may not have been very nice at the time, but I can tell you that as an adult I'm honored to have once meant so much to you."

"Uh-huh."

"Seriously. You may have been a late bloomer but look at you now. You're gorgeous! To think you once thought so highly of me is a real boost to my ego."

"Right." I roll my eyes so hard I feel the strain. "At least you're safe from me now," I tell him.

"Because you're no longer interested in me that way?" *Why did he have to ask that?*

I'm not going to come right out and tell him that's the reason because it's clearly not. I'm interested all right. "Because you've made it clear that you are never going to live in Elk Lake again so there's no point in pursuing the idea of us as a couple." My ice cream is going to turn to soup.

"What if I did live here?"

Why is he toying with me? "Are you?"

He shakes his head. "Probably not."

"So, there you have it. Let's move on, shall we?' I'm so agitated right now I could smack him with my spoon. Repeatedly.

"What do you want to talk about now?" he asks.

"I suppose I could tell you how I got a D in Geometry, unless of course you'd rather here about the time I broke my leg running from a cricket." *Why not air all my dirty laundry?*

Luke stands up and reaches out to take my hand. "How about if we go to the juke box and pick out a couple more songs to dance to. You, know"—he winks—"to add authenticity to the prom story you're going to tell your daughter someday."

I really do want to dance with Luke, but I'm overflowing with embarrassment for being such an awkward weirdo of a little girl who pined for him so relentlessly. Why couldn't I have been older? The fact that he remembers such humiliating things about me is beyond mortifying.

"I think I've danced enough," I tell him. "I should probably get going. I've got a big day tomorrow buying appliances."

"Lorelai." He says my name so tenderly I feel emotion prickle behind my eyes.

I pick up my ice cream and carry it across the room to the garbage before coming back to collect my coat.

"I'm sorry," Luke says. "I wasn't trying to embarrass you."

I don't have any idea how to respond to that. I wish I could have played it cool, but there are simply too many versions of me taking up space in my current twenty-eight-year-old body. And every one has spent way too long being hopelessly in love with Luke Phillips.

I offer a pathetic attempt at a smile. "Looks like I did a pretty good job of embarrassing myself," I tell him. "But that doesn't matter now. You've got your life, and I've got mine, and it's clear we're going in opposite directions."

Luke reaches out to take my hand, but I won't let him. Instead, I say, "Thank you for a mostly nice night." Then I turn and walk out of the ice cream parlor.

CHAPTER THIRTY

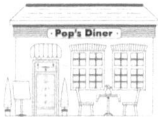

LUKE

I feel terrible for upsetting Lorelai so badly. I really wasn't making fun of her, although I guess I can see how it might have looked that way. She's just so different than she was, it's hard to even think of her as the same person.

Hurrying out of the ice cream parlor, I catch up to her and say, "I'll walk with you." She doesn't comment.

Once we get back to the diner, I tell her, "I'm parked out back. I guess I'll see you at home?"

Lorelai nods her head up and down but doesn't say anything else as she gets into her car. I feel awful as she pulls away. I truly thought she'd be able to laugh at the past by now. Once she's gone, I go back into the diner to pick up the food I'll need to make my dad french toast for breakfast. Then I head out to my car with determination to make one last stop before heading home.

At the market, I walk to the flower department and find several premade corsages in clear plastic clamshells in the refrigerator. I pick up a delicate one made with an assortment of pink roses and baby's breath.

Driving back to Lorelai's, I try to think of a way to apologize for making her feel so self-conscious, but I'm coming up dry. I park in the driveway next to her car and hurry up to the front door. It's unlocked so I don't have to use the key she gave me.

There's a light on in the living room, but other than that, there's no sign of life. Picking up my phone, I text Lorelai:

ME

Please come to the living room.

She ignores my text, so I try again:

ME

I have something for you.

She doesn't text back, but I hear some stirring from upstairs. Moments later, Lorelai walks downstairs. She's wearing a purple robe, the likes of which I've only seen my grandmother wear. "All snug and ready for bed, huh?" I ask her.

"Yup."

I walk toward her and hand her the corsage. "I figure you might want to press this so when you tell your daughter about prom you can show her proof."

Lorelai looks so sad, I'm afraid she's going to start crying. "I think she'll probably be looking for an actual photograph or something."

"Probably so," I agree. Then I gesture toward her robe and ask, "Any chance she'll buy this was all the rage?"

A small giggle escapes Lorelai, which seems to take her by surprise. "I'm going to go out on a limb and guess she'll be smarter than that. At least I hope she will be, but given her mother's history, maybe not." She looks so dejected I just want to wrap her in my arms.

"We could take a picture anyway …" I suggest.

"Luke." Lorelai walks past me and sits on the couch. As I join her, she says, "I'm sorry about how I acted tonight. You were wonderful. I was a total train wreck."

"No, you weren't," I assure her. She pegs me with a direct stare, so I confess, "I did some pretty embarrassing things as a kid, too."

"Like what?" She leans back so she can cross her arms.

"I once peed on our neighbor's foot because he wouldn't give me a cookie," I tell her. "Mr. Howard. He was eating an Oreo and wouldn't share so I expressed my displeasure."

"Please tell me you weren't fourteen." We both laugh at that.

"I was three, but I was mad."

"Anything else?" she wants to know.

"I told my third-grade teacher that I wanted to marry her and give her babies."

Lorelai's eyes open wide with delight. "How did that go over?"

"It was a whole big deal." I explain, "She sent me to the principal's office where I got interrogated about what I knew about making babies." Shrugging, I add, "I didn't know how they were made, so I told the principal you needed chocolate chips and butter."

Lorelai settles back into the cushions. "Thank you for trying to make me feel better. You are very nice, Luke. But I know what kind of kid I was and I'm sorry that I bugged you so much."

Scooting closer to her I tell her, "You were charmingly dedicated." Then I ask, "Now, I feel like there's something else we might need to do before our prom date is over."

She picks up her flowers. "You want me to put my corsage on?"

Shaking my head, I tell her, "I was thinking about a goodnight kiss. That's a pretty standard post-prom activity and for a truly authentic experience you'll need one of those."

"Luke." She moves to stand up, but I reach out and take her

hand. She tries to pull away again. "You don't have to kiss me, for Pete's sake."

"What if I want to?" I remember my first night here when Lorelai was drunk and thought we'd gone to the prom together. She seemed pretty determined to get a kiss. I've thought of that moment more times than I care to count. I may not have been interested when we were younger but that is no longer the case.

"I don't think … I mean … You don't… It's not like …"

The only way to progress is to stop her from talking. I do this by moving slowly so I don't scare her. Once my face is within inches of hers, I tell her, "I'm going to kiss you now."

But before I can, Lorelai launches herself the short distance between us and lays one on me. It's soft and sweet and so much nicer than I could have imagined. She quickly tries to pull out of my grasp like she can't believe what she just did, but I don't let her. Instead, I hold her close and tentatively deepen the kiss.

Lorelai is everything I could want in a woman except for the one small fact that she is not geographically desirable. I'm not sure how much time passes as we explore one another; I can only say that I enjoy every delicious second of our encounter.

When I finally release her, Lorelai makes no move to separate herself from me. Instead, she rests her head on my shoulder, and says, "That was very nice, thank you."

"Thank *you*," I tell her sincerely.

"I will always remember that kiss and I'll even tell my daughter about it." A noticeable blush covers her cheeks. "I won't go into detail."

"We don't have to stop yet," I tell her, hoping she likes the idea of continued canoodling as much as I do. But she surprises me by shaking her head.

"We'd better not," she says. "Don't get me wrong, I loved it, but that one kiss is going to have to hold me."

"Why is that?" I mean, if we both want more, why shouldn't we enjoy ourselves?

"Because I'm not going to move to Chicago and you're not

going to move back to Elk Lake. And as much as I'd like another kiss," she waggles a pointer finger between us, "there's really no point."

I disagree. But instead of saying that, I tell her, "You do have a lot going on in your life right now."

"So do you. You need to make things right with your dad and then you need to hightail it back to Chicago." Standing up, Lorelai adds, "I had a very nice evening Luke, thank you. I'm sorry I got a little moody there."

I start wondering if she didn't enjoy our kiss as much as I did. Which kind of concerns me. I've never had any complaints about my kissing, but maybe I'm not as good at it as I thought. "I had a great night, too," I tell her. "Really nice."

"Okay, then, goodnight."

She's about to make a beeline for the stairs so I hurry to say, "I won't be here for breakfast tomorrow. I'm cooking for my parents."

"No problem." She actually sounds relieved. "I have a big day."

"Will you be coming into Pop's tomorrow night?"

She shakes her head vigorously. "Probably not."

I get off the couch slowly. "I guess I'll see you around then."

That's all it takes for her to turn around and run up the stairs like the hounds of hell are nipping at her heels.

What just happened here? It suddenly feels like Lorelai is totally and completely over me, which is an odd thought after all these years. The truth is that she's stirred some feelings in me that I did not see coming.

Lorelai is nothing like the girl she was, and scarily, she's everything like the woman I someday see myself with. How can that be?

CHAPTER THIRTY-ONE

LORELAI

I barely slept a wink last night. I just replayed my evening with Luke on a loop. And let me tell you, that kiss got way more play than any other part of the night. My younger self would have climbed a mountain for a kiss like that. My older self is pretty jazzed, too. But as nice as it was, I can't let thoughts of being with Luke distract me from everything I have to take care of. That's why the best thing I can possibly do for myself is to keep out of his way.

I stay in bed until I hear the front door open and shut. Once I'm certain Luke isn't coming back inside for anything, I take a hot shower.

I don't bother to do more than towel dry my hair before throwing it up into a ponytail. Then I put on some old sweats and get ready to face my list for the day. When I get to the kitchen, I'm kind of sad that Luke didn't leave anything delicious for breakfast, but then I remember he's making breakfast for his parents.

After popping a Toaster Strudel into the toaster, I pour a cup of coffee and sit down at the kitchen table with my lists. With the bookshelves and closets packed, the house is already starting to look bare. Today, I plan to go through the kitchen and linen closets.

After eating, I get to work for an hour when I hear a knock at the front door. Opening it, I discover Allie standing there looking like she's just lost her best friend. "Are you okay?" I ask while pulling her inside. She's wearing holey jeans and a frayed sweater that I'm guessing she found in a rag bin.

Standing in my entryway, she responds, "I'm not great, to be honest."

. "What happened?" I lead the way into the living room before plopping down on the sofa. Allie follows suit.

"Brett is getting remarried," she announces.

"Brett, your ex?" I can't think of another Brett, but this seems incredibly fast.

She nods her head. "I just heard from a friend in the city that his new girlfriend is pregnant and they're going to elope to Vegas this weekend."

"Two things," I tell her. "The first being, what a pig! And the second, what if something happens to this baby, too?" I don't want to jinx a new life, especially one with such a turd of a dad, but Allie miscarried three times. These things do happen.

She shrugs. "I don't know. I suppose if they lose this baby, he'll leave her, too."

I have to know, "What did you ever see in that guy?"

Allie kicks off her shoes before pulling her feet onto the couch. "You know how you have a vision for your life? You picture reaching certain milestones by certain times and then you just think, okay, I'm at the place in my life where it's time to get married; have a family; buy a house, etc.?"

I know what she's saying, but I've never operated like that. While I've certainly thought about those things, none of them appeared to be imminent, so I never felt pressured to stay on any timeline. That's why I tell her, "Not really, no."

She stares at me disbelievingly. "You were never tempted to marry Michael because you thought it was time to get married?"

I shake my head.

"I don't believe you," Allie says.

"Why not? I left Michael."

"Didn't you ever wonder if you should just stay and take the next step?"

"No. But I did wonder how I lasted as long as I did."

Allie's brow wrinkles in confusion. "I don't think you're being honest with yourself, Lorelai."

"Why would I lie about wanting to stay with Michael?"

She shakes her head. "I don't think you're lying about your feelings toward him, but I don't think you're being honest about everything else."

Changing tactics, I ask her, "How many people our age do you know who move home with no plans for their future?"

"Just you," she says. "I think it's more common for people to never leave home than to come back."

"Exactly. So, I'm telling you the truth. I've never been tempted to stay with someone because I thought that was what I should do. Which is probably why I'm finding my current situation a bit challenging. My parents are telling me to create a plan and make it happen because it's time for me to move on, but I innately resist that kind of pressure."

"You must have hopes and dreams."

"I want to be happy," I tell her plainly. "I just don't know what the outside trappings of happiness look like." I've never really put this feeling into words before, but now that I'm saying it out loud, I realize how true it is.

"You want to get married someday, don't you?" She's clearly having a hard time accepting that I'm so different from her.

"I'd like to get married, yes. But marriage isn't the goal "

"The goal is happiness …" She sounds skeptical.

"Yeah, I mean, if I'm happy, then why do I need to fit into other people's definition of what that means? Can't I just figure it out for myself?"

"Is that what you're doing?" she wants to know. "Figuring it out for yourself while hiding away in Elk Lake?"

"That was mean," I tell her sharply.

"Maybe so, but isn't that what you're doing?"

Allie is volunteering some unpleasant opinions that I don't particularly appreciate. "First of all," I tell her. "I don't consider living in Elk Lake as hiding. I've been resting. Taking a break. You know, waiting for the next thing to come along."

"This break of yours could have gone on indefinitely had your parents never decided to sell."

Now I'm getting mad. "It would have gone on as long as it went on."

She arches her eyebrows like she's inspecting an alien life form. "The whole idea about being an adult is doing things that move your life forward." She itemizes, "For most of us that includes careers, marriage, homeownership, and having a family."

"I'm twenty-eight," I tell her plainly. "I'm not going to feel pressured to do things just because society tells me I should."

"Yes, but we have to grow up."

"You feel pressure to do these things," I say. When she nods, I add, "And yet, you and I are both in the same boat. We're both working jobs we didn't go to school for and we're both living with our parents. How is the way you went about this any better than the way I did?" I'm not saying that to be nasty, either. I really want to know how I'm the loser here.

"I grew up and did the things I was supposed to do," she says, sounding confused. "I didn't ask for my husband to leave me because I couldn't have a baby."

"Obviously not," I tell her. "But that's what happened. So again, I'd like to know how your choices have been better than mine?"

Allie stands up and starts pacing across the living room floor like she's trying to gather enough steam to launch herself into space. She suddenly stops and turns on me, wielding her pointer finger like it's a gun. "At least I tried."

"So have I," I tell her. "Up until very recently I had a job that I liked, and I've taken care of my parents' house while they're away."

"Everyone has to take care of the place they live," she retaliates.

Ignoring that comment, I say, "I know you're upset about Brett getting married, but that is not my fault."

"It's not my fault, either," she responds dejectedly.

"No, it's not, but I feel like you've come over here guns-a-blazing, looking for someone to blame your sadness on and that is not going to be me."

Allie inhales deeply before bursting into tears. "I'm sorry, Lorelai. I didn't mean half of the things I said to you. I really didn't. It's just that I've done everything right and I can't believe my life isn't working out like it should have."

I feel bad for Allie. "If you'd had a baby with Brett then you might never have found out his true character. Would you have wanted to remain ignorant to something like that?"

She scoffs. "Ignorance is bliss though, right?"

"You can't honestly be saying that you would have preferred to stay in the dark about the kind of man you married."

"Maybe he would have been a better man if I could have had a baby."

"Allison, character flaws like Brett's don't simply disappear because the person is never faced with challenges. If you'd had a baby and found out later that your husband was a cheat, then you'd spend the rest of your life feeling bad that your kid had such a rotten dad. At least now, you can meet someone a lot healthier and give your future family a better shot at success."

"*If* I meet someone," she says.

"You just have to take each day as it comes," I tell her. "Seriously, I was really scared when my parents told me they were selling, but the truth is, I think it was the best thing for me. It spurred me on and I'm starting to have ideas about a job that I'd really love to have."

"I thought you said you were happy working at the lodge."

"I was, but given my new circumstances, I can't keep working there so I have to find something else."

Allie throws her hands into the air. "I don't even have a plan anymore! I'm so far off schedule, I don't know how I'll ever get back on. My life is nowhere near where it should be."

"According to who?" I ask.

"According to me." She plops back down on the couch and rolls herself into a small ball.

"You need some pudding," I tell her. Then I get up and walk into the kitchen and make my friend a box of cookies and cream instant pudding.

I've always looked at other people and thought they had it all together, but now I'm starting to see there's nothing wrong with how I've lived my life. Bumps come no matter how much you think you're on track. Hard times affect everyone.

I'm happy with how my life is turning out, and happiness *is* the goal, no matter how that looks to other people.

CHAPTER THIRTY-TWO

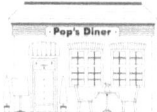

LUKE

I couldn't stop thinking of Lorelai last night. Memory after memory from our younger years popped into my head but this time I saw the past through her eyes. The girl worshipped me, and she made no bones about letting me know. In a typically thoughtless teenage way, I was annoyed by her adoration. I wish I could go back in time and give myself a swift kick in the butt. Not that anything could or would have happened given our age difference, but I sure as heck could have been nicer to her.

Lorelai was so upset last night that this morning I make the decision to pack up my things and move them over to my parents' house for the rest of my stay in Elk Lake. It's not that I don't want to see her. I find that's the problem. I don't want to cause her any more heartache than I already have.

I consider leaving her a note to thank her for letting me stay with her, but I think that might make her angry. I'll call her to thank her and see if she wants to meet up before I return to Chicago.

My dad is still sleeping when I walk into my parents' house. My mom leads the way to the kitchen before telling me, "Dad ate three bowls of soup last night and the equivalent of two whole sandwiches."

"He must have been on a hunger strike," I tease.

"He loved everything that you made for him," she tells me.

"Then why did he tell me to quit bringing him food when he was in the hospital?"

"Because you brought your food, not his. And your food makes him think he's not good enough, like you're the better chef."

"I've been training a long time," I tell her. I put the grocery sack I'm carrying on the counter before pulling a mixing bowl out of the cabinet. I take six eggs out of the refrigerator before cracking them into the bowl and adding some heavy cream and cinnamon. "I haven't made Dad's french toast in ages."

"Make a lot," she says. "I'm starving."

As she sits down at the kitchen table to keep me company, I ask, "How did Dad sleep last night?"

"He tossed around a bit, but once I gave him his pain meds, he knocked off."

"I talked to Jim about Dad's childhood," I tell her.

She nods her head. "He's a good man."

I whisk the egg mixture into a froth before saying, "I'm going to have to tell Dad that I know."

"I figured."

"So, you're fine with that?"

"I am. My first goal is peace in the kingdom, and I have not been very pleased the last couple of years."

"How do you want me to handle things? Do you want me to tell Dad that I just came across his album?"

She shakes her head. "Tell him the truth. But let him enjoy his breakfast first. He might as well get a last meal."

"That's pretty dramatic," I laugh.

"So's your dad."

We sit quietly while I cut thick slices of french bread before soaking them in the egg mixture. After the oven is preheated, I put the cooking sheet inside and set the timer for thirty minutes. Then I put bacon strips on the grill and make my dad's famous maple butter.

When everything's done, I assemble a tray and carry it into the living room. My dad's sitting up in bed with a smile on his face. "I smell french toast."

Laying the tray on his lap, I tell him, "I made it just the way you always did."

He looks skeptical. "Why didn't you try to make it fancy?"

Sitting down on the chair next to him, I tell him, "If I've learned anything it's that you don't mess with perfection. Your french toast has always been that."

Picking up his fork, he cuts into his food and takes a bite. "It's the cinnamon," he says. "You've got to add a lot of cinnamon."

I watch as he continues to enjoy his meal when my mom walks in. "I'm going to take a shower. Will you boys be okay without me?"

My dad looks panicked. "Don't be gone long."

She doesn't respond. Instead, she runs up the stairs like she doesn't want to be anywhere near us when I tell my dad what I know.

Once he's finished eating, I ask, "You want more?" He shakes his head. "Do you need to use the bathroom?" Another head shake.

"You don't need to stay," my dad says. "I'll be fine until your mom comes back."

"That's not how we're going to do this, Dad."

"Do what?"

"We're going to sit here and work things out. It's past time."

He shifts around nervously. "What do we have to work out?"

"Your anger with me," I practically yell at him. "I'd like to know why you're so mad at me."

"You know why," he says petulantly.

"I know you wanted me to work with you at Pop's, but you have to accept that's not the kind of food I want to make."

"Because you're too good for it," he hisses.

"No! Because I like making other stuff better. I like being creative."

When he doesn't respond, I tell him, "I know, Dad."

"I don't know what you think you know…" he starts to say, but the look on his face gives him away.

"I know about your childhood," I say as calmly as I can manage given the continued discord. "I know about your parents. I know about Bobby." Neither one of us says a peep after that. It's so quiet I fancy I can hear my own heart beating. I finally ask, "Did you hear me?"

His head barely moves up and down.

"Is there some reason you never told me?" I demand.

He offers a tentative shrug with the shoulder of his good arm. "What's to tell?"

"How about that my grandparents died and so did my uncle?" I cannot believe he's trying to act like this was no big deal.

"How would your life have been different had you known?" he asks. His voice is monotone like he isn't feeling any emotion whatsoever.

"I don't know, I might have felt like my dad wasn't a stranger to me."

"That's ridiculous," he counters. "We always had a great relationship."

"Until you decided to hate me."

Several long hard moments pass before he says, "I don't hate you. I'm just disappointed."

"Why would you be disappointed in me?" I demand. "It's a tribute to you that I followed in your footsteps."

"You're making your own path," he says. "You're not following mine."

"Just because I don't want to work at Pop's doesn't mean I haven't followed in your footsteps," I counter. "You were never disappointed in me when I was in business school," I remind him.

"I'm not disappointed in *you*," he says quietly.

"You just said that you were disappointed. You can't take that back now."

He shakes his head. "I said I was disappointed. You just assumed you were the reason."

I stand up and start to pace back and forth beside my dad's bed and demand, "What are you so upset about then?"

I don't know what I expect him to say, but I'm surprised when he starts crying. After a couple of minutes, he gestures for me to sit back down. He tells me, "My dad owned a restaurant called Pop's when Bobby and I were little."

What?! "How could you not have told me that?"

"He used to talk about how he wanted me and Bobby to work with him someday."

"That's nice," I say for lack of anything else coming to mind.

"It was, but like you, I wasn't interested."

"Are you serious?" If he didn't want to work with his dad, then why in the world would he expect differently from me?

"Bobby wanted to work with Dad. But that wasn't good enough. Dad wanted us all together."

"He didn't live long enough to see if that would happen," I say. "Maybe it would have."

"I don't think so." My dad explains, "I had other plans. I was going to move to South America and become a soccer star." I know my dad used to love to play soccer, but I had no idea he had such lofty dreams.

"Why didn't you then?" I demand.

"Because my parents died and then Bobby died."

I inhale sharply before saying, "I'm not following, Dad."

The look on his face is one of pure agony. "The day before my parents were killed in that car accident, I told my dad that I hated him and that I was never going to work in his stupid restaurant." The raw emotion in his voice hits me hard.

"How old were you?" I ask him.

"Ten." I can't imagine losing my parents so young.

"Dad," I tell him. "Kids say stupid things all the time. Do you remember how I tried to get you and mom to sell Kelsey after she was born so that I didn't have to share you?"

"You were only three," he says. "I was ten. I was old enough not to say something as horrible as I did."

"You were a *kid*," I remind him. "You were frustrated, and you just wanted your dad to be proud of you for who you are, not what he wanted you to be."

I can see the exact moment this concept hits him upside the head. Hammering it home, I tell him, "Like I want *you* to be proud of *me*."

"I am proud of you, Luke." He speaks so quietly I'm not really sure he said it.

"Then why are you so mad at me?"

He thinks for a minute. "I don't know. I guess …"—he takes a beat to put his thoughts together—"I guess I figured that if I made my dad's dream come true then I would somehow make things right with him."

My heart feels like it's in a vise. How has my father carried this pain around for so long and not seen that there is nothing for him to feel guilty about? "You raised kids. You know we get mad and say stupid stuff. You were just a kid yourself," I remind him.

"Maybe, but my parents died knowing that I said something awful. They died not knowing how sorry I was for doing that."

Standing up, I lean over and gently place my arms around my dad and let him cry on my shoulder. After several long minutes, I tell him, "Your parents forgave you immediately, Dad. It's what parents do."

His words come out as a hiccup. "But then Bobby died."

"That wasn't your fault, either," I tell him. "Jim said he was hit by a drunk driver."

"Ah, so Jim is the one who told you what happened."

I don't confirm or deny his assumption. That can be a fight for another day. "You didn't kill your brother, Dad," I affirm.

"I felt like it was *all* my fault," he says. "If I'd never said that horrible thing maybe my parents wouldn't have died, and neither would Bobby because he would have never gone to live with those other people."

"How have you been carrying this burden for so long?" I ask. "You were a kid. You weren't responsible for the bad things that happened to your family."

"I know that in here." He points to his head. Touching his heart, he adds, "In here it's a different story."

I walk into the kitchen and pour a glass of cold water. When I return to his bedside, I tell him, "Drink this. It'll help."

He smiles. "That's what I always told you."

"You were right, too. You were right about so much, Dad."

After he drinks his water, I take his glass back to the kitchen. My father has always seemed like such a big, strong, functioning human, yet he was being eaten alive by anguish and regret over something that simply wasn't his fault.

I have no idea how to help him heal from this, but I know one thing with great certainty: I will find a way because that's what family does for each other.

CHAPTER THIRTY-THREE

LORELAI

When I woke up this morning, I could tell something was different. The house felt empty, which it has not since Luke came to visit. Tiptoeing down the hall, I look into my room and discover all his things are gone. A wave of sadness fills me. He's already left, and he didn't say goodbye. I guess I can't blame him after how moody I was, but I'm still disappointed.

Before I can second guess myself, I pick up my phone and fire off a text to him.

ME

I see you've already left. I hope you have a safe trip back to Chicago.

He responds quickly.

LUKE

I'll be in town for a few more days, but I'm staying with my parents. I was going to call you later to thank you for everything.

ME

You're welcome.

LUKE

Would you like to meet me at Pop's for supper some night this week?

Before I can answer, my phone rings. It's Luke. "Hi," I say.

"Hi, yourself. Listen, I'm sorry about not saying goodbye in person, but I really would like to see you again before I go."

"When will that be?" I ask. It feels strange to know that Luke is going to be in Elk Lake, but he won't be staying with me.

"A few more days. My dad is recovering surprisingly fast, but I want to see him up and about before I go."

I suddenly feel strangely distant from Luke. "That's nice of you. Are things going well between you?"

"We worked it out this morning," he says. "We're going to be okay."

Walking into the kitchen, I sit down at the empty breakfast table. "I'm glad."

"So how about supper? How does Thursday night look? I'll tell you all about my dad then."

Thursday night is five nights away, so obviously Luke is in no hurry to see me. Which smarts. "I guess that would be fine," I tell him. What I really want to do is cry that our time together has ended before I knew it was ending. Although, had Luke stayed I might have thrown myself at him and begged him to love me. That would have been pathetic, so maybe it's best he slipped out unnoticed.

A thought suddenly hits me that if this is my last meal with Luke, I want it to be more special than another meal at Pop's. "I have a gift card for the dining room at the Elk Lake Lodge. How about if we go there instead?" I ask.

"I've been wanting to eat there!" he says enthusiastically.

"That sounds like a lot of fun. Just text me the time of our reservation and I'll meet you."

"Good, great, will do." I trip over my words like an idiot.

"I really appreciate everything you've done for me, Lorelai. You've been so accommodating." It's like I'm a dog and he's petting me on the head. *Good girl.*

"It was fun," I say, immediately regretting my choice of words. He's going to assume I'm talking about last night's kiss, so I amend that to, "I mean, it's been nice having another warm body at home with me." Great, now I sound like a perv, talking about his warm body.

Luke doesn't respond right away which makes me feel even more insecure. When he finally speaks, he says, "So let me know when our reservation is, okay?"

"Will do." I feel as awkward as I did when I was a little girl trying to impress him with my plastic-egg-stuffed bra. "Bye," I say quickly before hanging up. I have zero game. Nada. Ziltch.

I half expect Luke to text me back and tell me that dinner will no longer work, but he doesn't. I'm guessing he's nowhere near as sad as I am, which just goes to show that he doesn't care about me the way I care about him.

That's when I realize what a good thing it is that he's leaving. Once Luke is out of Elk Lake, there won't be any reason for me to lose focus. I will be onward and upward making a new life for myself. I cannot wait!

The days pass in the blink of an eye. Not only did I meet with Allie's dad, but he's already torn the wall down between the living room and dining room. It turns out that's not such a big project when the wall isn't loadbearing.

The painters came for two days and brought so many workers they've already painted the whole house.

Tomorrow the vinyl planking will be laid and then the following day, the new appliances will be delivered. After that, there won't be much else to do other than wait for the movers to load up my parents' belongings. I still can't believe they didn't want to be here to see the house before it changed so much.

The rest of today is spent in total upheaval as carpets are ripped up and carried out through the front door. Furniture moves from room to room as new carpets are laid, and more people come and go than were probably here all last year.

At five o'clock, the house is finally mine again and I begin the process of walking through and checking everything out. I'm ecstatic how everything looks so new. My room is a shock with all the remnants of my childhood either packed away or gotten rid of. But as I look at the blank slate, I can't help but feel excited for whoever is going to claim ownership of my childhood domain next.

My stomach growls reminding me that it's time to get ready for my dinner date with Luke. I've been so busy that I've hardly thought about him since our phone conversation. But now that I'm going to see him again, my nerves start to take over. What will we talk about? Will he try to kiss me again? Will I throw myself at him and beg him to make me his?

I hope I don't do the last thing, but honestly, I'm not sure I trust my ability to remain calm, cool, and collected around him. Reason seems to go out the window when I'm in his presence.

Going into my closet, I pull out a simple black dress. I've only worn it on a couple of occasions, but it can be dressed up or down depending on need. Tonight, I decide to accessorize with a wide black leather belt with a rhinestone buckle and large dangling rhinestone earrings. Why not leave Luke remembering me the way I want to be remembered? Like a total smoke show.

Walking into the lodge all dressed up, instead of in my work attire, feels nice. I can definitely see coming back here again sometime. I think about the gift card I have for a suite and wonder if

Allie would like to have a little staycation with me sometime. I know she could really use it. We've talked a couple of times on the phone this week and she's still devastated by her ex-husband's actions.

Trina spots me near the dining room and waves before hurrying toward me. After she gives me a hug, she says, "Lorelai! I'm so happy to see you. How are the renovations going?"

"The house looks brand new," I gush.

I spend a few minutes explaining the transformation, before she asks, "Can I come see it some time?" She notices my shocked expression before telling me, "A friend of mine in the city is trying to come up with some ideas to update his new brownstone. He just moved in, and he wants to give it a more modern feel."

"Any time you want," I tell her. "Just text me ahead of time so I can make sure I'm there."

I see Luke cross the lobby heading in our direction and my heart clenches. He looks amazing in his navy suit. He's not wearing a tie, but he looks sexier that way. Staring at his throat, I have the sudden urge to run up to him and kiss him. Luckily Trina turns around to see what I'm looking at, which effectively snaps me out of my daze and keeps me from making a fool of myself. "Hello!" she whispers under her breath. "Are you having dinner with *him*?"

Nodding my head, I tell her. "That's my brother's best friend. He's only in town for a short time."

"Girl, you need to jump on that." It doesn't sound like she's teasing either.

"I can't," I tell her. "He's going back to Chicago."

Before she can respond, Luke joins us. He leans in to give me a kiss on the cheek before saying, "Lorelai, you look beautiful." His voice is deep and complimentary making my stomach drop like I just hit a dip on a roller coaster.

"Thank you. You look very nice yourself." Then I gesture toward Trina. "This is my boss… I mean ex-boss…"

Trina stretches out her hand and says, "Lorelai and I are *friends*. We were lucky enough to have her work at the lodge with us. I'm Trina," she says.

Luke takes her hand, "Luke Phillips."

Trina's eyes open wider. "From Capon in Chicago?"

"Yes," Luke says proudly. "That's my restaurant."

"My fiancé and I love eating there!" she exclaims. "You have the best duck ravioli I've ever eaten."

Luke looks pleased. "It's the combination of dried cranberries and shitake mushrooms that really makes that dish."

"I don't know what's in that sauce," Trina says, "But I could roll in it."

Luke laughs. "I might add that to the description on the menu."

Trina smiles before telling the hostess, "Please give Lorelai and her friend the best table in the house."

"That's very nice," I say.

"With two honored guests like yourselves, we could hardly do less." Then she tells me, "I'll call you to make a plan for coming over."

The hostess leads the way through the dining room to a table located under the main chandelier. It's easy to tell this is prime seating, and I hope Luke is impressed that I can make this happen. Although, I'm sure he wasn't totally without influence. He *is* a rather famous chef.

Once we're both seated, our waiter comes over. "Trina would like to be in charge of your menu tonight if you're okay with that."

While I'm totally good with it, I worry that I only have two hundred dollars to spend. But who cares, if we go over, we go over. I'm determined to leave Luke with the best possible memory of me that I can.

Smiling at Luke, I tell him, "That sounds good to me. How about you?"

Luke hands the waiter our menus. "I'm looking forward to tonight."

The way he says that makes it sound like he's talking about something other than food.

I'm both excited and terrified at the same time.

CHAPTER THIRTY-FOUR

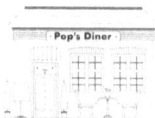

LUKE

Lorelai looks elegantly beautiful tonight. If our paths had crossed in Chicago, I would have been hard pressed not to have begged her to go out with me. And that's before I would have known what an exceptionally lovely woman she is.

Our waiter brings over two glasses of champagne. "The Veuve Clicquot pairs nicely with the pâté that will be out in a few moments."

Lorelai looks nervous, and when he leaves, she mumbles, "I feel like a country bumpkin telling you this, but I've never had pâté."

"You're in for a real treat then," I tell her. "When they pair it with champagne it means that it's delicate and creamy. Which is my favorite kind."

Lorelai takes a sip and immediately sneezes. She quickly explains, "It's the bubbles." *Could she be any more adorable?* I'm pretty sure the answer to that is no.

"How are things going at your house?" I ask her.

"It's been busy," she tells me. "In the few days that you've been gone it's changed so much you'd hardly recognize the place." She giggles before adding, "I even had a wall knocked out."

"Wow, you're taking your job seriously. What are your parents going to think when they find out you're tearing the place down?"

She shrugs. "It's hard to say. They'll either think it's fantastic or they'll never trust me with anything again. Either way, the house looks amazing, so I'm happy."

"Have you decided where you're going to go after it sells?" I want her to say that she's moving to Chicago, but she's made it clear that isn't going to happen.

"I looked at an apartment above the yarn shop," she says. "It's cute and I think it might be my perfect next step."

"You do love yarn."

"I do." Her eyes narrow as though trying to discern if I'm making fun of her.

"Do you remember that year you made all of those potholders and put them in your wagon to sell?" I try hard not to laugh because it was such a crazy sight. I mean, potholders door to door. You don't see that every day.

"I made eighty-two dollars doing that," she tells me proudly.

"Was that enough to cover the cost of the yarn?"

She teases, "Why? Are you thinking about getting a side hustle?" Then she explains, "I was seven, I didn't have to pay for my own yarn back then."

"What did you spend that kind of cash on?" I want to know. "More craft supplies? A red wagon upgrade?"

She shakes her head slowly. "I donated it to the animal shelter. That was when I started volunteering with them."

"You've been helping out at the animal shelter since you were seven?" I don't know why that surprises me, but it does. "Kids don't generally have philanthropic tendencies so young."

"I always wanted a dog or cat, but my dad was allergic so this was the only way I could spend regular time with animals."

"Have you ever had your own pet?" I say, thinking of my

childhood dog, Holly. I can't imagine her not having been a part of my life.

"I had a gerbil once, and a goldfish, but that's about it."

"Why haven't you gotten one now that you're grown?" I want to know.

Putting her champagne glass down, she tells me, "I guess I just haven't gotten around to it. Which I suppose is a good thing. I mean, my dad is still allergic, and I am living in his house."

"But you won't be for long," I tell her. "Maybe you'll get a friend soon."

"I might," she says with a bright smile on her face like the very thought makes her happy. "But I wouldn't want to leave a dog home alone all day."

"That's why I don't have one," I tell her. "They become such a part of the family, you'd feel like you were abandoning your child."

The waiter comes by and puts a plate down on the table between us. "Chicken liver pâté on brioche toast points with a side of onion marmalade."

"It looks wonderful," I tell him sincerely.

Lorelai seems more skeptical. When he walks away, she says, "I'm not a fan of liver."

"It's nothing like beef liver," I tell her. Picking up the dulled knife on the plate, I dab some of the pâté onto the toast before adding a small spoonful of the marmalade. I hand it to her. "Try it."

She hesitantly brings it up to her nose before taking a tentative bite. Her expression shifts from being doubtful to downright joyous. "Yum! It's earthy but kind of sweet at the same time."

Making myself a toast point, I tell her, "You only need one or two of these because it's rich, but it really is the perfect way to start a meal."

After eating two apiece in relative silence—we're both thoroughly engrossed in our food—the waiter comes back. He places a small plate in front of each of us. "Warm goat cheese salad on a bed of butter lettuce with dried cranberries, toasted pine nuts, and a honey and shallot vinaigrette."

"I've died and gone to heaven," Lorelai declares. "Pretend you don't notice if I get up and take my belt off."

I love how easily she can joke about herself. Most women would be too worried their date would think they were fat if they made a comment like that. Although, I suppose we're not really on a date, more's the pity.

Maybe that's why Lorelai can make fun so easily. Because she thinks of me like she does a brother. But then I remember that kiss from last week and know that can't be true.

Speaking of her brother, I ask, "Is Noah coming back before your parents sell the house?"

"He has to pick up all his stuff," she tells me. "But I don't think he'll stay for long. He's definitely not a small-town guy."

"I bet you could have some fun redesigning his apartment for him," I tell her. "Noah's space is nice, but the décor resembles what you'd think it would look like if a squatter had taken up residence."

"It's his use of take-out containers and piles of dirty clothes," she laughs. "He's been decorating with both for as long as I've known him."

After several minutes, the waiter returns with our entrées, interrupting our conversation. "For you, the filet mignon with a truffle sauce," he says, placing the plate in front of Lorelai. "And for you, sir, the duck confit."

"Thank you," I tell him, but my focus is entirely on Lorelai. She's beaming at her meal, her eyes sparkling in the candlelight. It's all I can do not to reach across the table and touch her.

"This is perfect," she says, her voice almost a purr.

"Maybe we can share."

She lowers her eyes coyly. "It's like you can read my mind."

"Maybe I can," I reply, trying to keep my tone light, but I can feel the tension tightening around us. Her comment about reading minds feels loaded, making me wonder if she knows just how often she's on my mind.

As we begin eating, the conversation flows easily, yet the air between us buzzes with unspoken words. I steal glances at her, captivated by the way she savors each bite, her lips parting slightly, her lashes brushing her cheeks as she closes her eyes in appreciation.

"You have a little sauce," I say, pointing to the corner of my own mouth to show her where. Without hesitation, she dips her napkin in water and wipes at the spot delicately.

"Better?" she asks, her voice soft, full of a playful challenge.

"Perfect," I whisper, feeling the electricity crackle between us.

The rest of the meal continues in this charged atmosphere, each brush of our hands as we reach for our glasses, each shared smile, intensifying the connection. By the time the dessert arrives — a decadent chocolate mousse—I'm almost dizzy from the heady mix of food, wine, and her nearness.

As we dig into the dessert, she looks at me, her gaze steady. "You know, if we keep eating like this, we might have to start running marathons."

"Are you a runner, too?" I ask.

With a small shake of her head, she answers, "Not unless you're chasing me with a butcher's knife with an intent to use it."

"Then we'll have to come up with another way to work off our meal." I belatedly realize my comment may have sounded a little R-rated, so I clarify, "We could find a dog to walk."

"Or," she counters, "we could just enjoy the moment and worry about the repercussions later."

Her smile is slow and knowing. As we savor the last bites, the tension transforms, morphing into something deeper, something undeniable. The waiter clears the plates, and for a moment, we just sit there, the weight of the unspoken hanging in the air between us.

I want to tell Lorelai how much I like her; how much I would like to date her for real, but considering her past feelings, I know that wouldn't be fair. She's made it clear she's never going to leave Elk Lake, so there's no point in making our inevitable goodbye harder than it will already be.

Lorelai breaks the tension by raising her hand to get the waiter's attention. When he comes over, she says, "I'll take the check."

"Trina has taken care of that for you." He adds, "She's covered the tip, as well, so you're good to go whenever you're finished."

Lorelai thanks him profusely before telling me, "That was an unexpected treat."

"Those are the best kind." My tone is heavy with innuendo, and I have to remind myself to pull it back.

Yet, as we stand and make our way to the exit, I can't help but wonder if things were different, if tonight could have signaled a new beginning for us.

But instead of dancing around the edges of what could have been, I know what I have to do.

CHAPTER THIRTY-FIVE

LORELAI

Holy cow! The tension over dinner was other-worldly. I came here expecting to maintain a friendly atmosphere while simultaneously making it clear that I no longer harbored any romantic feelings for Luke. I blew that spectacularly.

"Would you like to walk around for a bit?" I ask as we leave the restaurant. I tell Luke, "I can give you a tour." For effect, I bat my eyes once or twice as though suggesting we visit some dark corners where we can enjoy more kisses like we shared last week.

Instead of jumping at my offer, Luke looks at his watch, which makes me wonder if I'd imagined our chemistry. "I'm sorry, Lorelai, I really need to get going."

I want to demand to know where he can possibly have to go. His shift is over at Pop's—not that his dad's diner is still open. He can't possibly be needed at home, as his parents are probably already in bed.

As if he can feel my frustration, he explains, "I'm leaving early in the morning for Chicago. I need to pack up."

I want to know why he can't leave mid-morning, but I don't ask. Instead, I wait quietly for him to explain the tightness of his schedule. When he doesn't, I say, "Well, then you'd best be on your way."

He leans in as though he's going to kiss my cheek. My body immediately turns rigid with indignation. No way, buddy. You don't enjoy a meal like that and then refuse a tour only to put your lips on me. Not gonna happen. I pull away with enough force that I catch him unaware, causing him to stumble a few feet before regaining his balance.

"Have a good night, Luke," I say before quickly turning and walking away. I huff and grumble to myself all the way to my car. *What was that?* I know I claimed I wasn't interested in anything happening between us tonight, but that was before we actually ate together. That meal was one of the most erotic experiences of my life and we didn't even touch one another.

I'm so frustrated right now, I don't know what to do. Part of me wants to find Luke and demand to know what his problem is. But I've chased that man for too long. It's time for me to regain some lost dignity.

My brain flashes to the Valentine's Day I gave Luke a heart that I made out of a paper doily. The inscription read: *I love you with my whole heart.* I even put on lipstick and kissed the paper.

I cringe to think that most of my memories involving him are me declaring my undying love, and him looking for a way to get away from me. Like tonight! Gah! I'm so over being treated like a pesky little kid, I could kick a wall.

I sit in my car and wait for Luke to leave the lodge but he doesn't appear to be in as big of a hurry as he would have had me believe. Either that, or he's afraid to come out for fear I'd egg him. *Why didn't I bring a couple of dozen eggs with me?* Reminder: Take eggs along to all future dates in case it becomes clear the man I shared my evening with deserves to get pelted.

My phone beeps, so I look down to read the incoming text. It's from Luke.

LUKE

Lorelai, I had a lovely evening. Thank you so
much.

Bite me. But I don't send that because I don't want him to think he
matters enough to make me mad.

ME

The food was wonderful

LUKE

So was the company.

ME

Have a safe trip back to Chicago.

LUKE

Lorelai...

I turn my phone off before I can read anything more. I'm
embarrassed that I ever gave Luke the power to hurt me. If I could
go back in time, I'd warn my younger self not to let him break my
heart. But even as I consider such an outlandish idea, I know I
wouldn't have listened. Such is the pull of young love. You think
it's the most powerful thing in the world that you helplessly fall
to its destruction. *Talk about dramatic.*

Once I get home, I take off my dress and replace it with my
favorite granny nightie. Maybe I'll start a company where I design
comfort wear for hopeless spinsters. I remind myself there's
nothing wrong with being alone, so I correct that description to
snuggly garments for women smart enough not to let some man

rule their choices. I could call it something catchy like, "Forever Single," or "Man Kryptonite."

I am strong, talented, and I am going to make a great life for myself whether I share it with some man or not. Luke Phillips no longer has the power to make my heart hurt. I take back every loving gift I ever gave to him. I renounce all declarations of childish devotion. I relinquish any dreams of a future we might have shared. I am woman, hear me roar!

I'm worn out by the time I crawl into bed and all I want to do is cry. But I don't give into the urge. I've made some big changes in my life recently that include coming to terms with creating my own future. And a woman like that—one who's on the precipice of a great metamorphosis—does not cry for someone who won't give her the time of day.

As I drift into an uneasy sleep, a vivid dream begins to unfold. I see a version of myself unburdened by the sorrow Luke has left behind. I'm standing on a sun-drenched balcony overlooking Main Street in Elk Lake. The sky is a brilliant blue, and the air hums with possibility.

In this vision, I'm surrounded by friends who love and support me. Allie and Faith are there. And so is Trina. We laugh together in a way that heals old wounds and strengthens my will to own my happiness.

I don't know what I'm doing for a living but looking toward my living room, I see a large basket full of yarn. There are sketches on the dining room table full of imagined living spaces with swatches of colored fabric glued to the sides of the pages.

I may not envision myself living in exotic places like Paris, or Milan, or the serenely vibrant beaches of Bali, but I can see myself vacationing there.

Every step I take will be a step toward self-discovery. I will open myself up to love and I will fulfill my capacity for happiness. Will that look like everyone else's happy ending? Maybe not, but I will let my spirit soar freely, creating what it will without any barriers.

In this fantasy, the shadow of Luke no longer looms over me. My heart is mended and fortified, ready to embrace the world with renewed vigor. I feel an unwavering sense of fulfillment, a deep-seated peace that comes from knowing I am enough. My desires are my own to fulfill without the constraints of someone else's life.

When I wake, the dream lingers as a beacon of hope illuminating my path ahead. While my heart may still ache, that's not how my story will end.

I'm at the beginning of a new chapter, one where I reclaim my power and write my own destiny. I am Lorelai Riley, mistress of my own destiny, and I will find my happiness, with or without Luke Phillips.

CHAPTER THIRTY-SIX

LUKE

I lied to Lorelai about leaving today. I'm staying until the day after tomorrow so that I can cook supper for my parents at the diner. I didn't tell her that though because I knew after our dinner at the lodge I was in serious trouble. I was ready to throw caution to the wind and declare my interest to her regardless of the consequences, and that wouldn't be fair to her. She's made it clear what she wants, and my plans don't fit into her dreams.

My mom keeps to herself most of the day, seeming to realize how important it is for my dad and me to have uninterrupted time together. We talk about his childhood, and I learn all about his parents and Bobby. They sound like wonderful people, and it makes me sad that I never got to know them. I hear of my dad's favorite memories—which include a family trip to Disney World; his most cherished keepsake—a framed photo of them all in front of Space Mountain; and his biggest regret—never telling his dad how much he loved spending time at his diner.

The more we talk, the more I realize a significant part of my father's development was stunted by his careless words and the subsequent demise of his family. My heart aches for him and I want to wrap the little boy he used to be in my arms and assure him that everything will be okay.

Like so many, my dad is battling demons that invaded his life without invitation. Seeing him as a normal person is a novel experience. I've never thought of him as an ordinary human. From a childhood perspective, he was more like a legendary superhero who knew how to fix any problem that arose. I suppose my idolization has made his seeming disapproval of my life's choices even harder for me to understand.

Once my dad lies down for his afternoon nap—which has become a regular occurrence in his day—I take off for the diner to prepare for the evening meal. Despite my mom's concerns that he'd be angry when he learned I've been picking up the slack for him at Pop's, he was grateful and proud that his son had been there for him in his hour of need.

I've learned so much during this trip that it's going to take me a while to unpack it all. I've learned that while we don't live for others, we must always consider their feelings. Life, while often construed as a singular journey, is so much more than that. It's an adventure that, if lived right, includes compromise and concessions. Bending doesn't break us; it gives us more resilience and strength to handle whatever else might come.

Once I get to Pop's, I strap on an apron and think about what I can make for my dad. I consider something that he will love, while trying to come up with a twist that he might not have previously thought of. I want him to see there's a place where his style of cooking and mine can meet. By embracing our differences, we might actually broaden both of our repertoires.

Cooking for my parents at their diner is a curiously exciting feeling. I'm right where my dad has always wanted me to be, but he no longer seems to even care. Walking over to their table, I announce, "I've made a stuffed meatloaf for tonight's special."

"You know about my specials, huh?" The expression on his face is sheepish.

Giving him a knowing look, I tell him, "Tanya told me that

you served blackened catfish with garlic mashed potatoes." I wait a beat before adding, "Not coleslaw."

The color of his complexion deepens. "Everyone loved it. I'm sorry I gave you such a hard time."

I sit down next to my mom and ask, "Is this how you saw things working out between Dad and me?"

She shakes her head. "I could only hope, but you're both so relentlessly stubborn I was having doubts." Glaring at my dad, she demands, "How is it that you never told me that you didn't want to be in the restaurant business?" I'm surprised she didn't already know that. She must have overheard him tell me.

"I liked it after I got into it," he tells her. "Are you saying you would have preferred the life of a footballer's wife?"

"Soccer wife," she corrects him.

"They call soccer football everywhere in the world except the US," he reminds her.

My mom takes a sip of water before replying, "I'm glad this was our life. I like Pop's and Elk Lake has been the perfect place to raise the kids. I always felt like we were a key part of our community."

"What I want to know," I say looking at my dad, "is whether you copied the menu from your dad's restaurant here."

"A couple things for sure," he says. "But I like to think I put my own spin on them."

"That must be where I get it," I tease before asking, "What happened to your parents' restaurant? You know, after they passed."

"It was sold, and the proceeds went to the people who adopted me and Bobby. I think it was like a buyout for taking a kid they didn't want."

"You'd think someone would have taken both of you, then." My mom's tone is past judgmental and bordering on hostile.

"People want babies," my dad tells her. "It's not an easy task placing two adolescent boys." Changing the subject, he asks, "What comes with that meatloaf?"

"Caramelized onions and garlic mashed potatoes."

"You just can't get away from those mashed potatoes, can you?" he jokes.

"Just you wait until you try the onions," I tell him. "I caramelize them, then finish them off with root beer instead of wine."

My dad raises an eyebrow. "That doesn't sound like very fine dining to me."

"It's not. I learned a lot of stuff at culinary school and not all of it is fancy, as you like to call it."

"Well then, bring me the meatloaf!" he orders. My mom asks for the same.

Walking back into the kitchen, I tell Jim, "They both want the meatloaf."

"Good choice." He cuts two slices and puts them in a pan under the broiler to heat. "It's nice seeing your dad up and about again. It'll be nicer when he comes back to work."

"The doctor says he can start back next week, but he's got to take it slow."

"I might have to hire some help," Jim says. "Now that you're heading back to Chicago, I'm not sure we're going to be able to manage everything without you."

"That's a good idea. I'll be back in a few weeks to check on you," I tell him. "But I'm sure my dad would be happy for the extra help."

I get busy filling orders that are coming in, and I let my mind wander. I haven't even been home for three weeks, and I already feel myself slowing down. I expect readjusting to late hours at Capon might kick my butt. Even so, I am looking forward to getting back into my groove.

I plate my parents' order and then take it out to the dining room myself. I want to see my dad's face when he tries the onions. Putting their dishes down in front of them, I turn to my dad and declare, "I predict that you're going to beg me for the recipe."

He laughs. "You think, huh? You know I cook a pretty mean meatloaf."

"I know you do," I tell him. "But I think mine might be worth a cook off. We can serve some of each and let the customers decide which they like more."

"Are you challenging me?" My dad is trying to sound tough, but the truth is, I can tell he's excited at the prospect. This is probably the kind of lively competition our working together might have created.

I stand and watch while my dad cuts into his meatloaf. He takes a small bite and chews it thoughtfully before guessing, "Horseradish and Tabasco?"

"Yup. What else?"

He starts to list items. "Mushroom, spinach, and salsa! I like salsa in place of ketchup. Nice move."

I offer a small bow. "I should have known you would have caught that."

My mom rolls her eyes. "I'm starting to think that if you two ever did work together, I'd never see either of you. You'd be too busy competing."

My dad waves his fork through the air. "You don't have to worry about that. Luke is going home to Chicago, and I promised that we'd come up there and let him cook for us at Capon."

My mom positively beams with joy. "I'm glad to have my boys back together."

"I've been a real idiot, Luke," my dad says. "I promise to never pressure you about where you work again."

A feeling of warmth circulates through me. I love having my dad back. I just wish we hadn't lost so much time. "I'm still coming back to Elk Lake and we're going to have some throw downs. I'm thinking our first one should be meatloaf, but our second should be catfish."

"My money's on your dad for the catfish," my mom says loyally.

"How can you say that?" I want to know. "You've had my catfish at Capon."

She rolls her eyes. "I'll refrain from voting until I try them together," she says. "Now scoot. I want to enjoy my dinner, and I can't do that if you keep yapping."

As I walk back into the kitchen, an image of Lorelai pops into my head. I finally see why she likes living in Elk Lake so much. I've spent so much time away from home in the last several years, I forget how it feels to be so easily accepted. There's no need to prove yourself here. There's no pressure to be more.

Getting back on the line, I throw several burgers and chicken breasts on the grill while contemplating my future. Not too long ago, I thought I knew exactly what I wanted, and nothing was going to get in my way of having it. But now that my dad and I have mended fences, I finally see that there's more to life than leaving. Coming home has been pretty sweet, too, and I look forward to spending a lot more time here.

Which of course, brings me back to the topic of Lorelai ...

CHAPTER THIRTY-SEVEN

LORELAI

I've done a fabulous job revamping my family home. So much so, that I'm not sure my mom and dad will even recognize it when they see it in a few days.

When the doorbell rings, I hurry to open it. "Wait until you see!" I tell Anna, who's stopped by to check out the progress.

Pushing past me, she responds, "I can't wait." As soon as she walks into the entryway, she adds, "You took out that wall!" She's clearly as excited about the change as I am.

"I figured it was the easiest way to modernize the space."

Clapping her hands together, she declares, "I absolutely love it!" Then she walks into the living room. "The gas fireplace is a great addition, too. People love an easy fire, and they hate cleaning up ashes."

"Preach," I tease. "I just can't bring myself to go to all the effort to build a fire for just me, so I usually go without. But ever since I put in the gas, I light a fire all the time."

Anna shuffles through a stack of papers before handing them to me. "Here are the comps." Pointing to the top of the first page, she adds, "And here's where I think you should list."

My eyes pop open at the number. "Seriously? That much?" Not only am I delighted, but I'm suddenly nervous that with prices like these, I'll never be able to afford a home in Elk Lake.

As I follow her into the kitchen, she says, "The changes you've made have added a lot to the bottom line. I predict you'll more than triple your money back on those improvements."

Shaking my head, I tell her, "I can see why people flip houses now. I mean, I knew they made money, I just never realized they could make so much."

Running her hand over the navy cabinets, she tells me, "You don't make this much everywhere, but in a resort town, you can't lose. People don't mind spending money when they know their investment is secure."

"I wish I had the money to invest in a place to flip."

"Don't we all," she says. "That's the hardest part of the whole thing—making the mortgage payments until the reno is over and you can recoup your cash."

Walking up the stairs, Anna says, "You have a real eye for color. Most people paint everything the same shade of beige or white. I love the subtle varying shades you've used. If you're interested, I'd like to give some of my clients your number. I think you could really help them capitalize on their homes."

I feel a sense of pride fill me. I've been artistic for as long as I can remember but until now, I've never realized that it could be converted into a business. "I would really love that, Anna. Thank you."

"You changed the vanity!" Anna declares while walking into the hall bathroom.

"There was a deal at the hardware store," I tell her. "I couldn't resist."

"Did you do that in the main, as well?"

Nodding my head, I assure her, "It was a *screaming* deal."

"Let me see it," she says. "If it looks as good as this one, we may be able to add to the listing price." As we continue to walk around the upstairs, she says, "You've taken care of all the details.

The switch plates alone cost nothing but changing them out makes everything look so fresh. And I notice you replaced the closet pulls. So smart."

I'm seriously beaming at her praise. "I watch a lot of HGTV."

"So do a lot of people, but they don't seem to catch on how to do this stuff for themselves." She amends that to, "At least that's true for a lot of the sellers I've had."

"I talked to my parents this morning," I tell her. "They're coming home next week to check everything out and sign the paperwork."

Anna nods her head thoughtfully. "I'm guessing they'll have multiple offers in the first week of listing. We won't put it on the market officially until after Memorial Day when the season opens." She elaborates, "I predict a twenty percent increase based on the out-of-towners that will be interested in a vacation investment."

"That's crazy!" I declare. But even so, I can see that year-round Elk Lake residents might not be as interested in paying such a hefty price. But Chicagoans probably look at our inflated summer prices and still think they're a steal.

The doorbell rings again, so I tell Anna, "That's my friend. She wanted to come and see what I've done here. Go ahead and keep looking."

Running down the stairs, I open the door for my old boss. The first words out of her mouth are, "Your house is adorable! I love this neighborhood!"

"It's been a great place to live," I tell her before asking, "Are you and Heath looking to buy here in Elk Lake?"

She shrugs. "I think we eventually want to build, but we've been so busy getting the lodge going that we haven't settled on it yet."

"You live in one of the cottages at the lodge, right?"

"For now. Heath still spends a good deal of time in the city and we're not really sure what's next for us. I think I'd like to settle in Elk Lake, but a lot of that will depend on his next business venture."

Trina's fiancé is a billionaire, so I'm guessing he can do whatever he wants, but even though I'm not that financially sound, I still understand the need some people have to keep moving on.

Anna walks down the stairs and declares, "You've done an absolutely amazing job here, Lorelai!" She notices Trina. "Trina, how are you?"

Trina walks toward her and gives Anna a hug. "You look great!" she gushes. They have mutual friends—most notably Paige and Tim, who fell in love on the final season of *Midwestern Matchmaker*.

Anna laughs. "Twenty pounds of baby weight off and only twenty to go."

Trina announces, "When Heath and I start a family I'm going to make up for every diet I've ever gone on. I'm going to let myself eat anything and everything I want."

"It's a lot of fun," Anna says. "Except that once the baby comes, you have to deal with what you've done to yourself."

"You're gorgeous," Trina assures her, before telling her, "I have a friend in the city who just bought one of those magnificent old brownstones, but it needs a lot of work. I thought I'd see what Lorelai did here and then maybe get them together so she can help Chip with some ideas."

Anna tells her, "I was just telling Lorelai that I wanted to give her number to my clients who are selling. She's done an amazing job here!"

I love hearing how appreciated my talents are, especially when I never realized they were talents. Every change made to my parents' house just seemed like common sense to me. Leading the way into the living room, I sit down and announce. "Please feel free to keep singing my praises. The two of you are making my day."

Trina and Anna sit down with me, and Anna suggests, "You

might consider going to design school. I mean, you've done such a fantastic job here, but credentials will get you bigger clients."

I have never thought about design school, but the idea fills me with excitement. "I wonder if they have a school in Madison." As much as I don't want to go back there, I could probably stand it for however long it would take me to get some kind of certificate.

"If you're going to go to school," Trina says, "you should go in Chicago. They're more cutting edge."

While I've declared that I never wanted to live in Chicago, the thought of going to school there does not fill me with dread. I wonder why that is. But before I can put my feelings into words, an image of Luke pops into my head.

I'm immediately bombarded by a variety of feelings. I like Luke. I like him so much and I would love to date him. But even though he lives in Chicago, he's made it clear he will never move back to Elk Lake. And while I might be willing to go to school in the city, I know with certainty that I will be moving back home as soon as possible.

As such, what would be the point of getting in deeper with Luke if we are destined for such different futures?

The events of the rest of the day come and go, and I simply can't make sense of the whirlwind of emotions flooding my body. I'm hopeful, I'm nervous, I'm scared, but mostly I'm really excited about what the next chapter of my life will bring.

CHAPTER THIRTY-EIGHT

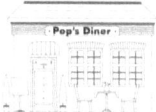

LUKE

Saying goodbye to my parents wasn't nearly as hard as I thought it would be. That's probably because I know we'll be seeing each other a lot more now. They promise that as soon as my dad is given the green light to go back to his regular schedule, they'll come and visit me in Chicago. When I asked what they'd do with the diner, my dad said that he'd close it if he had to. He feels bad about all the overtime that Jim has been working, and he's vowed to not lean on him so hard in the future.

As luck would have it, my car wouldn't start this morning. I had it towed to the mechanic and learned that my alternator needed replacing, so I decided to leave it in Elk Lake for repair and take the train back to the city. My mom dropped me off at the station, but she couldn't stay because she was going to take my place at the diner so Jim could take his dad to the doctor. The more I think about Jim, the more I realize he's been my family's guardian angel for as long as he's known us.

Sitting in the depot, I look around at the faces. Even though I don't know anyone here, they all look puzzlingly familiar to me. With their casual attire and placid expressions, no one seems to be in a great hurry. Yet, there's an underscored sense of motion as they are either getting ready to go into Chicago or they're waiting for someone who's visiting. If Norman Rockwell were still alive, he could sit in this depot and create one masterpiece after another of small-town America.

The ride home goes particularly quickly because I fall into a dead sleep. I wake up as the train pulls into Union Station. Looking around, I have a sort of otherworldly sensation like maybe I was never gone and the last three weeks were nothing more than a dream.

Picking up my phone, I check my text messages and read the newest one from my mom.

> MOM
>
> Hi, Honey! I hope you had a nice trip home. Your dad and I already miss you so much and we can't stop talking about coming to see you. Love, you, love you!!

So, it wasn't a dream after all. I take a cab to my apartment in Marina City which is across the river from Capon. As much as everything feels familiar, I still have a sensation like I'm an outsider and not coming home myself.

I hold my breath as I put my key into my front door lock. It's almost like I don't know what to expect. But then I open the door and everything looks the same. I credit my hectic work schedule for the incredible lack of personal style in my surroundings. Instead of having lived here for four years, it looks like I'm renting a furnished apartment that I'll only be in for a short time. After being at Lorelai's house and then with my parents, I realize it's time for me to make my apartment feel like a home. I just don't know where to start.

After turning up the heat, I plop down on my couch and look out onto the Chicago River. It's only three o'clock in the afternoon, but I feel like I want to go to bed for the night. I force myself to take a shower to wake up and then I change into my chef's pants and T-shirt before leaving the building and walking across the bridge to Capon. I've made this journey so many times I move like I'm on autopilot. Yet, there's still a strangeness to it that I find disconcerting.

The first person I see as I walk inside is Eve. She's standing at the hostess station talking on the phone. I overhear her say, "Yes, Mr. O'Neil. We have your table of twenty ready to go." She pauses a beat before adding, "We'd be happy to make it for thirty."

Hanging up the phone, my general manager stares at me with surprise in her eyes. "Luke! I didn't know you were coming back today. Why didn't you text and let me know?"

I walk over to her and offer her a quick hug. Eve is everything I used to think I was attracted to before our awkward attempt at dating. She's very tall, slender to the point of being all sharp angles. She's blonde and she's elegant above all else. She is physically nothing like Lorelai.

Lorelai is slightly above average in height, with red hair, pale skin, and a full enough figure that she doesn't look like she misses meals, let alone starve herself to achieve a feminine ideal. An ideal I realize I no longer find all that feminine. Lorelai is wholesome and real looking. To me, she's perfect.

"I wanted to pop in and surprise everyone," I tell her after pulling away.

"Worried we weren't surviving without you, huh?" She laughs loudly. "Did you happen to hear that a party of twenty just increased to thirty? It's been like that since you left. I swear, people are getting more social by the second." She cocks her head to the side and stares at me questioningly. "You look different."

"How so?" I ask.

Her eyes narrow like she's dissecting me. "It's hard to say. I mean, you still look like you, but the wrinkles around your eyes are less pronounced."

"Wrinkles? I don't have wrinkles. Laugh lines maybe…"

She scoffs. "You can call them laugh lines if you want, but I'm of a mind to call a spade a spade. As such, you have wrinkles."

She squints her eyes again, "But not as much as you used to. You look like you've been to a spa or something. Did you get Botox?"

"No, Eve, I did not get Botox." I can't believe she even asked that. "I've been sleeping more. Maybe that's the secret."

She takes my elbow and leads me over to the bar. "Sit down and tell me everything." She settles on a stool next to me.

"It was really great being back in Wisconsin," I tell her. "My dad and I talked a lot and we're in a good place now." I don't bother to go into the whole story. It's enough having lived it without rehashing it.

"How's he feeling?"

"He's on the mend," I tell her. "Luckily, he didn't do as much damage as he could have."

Looking around at the restaurant fills me with a sense of pride and awe. Capon has forty-eight tables varying from two- to six-tops. We push tables together for larger parties. On a weekend night, we'll turn the tables three times, sometimes four, depending on the lateness of the reservation.

"So, it's been busy," I say.

"Crazy busy. Seriously, Luke, if you ever wanted to expand, I think we could easily take double the reservations we currently do. I've been turning people away right and left."

"That's nice."

Apparently, I don't show the kind of excitement she's expecting, because she asks, "Who are you and what have you done with Luke Phillips?"

I snort laugh. "It's just really different at home," I tell her. "Maybe I lost my edge while I was gone."

"You do seem pretty relaxed." Curling her lip, she adds, "It's kind of spooky."

"The whole vibe of Elk Lake is pretty chill," I tell her. "How's the kitchen been working without me?"

Arching an eyebrow, she answers, "I know you want me to say that you're indispensable, and while you are wonderful, they didn't really miss you. The culinary school sent two bodies to fill in and the line cooks stepped up. They did so well, I think there might be a promotion or two in order."

Part of me thinks I should feel bad for not being missed more, but the truth is I'm glad for it. I've been carrying the success of Capon on my shoulders like a huge burden and it's been exhausting. Maybe that's how Bobby Flay does it. He actually trusts his staff to run with the ball without him micromanaging every detail.

"I think I'll stay long enough to get you through tonight's rush, but then I'll take off."

"You're leaving early?" Her shock makes it clear I've been a straight up workaholic.

"I think so," I tell her. "I've recently realized that I need a little more balance in my life. I might even take off two whole days a week."

She shakes her head in wonder. "Are you thinking about opening another place?"

"I'm thinking about a lot of things," I tell her. "I just need to regroup first."

A waiter waves toward Eve, so she stands up "Welcome home, Luke. It's good to have you back." I guess I am home, but having said that, it's a different kind of home than Elk Lake.

I have a lot to think about, but I don't really know where to start. I suppose that for tonight, I'll just jump back in and take it a step at a time. If it weren't for my parents and Lorelai, I wouldn't even be questioning what's next. But if mending fences with my dad taught me anything, it taught me that life should not be a solitary journey. And in order for that to be the case, I don't get to make all the calls.

Speaking of calls, it's all I can do not to pick up the phone and call Lorelai. I want to know how she's doing. I want to tell her all about Capon. But more than anything, I want to tell her how much I miss her and wish she were here.

CHAPTER THIRTY-NINE

LORELAI

I've spent the last week tying up all the house details. I've recovered the sofa with a canvas slipcover. I've reupholstered the dining room chairs with my handy-dandy staple gun, and I've purchased some new towels to hang in the bathrooms. When I was a kid, my mom used to call them "company towels," which essentially meant they were never to be used. In fact, the company towels from my childhood are still in the linen cabinet, and they're in the best shape of any of them. The only reason I bought new ones is because the colors are kind of dated.

My parents are coming home today, and I can't wait to show them the transformation of their home. I expect they'll not only be shocked but also excited by how much more money they're going to get because of all the upgrades.

At 1:15 on the nose, my mom texts that they've left the airport, and they should be home in forty-five minutes. I offered to pick them up, but she assured me that she and my dad are fine taking an Uber.

I hurry to take a shower and change into something nice before they arrive. I've even made a plate of sandwiches and some cookies that I baked from store-bought cookie dough. Which are perfectly edible even though my mom claims you can taste the chemicals. She and Luke have a lot in common.

On my way downstairs, I actually jump when I hear the doorbell ring. I'm surprised my parents got here so quickly because according to the Uber app, they're still twenty minutes away.

Opening the door, I stand there in shock. "Noah, what are you doing here?"

My brother pushes through the front door and drops a large duffle bag at my feet. "Are Mom and Dad here yet?"

"They should be here any minute," I tell him.

Walking into the living room, he says, "Then I'll tell you all at the same time. It's not a tale I care to repeat."

I have no idea what's going on, but I can tell it's not going to be a good story. "You want some lunch?" I ask him.

We walk toward the kitchen, and he doesn't even seem to notice that the wall between the living room and dining room has been removed. He doesn't even comment on the paint job in the kitchen. He merely asks, "You got any salami?"

"Open your eyes, Noah," I tell him.

He looks from his left to his right before answering, "My eyes are open."

"Do you notice anything different?"

Shrugging, he asks, "Did you clean? It looks clean.'

"Yes, I cleaned," I grumble. "But that's not what I'm talking about."

He sits at the kitchen table and slumps to the point where he's almost lying on it. "I'm tired, Lorelai. I've had a hard day. Heck, I've had a brutal week. I'm not in the mood to play guessing games."

He does seem particularly gruff, even for Noah, so I decide to let it go for now. "You want cheese on your sandwich?" He nods his head, so I open the refrigerator and get out the fixings. Then I build his sandwich the way I know he prefers. He likes three slices of bread, three slices of cheese, and enough salami that I don't know how he's going to bite through it all. Then there's lettuce and grain mustard. Putting it on a plate, I hand it over to him.

"How about chips?" he wants to know.

The only reason I don't pick up the bag and throw it at him is because he really seems out of sorts. So instead of resorting to violence, I merely open the bag, take out a handful, and add it to his plate. I watch as he eats in silence.

The next thing I know, I hear the front door open and my mom yell, "We're home, honey!"

My dad follows that up with, "This isn't our house! Where's the wall?"

Noah looks up from his lunch and says, "I knew something looked different."

Hurrying into the living room, I give both of my parents a big hug. Then I state the obvious, "I had the wall knocked down."

My dad looks like he's about to succumb to a heart attack, but my mom merely beams from ear to ear. "I love it!" she declares with feeling. "I mean, wow! It looks so much bigger in here."

"How much did it cost?" This from my dad.

I smile at him and in dulcet tones meant to soothe, I say, "Anna said you'll make back three times the cost, minimum. People want an open floor plan these days."

His expression transforms into a radiant smile, "I love it!"

"You should know that Noah is home," I tell them. "He's in the kitchen."

My mom nods her head. "He called and said he had something to tell us." She walks toward the back of the house and announces, "The kitchen is gorgeous!"

My dad and I quickly follow behind and my dad needs to know, "How much did *this* cost?"

"Three times the return in here, too."

"I love it!" he declares for the second time in as many minutes.

Noah looks up from his plate. "Hey."

"Hay is for horses," my dad tells him before nearly picking

him up by the scruff of the neck for a hug. Once my dad's done, he hands over his son so my mom can have a turn.

"Honey," my mom tells him. "You look like crap."

"Thanks, Mom." He disengages himself from her embrace before sitting back down. "I guess I might as well tell you all now."

"Tell us what?" I want to know. He clearly didn't get a personality transplant because he's as grumpy as ever.

"I lost my job," he says.

"You what?" My mom's in as much shock as any of us.

"I thought you were taking the team to first place this year. How did you lose your job?" my dad wants to know.

Noah exhales like he's blowing out birthday candles from across the room. "The school hired Holland Frame to be head coach."

"Really?" My dad suddenly seems very excited "How did they lure away a past NBA superstar to coach a high school team?"

"Holland's grandson goes to school there," Noah says.

My mom makes a cutting motion across her throat. "And just like that, they gave you the boot?"

Noah shakes his head. "They told me I'd be the assistant coach. They demoted me."

"Did they cut your pay?" my dad wants to know.

"No, but what does that have anything to do with it?" Noah demands.

I interject, "You got demoted but you kept your same salary, so what's the problem? How did you lose your job?"

"I quit!" my brother practically yells.

"Noah Riley." It's my mom's turn again. "Don't you dare tell me that you let your pride get in the way of gainful employment."

My brother bangs his fist on the table like a toddler demanding more Goldfish crackers. "My pride? I'll tell you about my pride. I single-handedly took that team from twentieth in the state all the way to third in three years. *I* did that. Holland Frame didn't."

"And so, you just walked?" my dad wants to know.

Noah shakes his head. "Not just like that. I told the superintendent that I would stay and allow Holland to be my assistant coach."

"Oh, dear," my mother says. "And of course they said no."

"Why of course?" Noah wants to know.

My dad pipes in with, "The NBA championship thing?"

"I brought the team up," my brother's voice raises again. "They are *my* team, not Holland's."

Leave it to my mom to cut to the chase. "So, you quit and came home to stay? That doesn't make any sense, honey. What could there possibly be for you here in Elk Lake?"

"It is still my home," he tells them. "At least until you sell it."

My dad nods his head sagely. "That's true. It is. But we're selling soon."

"There's something else," Noah says. All eyes are on him, so he adds, "Elk Lake High School has offered me a head coaching job."

"Elk Lake?" my mom asks.

My dad finishes her question, "High school?"

"Yes, Elk Lake High School," he tells them. "You might remember it because your children went there?"

"Their season is over," I volunteer. I know this because prom came early which means they didn't even make the playoffs.

"They've hired me for next year, but they want me to get going and start training next year's team." He smugly adds, "They have high hopes that with enough practice, I'll do for them what I did for my last school."

My mom looks very confused. "You'll only be able to stay until we sell."

"Unless I buy the house from you," Noah says.

"You want to buy our house?" You'd think my dad would like this idea more than he seems to.

"Maybe? I mean, why not?"

"What about your place in Chicago?" I ask.

"I can rent it out. I want to keep it for at least another five years before selling."

My mom makes eye contact with my dad and then motions him toward the living room. She tells me and Noah, "Don't move. We'll be back in a couple of minutes."

I have no idea what to say to my brother after they leave. so I tell him, "I'm sorry things aren't going your way."

He snorts but doesn't say anything else.

When my parents come back into the room, my dad looks kind of pale, but my mom seems determined. She addresses me first. "Lorelai, you did a beautiful job with the house."

"Thank you," I tell her. I like how her admiration feels.

"Your dad and I always knew you had a wonderful artistic flare, and we thought by letting you get the house ready for sale that you might discover a love of interior design."

"I have," I tell her. "In fact, I've been thinking about maybe taking some classes."

"Good," she says. "You can stay in Noah's house in Chicago while you decide if you like it."

"No, she can't!" my brother shouts. "I need a paying tenant, not a freeloader."

Nice, Noah, Way to make me like you. But I don't have a chance to say that because my dad decides to speak up. "You can stay here, Noah."

"Are you going to sell to me?" he wants to know.

My dad tells him, "We'll hold off selling the house for a year until you can decide if you want to stay in Elk Lake. If you do, we'll sell it to you next summer."

I raise my hand and bring my parents' attention back to me. "In this scenario, I'll be staying at Noah's rent free?"

"You still have to pay the utilities," my brother snaps. But then he softens and tells our mom and dad, "Thank you. I appreciate the help, because honestly, I don't know if I'm going to like working here."

"It's going to be a big change," my mom says. "But we believe in our kids so much that we want to do everything we can to help support you."

This seems to be an about-face from how it felt when they originally announced they were selling. "You told me I needed to get on a career path," I say. "And the whole time you were trying to lead me to that path?"

"Lorelai," my dad says. "You just needed a little push, is all."

"So, you don't need the proceeds of this house to survive?"

My dad laughs. "Honey, I bought bitcoin when it was only five thousand a coin."

I didn't know that. "How many coins did you get?"

"Four," my mom says proudly.

"And it's recently gone over a hundred thousand," Noah inserts. "Which means, you cleaned up!"

"We did pretty well," my dad agrees.

"That's amazing," I tell them. "I appreciate your help more than you will ever know."

My mom reaches out and takes my hand. Squeezing it, she says, "It's what being a parent is all about. Plus, you're worth our investment."

And just like that, I'm moving to Chicago to go to school, Noah's coming home, and my parents are going to play golf in Florida. I didn't see any of these changes coming, but the truth is, I know they're all for the best.

CHAPTER FORTY

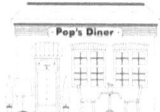

LUKE

I've been back in the city for a week, and I still don't feel like I'm in the groove of my old life. I roll over in bed when I hear my phone ring. Picking it up, I see that it's Jim.

Jim has never called me on the phone, so my first thought is that something has happened to my dad. "Hey, man, what's up? Is everything okay at home?"

"All's well here," he says. I immediately breathe a sigh of relief.

I still don't know why he's calling. "How's work?"

"Good."

"Your folks?"

"Really good."

It's like pulling teeth to get information out of him. "Not to be rude, but why did you call?"

"I wanted to let you know about an investment opportunity that has become available in Elk Lake."

"I appreciate that," I tell him. "But I plan to stay with my parents when I come back to visit."

"It's not a house," Jim says.

While I don't find it difficult to talk to Jim in person, a phone conversation appears to be an entirely different experience. "What is it?" I ask him.

"There's a restaurant in town that just went on the market."

I can't help the chuckle that bursts out of me. Jim appears to be picking up where my parents left off. "I'm good, Jim. I don't plan on opening a restaurant in Elk Lake."

"Don't you even want to know which restaurant it is?"

"Not particularly."

"It's called Pop's. You may have heard of it."

This catches me totally off guard. I thought my dad was going to work for another two years. "My parents are selling now? Why?"

"If I had to guess," Jim says, "It might have something to do with your dad's recent fall. Coming to terms with your mortality has a way of shocking your priorities."

"Are you going to buy it?" I ask. "I mean, honestly, Jim, you've worked there for so long, you're as responsible for Pop's success as my dad is."

"I already told you that I don't want to be the boss. Especially at this point in my life."

A heavy weight settles on my chest as I consider what it would be like without Pop's in the family. While I've never wanted to own it, I suppose I must accept that my feelings have changed a bit. Now that I know my dad's story, I realize that Pop's is a much bigger deal than I thought it was. Not only is my own history rich with memories, but it's also a tribute to my grandfather, a man I never had the pleasure of knowing.

With a sigh, I ask, "Who's listing the property?"

"Anna Tanaka from Elk Lake Realty," Jim says.

"Don't get your hopes up," I tell him.

Jim chuckles deep in his throat. "I got no hopes, son. I just wanted to make sure you knew what was up, so you didn't wind up with any regrets."

"Were my parents going to keep this a secret from me?" I want to know.

"They figured that now that you and your daddy have made up, they didn't want you to feel any pressure."

That's very considerate of them, but still, I'm glad Jim called me. "Thank you, Jim. I'll keep the secret."

"Good man," he says. "Now I gotta go." He hangs up before I can say anything else.

I immediately Google the phone number for Elk Lake Realty. Calling it, I ask for Anna. I don't have to wait for long. "Hello, this is Anna Tanaka."

"Anna," I say. "This is Luke Phillips. How are you?"

She seems oddly pleased that it's me. "I'm doing great, Luke! What can I do for you?"

"I just talked to Jim Parnicky from over at Pop's. He tells me my parents are selling the diner."

"I just left there," she says. "And yes, they're selling."

"They didn't tell me."

She doesn't comment on that. Instead, she asks, "Are you interested in knowing the price?"

"I am."

She gives me a number. I'm surprised it isn't bigger, but then again, whoever comes in will want to make their own changes. That will certainly raise their startup costs. Before I can second guess myself, I tell her, "I'll buy it."

"Do you want to place a counteroffer?"

"No. Offer full price, just don't tell them that I'm the one buying."

I can hear the excitement in her tone when she says, "What fun! Of course I'll keep your secret. I'll call them now and tell them that we have an offer."

"Thank you."

After hanging up with Anna, I start to wonder what I've done. But it doesn't take long to realize that buying Pop's is the right thing to do.

Capon has done really well without me, which makes it clear they don't need my constant attention. Not to mention that if I spend more time in Elk Lake then there's no reason that Lorelai and I can't date.

Suddenly feeling like a million bucks, I pick up the phone to call my folks. It's going to be hard not telling them that I not only know about Pop's, but I'm also the new owner. The phone rings four times before my dad answers. "Luke! Hi! Your mom and I were just talking about you."

"All good things, I'm sure," I joke.

"All good things," he assures me. "To what do we owe the honor of this call?"

"I just wanted to let you know that I'll be home in a couple of weeks. I thought I might stay long enough that we can have our meatloaf cook-off. Maybe even fit in the catfish one."

My dad sounds genuinely excited when he says, "I would love that! I wasn't going to hold you to it, though. I'm done pressuring you, son."

Now that I know he's selling Pop's, I'm certain he's telling me the truth. "I know that, Dad. But listen, I have a favor I need to ask if you don't mind."

"Just name it."

I spend the next few minutes explaining what I need him to do for me. Once I'm done, he says, "This is a big surprise coming from you." Little does he know, this isn't the biggest surprise on the horizon. And I can't wait to share that one with him, too.

CHAPTER FORTY-ONE

LORELAI

Noah's place is an absolute pit. Not only did he leave the refrigerator full of expired food, but he left wet towels on the bathroom floor. The whole place smells like mildew.

I open the sliding doors to the patio before grabbing a garbage bag and dumping all the trash into it. Even though Noah's apartment is gross, it's also charming in the way of pre-war buildings. The rooms are big, and the ceilings are high. Who knows, I might make a couple of minor design upgrades while I'm here.

I'm not sure if I'll get around to telling Luke that I'm in Chicago. It's only been ten days since he left Elk Lake and I'm still feeling pretty fragile as far as he's concerned. Plus, I'm going to be busy. I have an appointment at the design school this week, and tonight I'm meeting with Trina's friend, Chip. He wants me to tour his brownstone and brainstorm different things he can do to update it.

Looking at the clock, I realize I don't have a lot of time to get to Chip's apartment, so I quickly change into a nice skirt and blouse, before heading out to meet him. I don't know my way around

Chicago very well, so I'm not sure how long it will take to get from Wrigleyville to the Gold Coast.

It turns out that Chicago traffic is even worse than I thought it would be, and I wind up at Chip's ten minutes late. Knocking on his door, I admire the exterior of his home. It's downright elegant and I can only imagine what a shining star it was when it was built well over a hundred years ago.

A tall man wearing tennis whites opens the door. "Chip?" I ask. He's polished and handsome in the way of a movie star from the nineteen forties.

"Lorelai!" he declares enthusiastically. "Come in!"

I follow him into his home and let out a low whistle. "Wow." I thought the ceiling height of my brother's place was impressive, but this is crazy. "Your ceiling must be twelve feet high."

"It's great, isn't it?" He rubs his hands together enthusiastically. "Wait until you see the upstairs. I want to keep its charm, but I'm not a fan of fussy Victorian decor."

"I hope you plan on keeping the crown molding," I say as I look up and admire the decorative trim. The chandelier medallions are also out of this world!

"Definitely keeping the molding," he says. "My husband Bob loves all of those touches and he'd murder me if I even suggested changing them. But I still want to hear what you think we can do with the place to make it a little less feminine."

I spend the next three hours talking ideas with Chip. I fantasize that he'll give me a credit card like my dad did and tell me to go nuts, but I don't want to be greedy. I'm just happy to have anything to do with conceptualizing a future for this beautiful home.

After we discuss all of the possibilities, including turning the butler's pantry into a serviceable bar, and reconfiguring a smaller bedroom upstairs to be used as the master closet, Chip announces, "I'm starving. How would you like to join me for dinner?"

"I don't want to put you out," I tell him. I like Chip so much and am really enjoying spending time with him.

I know he's a kindred spirit when he says, "I'm not cooking. I'm suggesting we go out and eat like civilized people."

"Then I'm in," I say happily.

Chip escorts me to the living room sofa. "I'll just go change and call a car."

Several minutes later, he comes back and announces, 'Bob has a late meeting but said to tell you that he can't wait to meet you." He accurately reads the questioning expression on my face, because he adds, "That's if you'll take the job."

I'm about to blurt out that I'll do it for free, but I manage to keep that information to myself. I'm still going to need money for design school.

Chip leads the way out the front door and down to the waiting Uber. He opens the back door for me before running around and getting in on the other side. Once he's settled, he gives the driver an address. Then he asks me, "How long are you planning on being in the city?"

"I'm not sure yet," I tell him. "I have an interview tomorrow." I don't tell him it's at the design school because I don't want to jinx my chances of getting in. "But I will definitely be here long enough to help you and Bob out."

He reaches over and takes my hand. "You're a doll! Trina told us you did amazing work at your parents' house, and I just know you're the right fit for us."

The driver turns onto State Street, and I feel a rush of excitement. When I was little, my mom used to bring me and Noah to Marshall Field's to meet Santa and to have brunch. It's a wonderful core memory.

When the car pulls over, Chip says, "I hope you're in the mood for the best meal of your life."

"I'm always in the mood for that," I laugh.

"Good, because as far as I'm concerned, Capon has the best food in town."

"Capon?" I nearly choke on my own spit.

"Have you heard of it?" He leads the way down the river front path.

"I, um ... have. In fact, the owner is my brother's best friend."

"You'll have to introduce me if he's there!" Chip gushes. "Bob is going to be so jealous that I met Luke Phillips before him."

I subconsciously start to walk slower. I have no idea how to act around Luke. The last time I saw him, he refused to so much as let me show him around the Elk Lake Lodge. I mean, he bolted out of there like someone had set fire to his socks.

Chip slows his stride down to the near crawl I'm moving at and asks, "Would you prefer eating somewhere else?"

That's when I realize that I want to see Luke. I want to show him that I'm in Chicago and I'm doing well. Great, in fact! "No, no," I say. "Let's go."

As we near Capon, I realize that Luke's restaurant is every bit as impressive as he said it was. There's no outdoor dining at this time of year, but I immediately know that I'd love to eat here sometime in the summer. You simply can't beat the river view.

Chip holds the door for me and I walk in. The inside is as gorgeous as the outside. It feels wide open and airy while still giving you the sense that you've walked into an intimate setting. I'm going to have to study all the details so I can learn how they've managed such a feat.

The hostess is a tall blonde woman that I'm guessing was a super model in her last incarnation. She's slender and absolutely stunning. I'm instantly jealous.

"Hello," she greets us with a blinding smile, showcasing her perfect Chiclet teeth. "May I have a name for your reservation?"

"Chip Greenberg," Chip says.

She looks at her book before picking up two menus. "Please follow me." She seats us at a table in front of the window. "Your waiter will be right with you. Enjoy your meal."

Before she can walk away, Chip says, "My friend here knows Luke Phillips. We were hoping we might be able to say hello to him."

Heidi Klum's look-alike eyes me up and down with interest before asking, "May I get your name?"

"It's Lorelai," I tell her. "Lorelai Riley. I'm from Elk Lake, Wisconsin."

She looks like I just told her that my name was Ed McMahon and she just won the Publishers Clearing House. "Really? Well, Lorelai, you're in luck. Luke just came home from Elk Lake last night."

Wait, what? He was in Elk Lake last night and he didn't let me know? *I* was in Elk Lake last night. I suddenly have the urge to run away. The only reason I don't is because I'd probably wind up tripping over my own feet and face planting on the ground, maybe chipping my front teeth for kicks.

After she walks away, Chip picks up the wine menu and says, "This is exciting!"

Exciting like meeting a ninja in a dark alley. "Yes, so lucky that Luke is here." I don't sound the least bit delighted. With any luck, Luke will be so busy that we'll be gone before he can come out.

But as my luck would have it, that doesn't appear to be the case. Turning my head slightly to the right, I watch the kitchen door swing open and Luke walk out. He makes his way to our table in record time, all the while wearing a very confused expression on his face. The first words out of his mouth are, "Lorelai, what are you doing here?"

CHAPTER FORTY-TWO

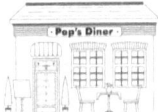

LUKE

I've thought about Lorelai a lot since I last saw her. I mean, a lot. I spent the last four days in Elk Lake—I had to pick up my car—and it was all I could do not to call her. I did find myself driving down her street once or twice. It was like my car had a mind of its own and I had no choice but to let it take me where it wanted to go.

I'm drawn by an undeniable force as I walk across the dining room at Capon. Stopping at her table, I realize Lorelai is even more beautiful than I remember her being. "Lorelai, what are you doing here?"

She looks up and stares at me like I'm a phantom. "Luke. Hello."

"Hello." I repeat, "What are you doing here?"

She shrugs nonchalantly before answering, "Eating, I hope."

I don't like the chill coming off her. Not one bit. "I mean, what are you doing in Chicago?"

"Oh, that." She releases a nervous laugh. "I'm here with my friend Chip."

For the first time I notice she's not alone and I turn to her dinner partner. *Chip* is unexpected. He's hands down the most handsome guy I've ever seen, which is alarming. "You're on a date?" *She's on a date?*

Lorelai takes a long sip of her water before answering me. In fact, she must set a world record for taking her time. She eventually says, "I'm helping Chip out."

"By dating him?" I demand heatedly.

"By helping me design my home," Chip interjects. Then he stands up, all eight feet of him—not really but he's taller than I am. Putting his hand out, he says, "Chip Greenberg. I'm one of your biggest fans."

Now this is a conundrum. I love happy customers, just not really good-looking ones eating with Lorelai. I tentatively shake his hand. "Luke Phillips. It's nice to meet you." *Lies.*

"My husband and I eat here at least twice a week," he offers.

Husband? Yes! Chip is gay! Talk about good news. I'm suddenly quite happy to make his acquaintance. Even though no one asks me to join them, I still pull up a free chair and sit down. "So, Chip," I say. "Tell me how you know Lorelai."

"Our mutual friend, Trina Rockwell, introduced us."

Lorelai doesn't seem overly pleased that I've joined them. "How long are you in town for?" I ask her.

"I don't know," she says evasively. "I have some things to do here before I go back to Elk Lake."

"So, you haven't moved here?" I want to know.

"No." She doesn't offer anything else. Then she says, "I hear you've been in Elk Lake." The accusation in her tone is clear. I was in Elk Lake, and I didn't call her.

"I was," I tell her. "I have some exciting news."

She visibly rolls her eyes, but she doesn't ask what my news is, so I volunteer, "I just bought Pop's." I wish I'd had a camera trained on her face when I said that. Her expression is priceless.

"You what? Why did you buy Pop's?"

"My dad was selling it."

"Yes, but you don't want to live in Elk Lake."

"Who told you that?" I ask. I know I'm yanking her chain a little, but this really is a delicious moment.

"*You* told me that," she practically yells. "In no uncertain terms. Repeatedly. You told me that you wanted to stay in Chicago."

"You told me that you never wanted to come to Chicago, but here you are," I retaliate.

She opens her mouth like she's going to reply, then she closes it, before opening it once again. "Yes, but …"

I shrug. "I guess we both changed our minds."

"Yes, but …"

"Unless of course you aren't going to be here for long."

Lorelai's head looks like it's going to explode. "I don't know how long I'm going to be here."

"You came to help Chip." I can't help but wonder if there's another reason she's here. A reason that might be me.

Her head bobs up and down. "I did."

"Is he the only reason?" I can see Chip out of my peripheral vision and his focus keeps moving back and forth between us like he's watching a ping pong match.

"I … no … I mean …" She is so adorably flustered that all I want to do is pull her into my arms and kiss her.

With the worst timing ever, Eve walks over and announces, "Luke, table forty would like a word."

Annoyed by the interruption, I tell her, "I'm kind of busy."

"It's Jerry Reinsdorf," she says.

I turn to Lorelai and tell her, "He owns the Chicago Bulls. I'm doing a special event for them next week."

"You'd better go, then." She makes a shooing movement with her hands.

Once I'm standing, I address both her and Chip. "I would like to send you food of my choice, if you're okay with that."

"That sounds wonderful!" Chip exudes.

Lorelai merely says, "Fine by me."

I know she's mad at me. But now that I've bought Pop's and plan on spending half my days in Elk Lake, this is my chance to woo her. Even if she decides to stay in Chicago, I'll be here, too.

I make a quick stop at Jerry's table before going back into the kitchen. I'm going to make Lorelai the best meal she has ever had in her life. I start out with a candied beet and feta salad. On the side of her plate, I use a balsamic reduction and write the words, "Will you …" Then I send the first course out.

The second course is my famous chicken pot pie with truffles and water chestnuts. On that plate, I write the words, "Go out …"

The third course is a chocolate mousse dome featuring a trio of mousses with a mirror glaze. I finish my request in fudge sauce. "With me, please?"

My plan is to give her a few minutes to cobble the message together into one cohesive request before going out to see what her answer is. I watch the clock for five minutes, before charging through the kitchen doors in a near military march as I head to Lorelai's table. When I get there, I look down and discover that the waiter put the dessert with the message in front of Chip.

He looks up expectantly, so I tell him, "I think you got the wrong plate."

"Really?" It's clear he's faking shock as he asks, "You weren't asking me out on a date?"

"I, uh … well … no," I tell him. "I was asking Lorelai."

She breaks her silence by saying, "You want to date me? Why?"

"Lorelai." I get down on one knee in front of her. I belatedly realize this is the same posture I might use if I were proposing. "I bought Pop's so that I would be in Elk Lake more."

"You didn't do that for me," she states almost bitterly.

"Part of the reason I did that was so that we could see what might happen between us. I like you so much. I think you're the loveliest, kindest, most beautiful woman in the world, and more than anything, I want to see what might happen if we give us a chance."

Her eyes fill with unshed tears and I can't tell if they're tears of joy or something else. "Luke …"

"Please, Lorelai," I beg. "I have enjoyed getting to know you so much as an adult. I admire you, I respect you, I want to get to know everything about you. And I want to kiss you. There needs to be a lot of kissing."

Blinking rapidly to staunch the moisture in her eyes, she asks, "Will you eat Toaster Strudel with me?"

"God, no," I tell her. "But honestly, I'd do almost anything else."

The tension eases from her face and she offers me the slightest smile. "I might be in Chicago for a while."

"Luckily, I have a restaurant here, too," I tell her. "So, wherever you are, I can be in the same place."

Lorelai doesn't answer right away. In fact, she takes so long that Chip interjects, "For the love of God, woman, date the man! If it weren't for Bob, I'd go out with him myself!"

Going for levity, I smile at Lorelai and ask, "So what's it going to be? You and me, or me and Chip?"

She laughs heartily before answering, "For Bob's sake, I'll agree to date you."

"You won't be sorry," I tell her. Then I lean in slowly and say, "I'm going to kiss you now." But she doesn't give me the chance. Instead, she hops onto my lap and throws her arms around my neck and lays one on me. It is the sweetest, most passionate kiss. It's full of hope, and promise. When we finally break apart, I ask, "Will you let me take you home tonight? I have a surprise for you."

"A surprise?" she wants to know.

Chip stands up and declares, "It's not that I mind being a third wheel, but I think things might move a little faster if I go."

He takes his wallet out, so I motion for him to put it away.

"Your dinner is on me," I tell him. "And let me know the next time you and Bob come in. I'd love to meet him."

"Thank you," Chip says. Then he winks at Lorelai, and adds, "I'm going to need to know what that surprise is. Call me tomorrow."

Once Chip is gone, I tell Lorelai, "Thank you. I promise you won't be sorry."

I can't help but laugh when she says, "I'd better not be ..."

CHAPTER FORTY-THREE

LORELAI

Luke and I walk hand in hand next to the river. I don't think I've ever been party to such a romantic moment. He stops walking and turns to look at me before kissing me again. I could really get used to this.

"Do you mind if we stop off at my apartment first? That's where the surprise is."

I arch an eyebrow in response. "That sounds like a line," I tell him.

He shakes his head. "Not a line. It's a G-rated surprise."

"Toaster Strudel?" I tease.

"Girl, I'm going to make you real strudel one of these days and you are going to love it so much that you will never touch Toaster Strudel again."

Crossing the bridge, Luke leads me toward the first of the two icon towers in Marina City. "I didn't know you lived here."

"It's how I knew I wanted my restaurant to be on the river. You can see Capon from my place."

Walking into the building, he leads me to the elevator and pushes the button for the twenty-fourth floor. We kiss again when the doors close and I start to think I wouldn't mind at least a PG surprise. When the elevator stops, Luke takes me by the hand. We stop at the third door on the right and he takes his key out. Before he can put it into the lock, I hear a dog bark.

"You got a dog?" I demand. "You said that you couldn't get a dog because you weren't home enough."

"I never leave her for more than three hours," he tells me. Then he says, "But she's not mine. I'm keeping her for a friend."

A wave of jealousy washes over me so intensely it catches me off guard. "What kind of friend?" I ask cautiously.

"She's a really good friend."

"She?" Now I am simmering. "What are you doing asking me out if you have a *friend* like that?"

"Don't get mad yet," he says. Then he opens the door and we're both assaulted by his charge.

"Penelope?" I practically burst into tears as the doodle does her happy dance around me. Then I turn to Luke. "What are you doing with Penelope?"

"I picked her up when I was in Elk Lake last week."

"For who? Who's your friend?"

A slow smile overtakes him. "You are my friend, Lorelai. I knew you were going to have to leave your parents' house, and I know you wanted Penelope. I didn't want someone else to get to her first. My parents said you could drop her off with them whenever you want."

Honest to goodness tears start to stream down my face. "You got her for me?"

"I did."

"My parents aren't selling the house until next year," I tell him.

"Doodles are hypoallergenic," he responds.

I'm so full of emotion I swear I'm going to burst. "Noah is staying at my parents' house now, too."

He looks shocked. "Why?

"It's a bit of a story," I tell him. "But the long and short of it is that he's the new basketball coach of the Elk Lake Crappies."

Luke laughs. "I keep hoping someone will change that name."

"It is pretty bad," I agree. "But crappies are delicious fish, so you just have to keep reminding yourself of that."

"I cannot see your brother in Elk Lake to save my life."

"You couldn't see yourself there, either," I remind him. "But now you've bought a restaurant there."

He nudges into my side. "You're there. That's the real draw."

That's when I get the best idea ever. "Luke, my best friend from high school

was Allison Scott. Do you remember her?"

"Maybe? I mean, I knew you had one friend around more than any other."

"That was Allie," I tell him. "And Allie is back home."

"And?" He's clearly not putting this together.

"Allie had as big of a crush on Noah as I had on you."

"Are you suggesting we get even with your brother for helping us get together?"

"I absolutely am," I tell him.

"I love how karma works. And I hope it works out as well for Noah as it has for us." And with that he kisses me again and again.

As much as I spent my childhood dreaming of a life with Luke, I never thought it would happen. And when I least expected it, he knocked on my door and swept me off my feet. I don't know whether we're going to live here or in Elk Lake, I just know one thing for sure. I want to be wherever Luke is.

Life is too short not to be surrounded by the people you love. And even though I'm not going to say the words yet, I love Luke. I always have, and I always will.

Now, to make sure things turn out as well for Noah and Allie.

EPILOGUE

LORELAI

Luke and I have been dating for a little over a year now and things have been going great. We stayed in Chicago for the first six months, except for weekends. I'm taking the rest of my design classes online so that we could go back to Elk Lake.

Noah is still at my parents' house, so I rented an apartment in town. I could have stayed with him, but I don't want to cramp his style. Also, I really don't want to be cast in the role of his maid and if I know my brother like I think I do, that's how he would treat me. I do take Penelope over once in a while though, so she can play in the backyard.

As luck would have it, that cute apartment over the Yarn Barn was vacant again when I was looking, so that's where Penelope and I live. They love her at the yarn shop and get pretty excited when I bring her downstairs to help me pick out supplies. They've even bought treats for her for when she visits.

"Penelope!" I call to her as soon as I walk into the apartment. Even though she's napping in a sunbeam, she rouses herself to greet me. "Let's go see Luke," I tell her. Her tail starts to swish with vigor.

After leashing her up, we walk down the street to Pop's. Luke and his dad are having one of their famous throw downs tonight. This time it's fish tacos, which are a favorite of mine no matter which of the Phillips men is making them.

Walking through the front door, I tell Penny, "You be good and no eating off of plates." If I know Luke, she won't have a chance to because he will have already given her something special.

Luke's mom spots me right away and hurries over. "Lorelai!" She gives me a hug before crouching down to pet Penelope. "How's my grand-dog? How's my little girl?" she asks excitedly. Sometimes when Luke and I go into the city for a couple of days, Penny stays with John and Brenda. She loves them almost as much as she loves us.

Brenda leads the way to a booth by the window and announces, "We're sitting here. I figure this way Penelope can sit on the seat next to me." Penny whines with pleasure. Surely, there was never an animal as loved as she is.

As soon as I'm seated, the bell rings over the front door so Brenda hurries off to seat the next guests. This time it's Luke and Noah's other friend from high school, Tony. He's with his husband and their daughter Raven, who is the cutest little girl in the world.

I look around the restaurant and realize that I know nearly everyone here. Faith and Teddy are a few tables over with their daughters. Anna and her family are seated at the table next to them. Paige and Tim are here, and so are Trina and Heath. Chip and Bob have become very good friends of ours, as well. They wanted to come out for the weekend, but they're on standby waiting for their daughter to be born.

Luke comes out of the kitchen and whistles to get everyone's attention. "Good evening, folks. You all look familiar, so you know how this is done. The servers will bring you each one of my tacos and one of my dad's. You choose your favorite and mark it on the card and we'll take twenty-five percent off everything you order. Now who's ready for a taco showdown?!"

The dining room erupts in cheers of excitement, but Luke doesn't go back to the kitchen. Instead, he adds, "Tonight is a tiny bit different than our other cook-offs." We all wait expectantly for him to explain. Walking over to me, he leans down and tenderly kisses me on the mouth before Penelope whines for her fair share of attention.

Luke ruffles her ears before declaring, "I think you all know Lorelai." The crowd cheers again. "Lorelai and I have been a couple for a full year now." Hoots fill the air. "But even though we've only been dating for a year, we've known each other most of our lives."

I'm a little embarrassed that he's introducing me like this. I mean, everyone knows me, but it's still sweet. Luke drops to one knee in front of me and before I know what's happening, he says, "Lorelai, I love you with my whole heart. I was wondering if you might do me the honor of becoming my wife."

Brenda and John are standing together and nearly jumping up and down with excitement. That's when I see that Noah has come into the restaurant as well. I'm glad Luke waited for him. If I know Luke, I'm sure he tried to get my parents here, but they're currently in Europe. They've been traveling more than ever and having a great retirement.

My heart is full of so much joy, I'm not sure how I'm containing it all. "Luke." I reach out a hand to bring him closer to me. He stands up and scoots into the booth next to me. Leaning into his side, I whisper in his ear, "I would love to be your wife."

"What did she say?" a lone voice in the crowd shouts out.

"She said yes!!!" Luke hollers back.

The crowd starts to chant, "Kiss, kiss, kiss!!!"

Luke leans over and claims my mouth in the most soul-searing way. "You're my home, Lorelai. Whether that's in Elk Lake, or Chicago, or Siberia."

"It's in Elk Lake," I assure him with a smile. "It will always be here."

My biggest dreams in life are coming true. I guess some girls might have given up on Luke, but I knew with my whole heart this man was meant for me. Now, at long last, we are going to be one. I truly am the luckiest woman in the world!

Allie comes over to our table and says, "Congratulations, you two. You're going to make each other so happy. I just know it."

"Speaking of happy," my eye strays in my brother's direction, "anything you want to tell me?"

"I might have a story." She smiles coyly. "But that's for another day …"

Allie and Noah's story is coming soon! Preorder *Pity Please* now.

If you haven't read the first book in the series, here's a teaser for *Pity Date*.

PITY DATE TEASER:

FAITH

Anna and I have been planning our weddings since we were in Pull-Ups at the Little Sunshine Preschool on Maple Street. Of course, we're going to be each other's maid of honors. To be precise, I'll be Anna's maid of honor when she gets married next month, and she'll be my matron of honor, seeing as how she's getting hitched first. Not that I'm officially planning my wedding. Not yet. I have an inkling of who my groom might be, but nothing's set in stone.

My prospective fiancé is none other than Astor Hill. Not only is he Anna's fiancé's best friend from law school and office mate, but we're walking up the aisle together for the ceremony. We haven't been a couple that long, but as you near your thirties—and I'm twenty-nine and three quarters— most of us have dated enough toads to know when we're being courted by a real prince. Astor is a real prince if there ever was one. *His name alone, am I right?*

"Faith, are you coming out or not?" Anna yells through the curtain of my changing cubicle. That's when I realize I haven't even taken off my street clothes yet, let alone put on the bridesmaid dress.

I start to fumble with the button on my jeans. "I'm almost ready."

"Are you daydreaming about Astor again?" she teases. "Girl, you've been nonstop mooning over that man since your first date. I'm starting to think you might be the next one to the altar."

I subconsciously put my hand to my heart in a gesture of pure, unadulterated, "Who, me?" Astor hasn't mentioned taking our relationship to the next level, but that doesn't mean he's not thinking about it. He lives in Chicago, and I live in Elk Lake, Wisconsin, which means we only see each other on the weekends.

But as absence makes the heart grow fonder, it's been a very workable arrangement. Especially since it's only temporary.

Astor and I met on a blind date nearly ten months ago while I was visiting Anna. We hit it off so spectacularly that I've taken the train down to Chicago most weekends since. It's just over two hours from my door to his.

Ripping off my t-shirt, I gingerly step into the pool of silver *poult-de-soie* at my feet. As I pull the sheath dress up, it gets stuck on my hips. "Crap," I grumble under my breath. One of the benefits of falling in love is that my appetite for food has decreased considerably, which is obviously the reason I made such a rookie mistake as to think I could get into this dress the same way a supermodel might. While my hips have shrunk a size since Astor and I have been together, they have a ways to go before making the pull-up maneuver possible.

"How's the house hunt?" I ask. Anna met Christopher when she was a realtor in Chicago. She sold him his condo. Once they got engaged, they decided he would hang his shingle in Elk Lake and the two of them would get busy starting a family. When she's not planning the wedding, she's looking for their first home as a married couple, as well as office space that will suit Chris's lawyering needs. Astor is planning to join the mass migration to Elk Lake and set up shop with him. For this reason alone, it would appear he sees a future with me.

"I've found a couple places that I like but neither one of them is perfect. The one on Elk Lake is slightly preferable. Three bed, two bath, its own dock."

"You've always wanted to live on the lake," I remind her. *I've* always lived on the lake. Actually, I'm still in the house I grew up in. My parents bought a condo in Boca several years ago, so I've got the place all to myself. Which, honestly, is the only reason I'm still there. My mom is too much of a control freak to cohabitate with on an ongoing basis.

"It's the old Turner house down the road from you."

"I love that place! All it needs is a good coat of paint and maybe a new porch."

"And a new roof, and potentially a new septic ..." she groans.

"Oh boy, that sounds like a lot." As I put the dress over my head and scooch the silk material down my hips, I decide that two more pounds ought to be enough for this confection to be a perfect fit. I could manage it now, but I wouldn't be able to eat supper and I'm really looking forward to the meal I helped Anna pick out—prime rib or wide-mouth bass served with prosciutto wrapped asparagus, balsamic glazed new potatoes, and the triple layer Black Forest cake I'm making for their wedding cake. *Seriously yummy.*

"Yeah, but it's a steal," she says. "I'm going to show it to Chris over the weekend and see what he thinks."

"Has Chris said anything about Astor popping the question?" I ask, trying my best not to sound as hopeful as I've started to feel.

"No, but that doesn't mean anything. You know men, they don't talk like we do." *Life would be so much easier if they did.*

My heart races like I just hurdled over the twenty-yard buffet at the Rib Barn. "I don't suppose there's any way you could ask?"

"Chris?"

"Of course, Chris. I don't want you asking Astor," I practically hiss. The disaster potential of approaching an unsuspecting man with such a question is seriously staggering.

The next thing I know I hear what I suspect is Chris's phone ringing. "I didn't mean now!" I holler.

Instead of hanging up, Anna pushes her way into my dressing room and sits down on the chair wedged in the corner. "Hey, babe, what's up?" Chris's deep voice is a near baritone which is odd as he's rather slightly built. It's kind of a Rick Astley situation. You know, that singer from the eighties. How *that* ginger isn't a giant Black man is anyone's guess. Chris is a moderately statured Japanese-American with a flat Midwestern accent that belies his genetics.

"Faith and I are at the bridal boutique for a fitting. I just got done and I thought I'd call you and tell you how much I love you."

"I love you too, babe." He sounds distracted which is par for the course. Lawyers aren't known for having vast amounts of free time to chit chat during business hours. "Is there anything else? I have an important meeting in ten minutes. I need to jet."

Anna jumps right in. "Has Astor said anything about Faith? You know, about asking her a big question?"

My face heats up to the point where a glance in the mirror confirms I've taken on the color of a steamed beet. My complexion matches the auburn highlights in my hair.

"I'm not on speaker phone, am I?" Chris's question prompts a flock of butterflies to take flight in my lower abdomen.

My friend shakes her hands in the air like she's wielding a pair of imaginary pompoms. *Oh. My. God. This is it. I'm about to find out what my future holds and I'm not sure I'm ready.* No, I'm ready. I'm so very ready. How much fun will it be to have a practice run up the altar at Anna and Chris's wedding knowing we'll be next? I make a mental note to catalogue every detail of this moment so I can accurately write about it in my journal tonight. *"Dear Diary, this afternoon my whole life changed ..."*

"Nope, not on speaker," Anna lies with a twinkle of anticipation in her eyes. Her body practically vibrates with excitement. Meanwhile, I lean against the mirror to keep my knees from buckling.

"It's like this, A," he says after exhaling what feels like the longest breath in history. I'm suddenly not sure good news is forthcoming. "Astor's been waiting until after the wedding, so he doesn't make things uncomfortable for us."

Anna barely lets him finish his sentence before announcing, "I wouldn't be uncomfortable if they got engaged before our wedding. Would you?"

"Um, no." Chris clears his throat loudly. "But Astor's not going to ask Faith to marry him."

"But you just said ..." She looks at me with panic in her eyes and makes a motion to take him off speaker. I shake my head fiercely. I want to hear what Chris has to say. I *need* to hear it.

"Astor isn't going to ask Faith to marry him because he's going to break up with her."

"Excuse me?" Anna shouts. *Shouts.* "Break up with her? Why? They're perfect together!"

"He's met someone else." That one sentence obliterates all my emotional reserve, and the wall is no longer strong enough to hold me up. I fall to the floor like a discarded corn husk. The seams of my dress strain against themselves as though my body has become allergic to it and is swelling in an attempt to burst free.

"No!"

"Tiffany started working in our office last month. She and Astor have been practically inseparable ever since," he informs her.

"While he's been with Faith? That bastard! That no-account son of a bitch!" Even my friend's staunch support and anger isn't enough to pop the strange balloon of suspended reality that's formed around me like a protective shield.

A feminine voice interrupts her tirade. "Is there something I can help you with in there?" Missy Corner asks. Missy went through grade school and high school with me and Anna. She opened a bridal boutique with her mother the minute she graduated from college in hopes the karma of the whole thing would find her standing at the altar in record time. So far, she's as single as I apparently still am.

"No, Missy. We're fine," Anna tells her.

Suddenly, my skin feels like an army of fire ants are on the march to do battle with my nervous system. I'm hot and prickly and most decidedly *not* fine.

"Look, A, I've got to go. Let's talk about this tonight, okay?" Chris signs off, leaving me and Anna to stare at each other like we've just been told the nuclear button in the Oval Office has been pushed and we only have minutes before the end of the world.

The end of *my* world, anyway.

Read it now!

ABOUT THE AUTHOR

USA Today Bestseller Whitney Dineen is a rock star in her own head. While delusional about her singing abilities, there's been a plethora of validation that she's a fairly decent author (AMAZING!!!).

After winning many writing awards and selling nearly a kabillion books (math may not be her forte, either), she's decided to let the voices in her head say whatever they want (sorry, Mom). She also won a fourth-place ribbon in a fifth-grade swim meet in backstroke. So, there's that.

Whitney loves to play with her kids (a.k.a. dazzle them with her amazing flossing abilities), bake stuff, eat stuff, and write books for people who "get" her. She thinks french fries are the perfect food and Mrs. Roper is her spirit animal.

Join her newsletter for news of her latest releases, sales, and recommendations. If you consider yourself a superfan, join her private reader group, where you will be offered the chance to read her books before they're released.